S0-BAD-758

THE AFFIRMATION

Also by Christopher Priest in Gollancz

The Separation
The Prestige
The Glamour
The Extremes

THE AFFIRMATION

Christopher Priest

Copyright © Christopher Priest 1981, 2006

All rights reserved

The right of Christopher Priest to be identified as the author of
this work has been asserted by him in accordance with the
Copyright, Designs and Patents Act 1988

First published in Great Britain in 1981 by
Faber and Faber

This edition published in Great Britain in 2006 by
Gollancz
An imprint of the Orion Publishing Group
Orion House, 5 Upper St Martin's Lane, London WC2H 9EA

A CIP catalogue record for this book is available
from the British Library

ISBN 0 575 07577 5

Typeset at The Spartan Press Ltd,
Lymington, Hants

Printed and bound in Great Britain by
Mackays of Chatham plc, Chatham, Kent

www.orionbooks.co.uk

TO M.L. AND L.M.

CHAPTER 1

This much I know for sure:

My name is Peter Sinclair, I am English and I am, or I was, twenty-nine years old. Already there is an uncertainty, and my sureness recedes. Age is a variable; I am no longer twenty-nine.

I once thought that the emphatic nature of words ensured truth. If I could find the right words, then with the proper will I could by assertion write all that was true. I have since learned that words are only as valid as the mind that chooses them, so that of essence all prose is a form of deception. To choose too carefully is to become pedantic, closing the imagination to wider visions, yet to err the other way is to invite anarchy into one's mind. If I am to reveal myself then I prefer to do so by my choices, rather than by my accidents. Some might say that such accidents are the product of the unconscious mind, and thus inherently interesting, but as I write this I am warned by what is to follow. Much is unclear. At this outset I need that tedious quality of pedanticism. I have to choose my words with care. I want to be sure.

Therefore, I shall begin again. In the summer of 1976, the year Edwin Miller lent me his cottage, I was twenty-nine years old.

I can be as certain of this as I am of my name, because they are both from independent sources. One is the gift of parents, the other the product of the calendar. Neither can be disputed.

In the spring of that year, while still twenty-eight, I came to a turning-point in my life. It amounted to a run of bad luck, caused by a number of external events over which I had little or no control. These misfortunes were all independent of each other, yet because they all came together in the space of a few weeks it seemed as if they were part of some terrible conspiracy against me.

In the first place, my father died. It was an unexpected and premature death, of an undetected cerebral aneurysm. I had a good relationship with him, simultaneously intimate and distant; after the death of our mother some twelve years earlier, my sister Felicity and I had been united with him at an age when most adolescents are resisting their parents. Within two or three years, partly because I went away to university, and partly because Felicity and I became alienated from each other, this closeness had been broken. The three of us had for several years lived in different parts of the country, and were together only rarely. Even so, the memories of that short period in my teens lent an unspoken bond between my father and me, and we both valued it.

He died solvent but not rich. He also died intestate, which meant that I had to be involved in a number of tedious meetings with his solicitor. At the end of it all, Felicity and I each received half of his money. It was not large enough to make much difference to either of us, but in my case it was sufficient to cushion me from some of what followed.

Because, in the second place, following a few days after the news of my father's death, I heard that I was soon to be made redundant.

It was a time of recession in the country, with inflating prices, strikes, unemployment, a shortage of capital. Smugly, with my middle-class confidence, I had assumed my degree would insure me against any of this. I worked as a formulation chemist for a flavour house, supplying a large pharmaceutical company, but there was an amalgamation with another group, a change of policy, and my firm had to close my department. Again, I assumed that finding another job would be a mere technicality. I had qualifications and experience, and I was prepared to be adaptable, but many other science graduates were made redundant at the same time and few jobs were available.

Then I was served notice to quit my flat. Government legislation, by marginally protecting the tenant at the expense of the landlord, had disrupted the forces of supply and demand. Rather than rent property, it was becoming more advantageous to buy and sell. In my case, I rented an apartment on the first floor of a large old house in Kilburn, and had lived there for several years. The house was sold to a property company, though, and almost at once I was told to get out. There were appeal procedures, and I embarked on them, but with my other worries at the time I did not act promptly or effectively enough. It was soon clear I should have to vacate. But where in London could one move to? My own case was far from untypical, and more and more people were hunting for flats in an ever-shrinking market. Rents were going up quickly. People who had security of tenure stayed put, or, if they moved, transferred the tenancy to friends. I did what I could: I registered with agencies, answered advertisements, asked my friends to let me know if they heard of a place coming free, but in all the time I was under notice to quit I never even got so far as to look at any places, let alone find somewhere suitable.

It was in this context of circumstantial disaster that Gracia and I fell out. This, alone of all my problems, was one in which I played a part, for which I bore some responsibility.

I was in love with Gracia, and she, I believe, with me. We had known each other a long time, and had passed through all the stages of novelty, acceptance, deepening passion, temporary disillusionment, rediscovery, habit. She was sexually irresistible to me. We could be good company to each other, complement our moods, yet still retain sufficient differences from each other to be surprising.

In this was our downfall. Gracia and I aroused non-sexual passions in each other that neither of us had ever experienced with anyone else. I was normally placid, yet when I was with her I was capable of degrees of anger and love and bitterness that always shocked me, so powerful were they. Everything was heightened with Gracia, everything assumed an immediacy or importance that created havoc. She was mercurial, able to change her mind or her mood with infuriating ease, and she was cluttered with neuroses and phobias which at first I found endearing, but which the longer I knew her only obstructed everything else. Because of them she was at once predatory and vulnerable, capable of wounding and being wounded in equal measure, although at different times. I never learned how to be with her.

The rows, when we had them, came suddenly and violently. I was always taken unawares, yet once they had started I realized that the tensions had been building up for days. Usually the rows cleared the air, and we would make up with a renewed closeness, or with sex. Gracia's temperament allowed her to forgive quickly or not at all. In every case but one she forgave quickly, and the one time she did not was of course the last. It was an awful, squalid row, on a street corner in London, with people walking past us trying not to stare or listen, with Gracia screaming and swearing at me, and I stricken with an impenetrable coldness, violently angry inside but iron-clad outside. After I left her I went home and was sick. I tried to ring her, but she was never there; I could not get to her. It happened while I was job-hunting, flat-hunting, trying to adjust to the death of my father.

Those, then, were the facts, insofar as my choice of words can describe them.

How I reacted to all this is another matter. Nearly everyone has to suffer the loss of a parent at some point in life, new jobs and flats can be found in time, and the unhappiness that follows the end of a love-affair eventually goes away, or is replaced by the excitement of meeting another person. But for me all these came at once; I felt like a man who had been knocked down, then trodden on before he could get up. I was demoralized, bruised and miserable, obsessed with the accumulating unfairness of life and the crushing mess of London. I focused much of my distemper on London: I noticed only its bad qualities. The noise, the dirt, the crowds, the expensive public transport, the inefficient service in shops and restaurants, the delays and muddles: all these seemed to me symptomatic of the random factors that had disrupted my life. I was tired of London, tired of being myself and living in it. But there was no hope in such a response, because I was becoming inward-looking, passive and self-destructive.

Then, a fortunate accident. Through having to sort out my father's papers and letters, I came in contact again with Edwin Miller.

Edwin was a family friend, but I had not seen him for years. My last memory, in fact, was of him and his wife visiting the house while I was still at school. I must then have been thirteen or fourteen. Impressions from childhood are unreliable: I remembered Edwin, and other adult friends of my parents, with an uncritical sense of liking, but this was second-hand from my parents. I had no opinions of my own. A combination of schoolwork, adolescent rivalries and passions, glandular discoveries, and everything else of that age, must have been making a more immediate impression on me.

It was refreshing to meet him from the vantage of my own adulthood. He turned out to be in his early sixties, suntanned, wiry, full of an unassumed friendliness. We had dinner together at his hotel on the edge of Bloomsbury. It was still early spring, and the tourist season had barely begun, but Edwin and I were like an island of Englishness in the restaurant. I remember a group of German businessmen at a table near ours, some Japanese, some people from the Middle East; even the waitresses who brought us our portions of roast topside beef were Malaysian or Filipino. All this was emphasized by Edwin's bluff, provincial accent, reminding me irresistibly of my childhood in the suburbs of Manchester. I had grown used to the increasingly cosmopolitan nature of shops and restaurants in London, but it was Edwin who somehow underlined it, made it seem unnatural. I was aware all through the meal of a distracting nostalgia for a time when life had been simpler. It had been narrower, too, and the vague memories were a distraction because not all of them were pleasant. Edwin was a kind of symbol of that past, and for the first half-hour, while we were still exchanging pleasantries, I saw him as representing the background I had happily escaped when I first moved back to London.

Yet I liked him too. He was nervous of me – perhaps I also represented some kind of symbol to him – and compensated for this by too much generosity about how well I had been doing. He seemed to know a lot about me, at least on a superficial level, and I presumed he had got all this from my father. In the end his lack of guile made me own up, and I told him frankly what had happened to my job. This led inevitably to my telling him most of the rest.

'It happened to me too, Peter,' he said. 'A long time ago, just after the war. You'd have thought there were a lot of jobs around then, but the lads were coming back from the Forces, and we had some bad winters.'

'What did you do?'

'I must have been about your age then. You're never too old for a fresh start. I was on the dole for a bit, then got a job with your dad. That's how we met, you know.'

I didn't know. Another residue of childhood: I assumed, as I had always assumed, that parents and their friends never actually met but had somehow always known one another.

Edwin reminded me of my father. Although physically unalike they were about the same age, and shared some interests. The similarities were mostly my creation, perceived from within. It was perhaps the flat northern accent, the intonation of sentences, the manneristic pragmatism of an industrial life.

He was just as I remembered him, but this was impossible. We were both fifteen years older, and he must have been in his late forties when I last saw him. His hair was grey, and thin on the crown; his neck and eyes were heavily wrinkled; there was a stiffness in his right arm, which he remarked on once or twice. He could not possibly have looked like this before, yet sitting there in the hotel restaurant with him I was reassured by the familiarity of his appearance.

I thought of other people I had met again after a period of time. There was always the first surprise, an internal jolt: he has changed, she looks older. Then, within a few seconds, the perception changes and all that can be seen are the similarities. The mind adjusts, the eye allows; the ageing process, the differences of clothes and hair and possessions, are edited out by the will to detect continuity. Memory is mistrusted in the recognition of more important identifications. Body-weight might differ, but a person's height or bone-structure do not. Soon it is as if nothing at all has altered. The mind erases backwards, re-creating what one remembers.

I knew Edwin ran his own business. After a few years working for my father he had set up on his own. At first he had taken on general engineering jobs, but eventually set up a factory that specialized in mechanical valves. These days his principal customer was the Ministry of Defence, and he supplied hydraulic valves to the Royal Navy. He had intended to retire at sixty, but the business was prospering and he enjoyed his work. It occupied the major part of his life.

'I've bought a little cottage in Herefordshire, near the Welsh border. Nothing special, but just right for Marge and me. We were going to retire down there last year, but the place needs a lot of doing up. It's still empty.'

'How much work is there to do?' I said.

'Mostly redecorating. The place hasn't been lived in for a couple of years. It needs rewiring, but that can wait. And the plumbing's a bit antiquated, you could say.'

'Would you like me to make a start on it? I'm not sure I could take on the plumbing, but I'd have a go at the rest.'

It was an idea that was sudden and attractive. An escape from my problems had presented itself. In my recently acquired hatred of London, the countryside had assumed a wistful, romantic presence in my mind. Talking about Edwin's cottage, that dream took on a concrete shape, and I became certain that if I stayed in London I would only sink further into the helplessness of self-pity. Everything became plausible to me, and I tried to talk Edwin into renting me his cottage.

'I'll lend it to you free, lad,' Edwin said. 'You can have it as long as you need it. Provided, of course, you do a spot of decorating, and when Marge and me decide it's time to give it all up, then you'll have to look for somewhere else to go.'

'It'll be for just a few months. Long enough to get myself back on my feet.'

'We'll see.'

We discussed a few details, but the arrangement was finalized in a matter of minutes. I could move down there as soon as I liked; Edwin would mail me the keys. The village of Weobley was less than half a mile away, the garden would have to be looked at, it was a long way to the nearest mainline railway station, they wanted white paint downstairs and Marge had her own ideas about the bedrooms, the phone was disconnected but there was a call-box in the village, the septic tank would have to be emptied and perhaps cleaned out.

Edwin almost forced the house on me once we had convinced each other it was a good idea. It was worrying him while it was empty, he said, and houses were made for living in. He would fix up with a local builder to come in and repair the plumbing, and do some rewiring, but if I wanted to feel I was earning my stay I could do as much of the work as I wished. There was only one proviso: Marge would want the garden done a certain way. They might come down and visit me at weekends, to lend a hand.

In the days that followed this meeting I began to act positively for the first time in several weeks. Edwin had given me the spur, and I moved forward with purpose. Of course I could not move down to Herefordshire straight away, but from the moment I left him everything I did was directly or indirectly towards that end.

It took me a fortnight to free myself of London. I had furniture to sell or give away, books to find a home for, bills to pay and accounts to close. I wanted to be unencumbered after my move; from now on I would have around me only the minimum of things I would need. Then there was the actual move; a rented van and two return trips to the cottage.

Before finally leaving London I made several renewed efforts to locate Gracia. She had moved, and her former flatmate almost slammed the door in my face when I called round to the old address. Gracia wanted never to see me again. If I wrote to her the letter would be forwarded, but I was told not to bother her. (I wrote to her anyway, but no reply came.) I tried the office where she had worked, but she had moved from there too. I tried mutual friends, but either they did not know where she was or else they would not tell me.

All this made me deeply restless and unhappy, feeling that I was unfairly treated. It was a stark reminder of my earlier sense that events were conspiring against me, and much of my euphoria about the cottage was dispelled. I suppose that I had subconsciously imagined moving to the countryside with Gracia, that away from the stresses of city life she and I would not argue, would develop the mature love we had for each other. This buried hope had remained as I organized the details of my move, but with her total repudiation of me at the last minute, it was brought home to me that I was totally alone.

For a few exciting days I had seen myself at a new beginning, but by the time I was finally settled in the cottage all I could think was that I had reached an end.

It was a time for contemplation, for inwardness. Nothing was what I wanted, but all of it had been given to me.

CHAPTER 2

The cottage lay in agricultural countryside, about two hundred yards down an unmade lane leading off the road between Weobley and Hereford. It was secluded and private, being surrounded by trees and hedges. The house itself was on two storeys, slate-roofed, whitewashed, mullion-windowed and stable-doored. It had about half an acre of garden, running down at the back to a clean-flowing brook. The previous owners had cultivated fruit and vegetables, but everything was now overgrown. There were small lawns behind and in front of the house, and several flowerbeds. By the brook was an orchard. The trees needed pruning, and all the plants and flowers would have to be cut back and weeded.

I felt possessive of the cottage from the moment I arrived. It was mine in every sense except legal ownership, and without meaning to I began to make plans for it. I imagined weekend parties, my friends driving down from London to enjoy good country food and rural peace, and I saw myself toughening up for the rigours of a less civilized existence. Perhaps I would get a dog, gum-boots, fishing equipment. I determined to learn country crafts: weaving, woodwork, pottery. As for the house, I would soon transform it into the sort of bucolic heaven most townsmen could only dream about.

There was much to be done. As Edwin had told me, the wiring was ancient and inefficient; only two power-sockets worked in the whole house. The pipes gave out a loud knocking whenever I ran the taps, and there was no hot water. The lavatory was blocked. Some of the rooms were damp; the entire place, inside and out, needed repainting. The floor in the downstairs rooms showed signs of woodworm, and upstairs there was a damp-rot in the roof beams.

For the first three days I worked hard at settling in. I opened all the windows, swept the floors, wiped down shelves and cupboards. I poked a long piece of wire down the lavatory, and afterwards peered cautiously under the rusting metal lid of the septic tank. I attacked the garden with more energy than expertise, pulling up by its roots anything I thought might be a weed. At the same time, I made myself known to the general store in Weobley, and arranged for weekly deliveries of groceries to be made. I bought all sorts of tools and utensils I had never needed before: pliers, brushes, a putty-knife, a saw, and for the kitchen a few pots and pans. Then the first weekend arrived. Edwin and Marge came to visit me, and at once my energetic mood vanished.

It was obvious that Edwin's generosity was not shared by Marge. When they arrived I realized that Edwin had been made to regret his friendly offer to me. He stayed apologetically in the background while Marge took control. She made it clear from the outset that she had her own plans for the cottage, and they did not include someone like me living there. It was nothing she said, it was just implicit in her every glance, every comment.

I barely remembered Marge. In the old days, when they had visited us, it was Edwin who had been dominant. Marge then had been someone who drank tea, talked about her back trouble and helped with the washing up. Now she was a plump and prosaic person, full of conversation and opinions. She had plenty of advice on how to clean the place up, but did none of it herself. In the garden, she did more, pointing out what was to be saved, what to be sacrificed to the compost heap. Later, I helped them unload the numerous pots of undercoat and paint they had brought in the car, and Marge explained exactly which colours were to go on which walls. I wrote it all down, and she checked it through.

There was nowhere they could stay in the house, so they had to take a room over the pub in the village. On the Sunday morning, Edwin took me aside and explained that because of a strike of petrol-tanker drivers there were long queues at the motorway filling stations, and if I didn't mind they would leave soon after lunch. It was the only thing he said to me all weekend, and I was sorry.

When they were gone I felt dispirited and disappointed. It had been a painful, difficult weekend. I had felt trapped by them: my gratitude to Edwin, my awkward realization that he had got into hot water with Marge because of it, my continual urges to justify and explain myself. I had had to please them, and I hated the unctuousness I heard creeping into my voice when I spoke to Marge. They had reminded me of the temporary nature of my residence in the house, that the cleaning up and repairs I was starting were not in the end for myself, but a form of rent.

I was sensitive to the slightest upset. For three days I had forgotten my troubles, but after the visit I rehearsed my recent preoccupations, particularly my loss of Gracia. Her disappearing from my life in such a way – anger, tears, unfinished sentiments – was profoundly upsetting, especially after so long a time together.

I started to brood about the other things I had left behind me: friends, books, records, television. I grew lonely, and acutely aware that the nearest telephone was in the village. I waited illogically for the morning mail to arrive, even though I had given my new address to only a few friends and expected to hear from none of them. While in London I had been extensively aware of the world, through reading a daily newspaper, buying several weekly magazines, keeping in touch with friends and listening to the radio or watching television. Now I was cut off from all that. It was through my own designs, and yet, unreasonably, I missed it all and felt deprived. I could of course have bought a newspaper in the village, and once or twice I did, but I discovered my needs were not external. The emptiness was in myself.

As the days passed my gloomy preoccupations intensified. I became careless of my surroundings. I wore the same clothes day after day, I stopped washing or shaving and I ate only the simplest and most convenient food. I slept late every morning, and for many of the days I was plagued by headaches and a general stiffness in my body. I felt ill and looked ill, although I was sure there was nothing physically wrong with me.

It was by now the beginning of May, and spring was advancing. Since I had moved into the cottage the weather had been mostly grey, with occasional days of light rain. Now, suddenly, the weather improved: the blossom was late in the orchard, the flowers began to open. I saw bees, hoverflies, a wasp or two. In the evenings, clouds of gnats hung around the doorways and under the trees. I became aware of the sounds of birds, especially in the mornings. For the first time in my life I was sensitive to the mysterious organisms of nature; a lifetime in city apartments, or uncaring childhood visits to the countryside, had ill prepared me for the commonplaces of nature.

Something stirred inside me, and I felt restless to be free of my introspection. Yet it continued, a counterpoint to the other gladness.

In an attempt to purge both the restlessness and the depression, I made a serious attempt to start work. I hardly knew how I should begin. In the garden, for instance, it seemed that no sooner had I weeded one patch than what I had done a few days before became just as overgrown and untidy. In the house, the work of redecoration was one that had apparently endless ramifications. It would be a long time before I could start painting, because there were so many preliminary repairs to make.

It helped me to imagine the results. If I could summon an image of the garden, pruned, tidied, blooming, then it gave me an incentive to start. To visualize the rooms newly painted, made clean and tidy, was in a sense half the work already done. This was a discovery, a step forward.

In the house, I concentrated on the downstairs room where I had been sleeping. This was a long, large room, running the depth of the house. At one end, a small window looked out towards the garden, hedge and lane at the front; at the other end, a much wider window gave a view of the back garden.

I worked hard, encouraging myself with my imaginative vision of how the room would be by the time I finished. I washed the walls and ceiling, repaired the crumbling plaster, scrubbed down the woodwork, and then applied two coats of the white emulsion Edwin and Marge had brought. When the woodwork was painted, the room was transformed. From a dingy, temporary hovel it had become a light, airy room in which one could live in style. I cleaned up the paint-splashes thoroughly, stained the floorboards and polished the windows. On an impulse I went into Weobley and bought a large quantity of rush matting, which I spread across the floor.

What most excited me was the discovery that what I had imagined for the room had come to be. The conception of it had influenced its execution.

I sometimes stood or sat in that room for hours on end, relishing the cool tranquillity of it. With both windows opened a warm draught passed through, and at night the honeysuckle that grew beneath the window at the front released a fragrance that until then I had only been able to imagine from chemical imitations.

I thought of it as my white room, and it became central to my life in the cottage.

With the room completed I returned to my introspective mood, but because I had had something to do for the last few days, I now found that my thoughts were more in focus. As I pottered about the garden, as I started the decoration of the other rooms, I contemplated what I was doing with my life, and what I had done with it in the past.

I perceived my past life as an unordered, uncontrolled bedlam of events. Nothing made sense, nothing was consistent with anything else. It seemed to me important that I should try to impose some kind of order on my memories. It never occurred to me to question why I should do this. It was just extremely important.

One day I looked in the bloom-spotted mirror in the

kitchen and saw the familiar face staring back at me, but I could not identify it with anything I knew of myself. All I knew was that this sallow, unshaven face with dull eyes was myself, a product of nearly twenty-nine years of life, and it all seemed pointless.

I entered a period of self-questioning: how had I reached this state, this place, this attitude of mind? Was it just an accumulation of bad luck, as the ready excuse seemed to be, or was it the product of a deeper inadequacy? I began to brood.

At first, it was the actual chronology of memory that interested me.

I knew the order of my life, the sequence in which large or important events had taken place, because I had had the universal experience of growing up. Details, however, eluded me. Fragments of my past life – places I had visited, friends I had known, things I had accomplished – were all there in the chaos of my memories, but their precise place in the order of things had to be worked at.

I aimed initially at total recall, taking, for example, my first year at grammar school, and from that starting point trying to attach the many surrounding details: what I had been taught that year, my teachers' names, the names of other children in the school, where I had been living, where my father had been working, what books I might have read or films seen, friendships made or enmities formed.

I muttered to myself as I worked at the decorating, telling myself this inconsequential, rambling and incoherent narrative, as muddled then as the life itself must have been.

Then form became more important. It was not enough merely to establish the *order* in which my life had progressed, but the relative significance of each event. I was the product of those events, that learning, and I had lost touch with who I was. I needed to rediscover them, perhaps relearn what I had lost.

I had become unfocused and diffuse. I could only regain my sense of identity through my memories.

It grew impossible to retain what I was discovering. I became confused by having to concentrate on remembering, then retaining it. I would clarify a particular period of my life, or so I thought, but then in moving on to another year or another place I would find that either there were distracting similarities, or I had made a mistake the first time.

At last I realized I should have to write it all down. The previous Christmas Felicity had given me a small portable typewriter, and one evening I retrieved it from my heap of possessions. I set up a table in the centre of my white room. I started work immediately, and almost at once I was discovering mysteries about myself.

CHAPTER 3

I had imagined myself into existence. I wrote because of an inner need, and that need was to create a clearer vision of myself, and in writing I *became* what I wrote.

It was not something I could understand. I felt it on an instinctive or emotional level.

It was a process that was exactly like the creation of my white room. That had been first of all an idea, and later I made the idea real by painting the room as I imagined it. I discovered myself in the same way, but through the written word.

I began writing with no suspicion of the difficulties involved. I had the enthusiasm of a child given coloured pencils for the first time. I was undirected, uncontrolled and entirely lacking in self-consciousness. All these were to change later, but on that first evening I worked with innocent energy, letting an undisciplined flow of words spread across the paper. I was deeply, mysteriously excited by what I was doing, and frequently read back over what I had written, scribbling corrections on the pages and noting second thoughts in the margins. I felt a sense of vague discontent, but this I ignored: the overwhelming sensation was one of release and satisfaction. To write myself into existence!

I worked late, and when eventually I crawled into my sleeping-bag, I slept badly. The next morning I returned to the work, letting the decoration stay unfinished. Still my creative energy was undiminished, and page after page slipped through the carriage of the typewriter as if there was nothing that could ever obstruct the flow. As I finished with them I scattered the sheets on the floor around the table, imposing a temporary chaos on the order I was creating.

Inexplicably, I came to a sudden halt.

It was the fourth day, when I had upwards of sixty sheets of completed draft around me. I knew each page intimately, so impassioned was my need to write, so frequently had I re-read my work. What lay unwritten ahead had the same quality, the same need to be produced. I had no doubts as to what would follow, what would be unsaid. Yet I stopped halfway down a page, unable to continue.

It was as if I had exhausted my way of writing. I became acutely self-conscious and started to question what I had done, what I was going to do next. I glanced at a page at random, and all at once it seemed naïve, self-obsessed, trite and uninteresting. I noticed that the sentences were largely unpunctuated, that my spelling was erratic, that I used the same words over and over, and even the judgements and observations, on which I had so prided myself, seemed obvious and irrelevant.

Everything about my hasty typescript was unsatisfactory, and I was stricken by a sense of despair and inadequacy.

I temporarily abandoned my writing, and sought an outlet for my energies in the mundane tasks of domesticity. I completed painting one of the upstairs rooms, and moved my mattress and belongings in there. I decided that from this day my white room would be used solely for writing. A plumber arrived, hired by Edwin, and he started to fix the noisy pipes, and install an immersion heater. I took the interruption as a chance to rethink what I was doing, and to plan more carefully.

So far, everything I had written relied entirely on memory. Ideally, I should have talked to Felicity, to see what she remembered, perhaps to fill in some of the minor mysteries of childhood. But Felicity and I no longer had much in common; we had argued many times in recent years, most recently, and most bitterly, after our father's death. She would have little sympathy for what I was doing. Anyway, it was *my* story; I did not want it coloured by her interpretation of events.

Instead, I telephoned her one day and asked her to send me the family photograph albums. She had taken in most of my father's possessions, including these, but as far as I knew she had no use for them. Felicity was undoubtedly puzzled by my sudden interest in this material – after the funeral she had offered the albums to me, and I had said no – but she promised to mail them to me.

The plumber left, and I returned to the typewriter.

This time, after the pause, I approached the work with greater care and a desire to be more organized. I was learning to question my subject matter.

Memory is a flawed medium, and the memories of childhood are frequently distorted by influences that cannot be understood at the time. Children lack a world perspective; their horizons are narrow. Their interests are egocentric. Much of what they experience is interpreted for them by parents. They are unselective in what they see.

In addition, my first attempt had been not much more than a series of connected fragments. Now I sought to tell a story, and to tell it in such a way that there would be an overall shape, a scheme to the telling of it.

Almost at once I discovered the essence of what I wanted to write.

My subject matter was still inevitably myself: my life, my experiences, my hopes, my disappointments and my loves. Where I had gone wrong before, I reasoned, was in setting out this life chronologically. I had started with my earliest memories and attempted to grow on paper as I had grown in life. Now I saw I had to be more devious.

To deal with myself I had to treat myself with greater objectivity, to examine myself in the way the protagonist is examined in a novel. A described life is not the same as a real one. Living is not an art, but to write of life is. Life is a series of accidents and anticlimaxes, misremembered and misunderstood, with lessons only dimly learned.

Life is disorganized, lacks shape, lacks *story*.

Throughout childhood, mysteries occur in the world around you. They are mysteries only because they are not properly explained, or because of a lack of experience, but they remain in the memory simply because they are so intriguing. In adulthood, explanations often present themselves, but by then they are far too late: they lack the imaginative appeal of a mystery.

Which, though, is the more true: the memory or the fact?

In the third chapter of my second version I began to write of something that illustrated this perfectly. It concerned Uncle William, my father's older brother.

For most of my childhood I never saw William . . . or Billy, as my father called him. There had always been something of a cloud to his name: my mother clearly disapproved of him, yet to my father he was something of a hero. I remember that from quite early on my father would tell me stories of the scrapes he and Billy had been in as children. Billy was always getting into trouble, and had a genius for practical jokes. My father grew up to become a respectable and successful engineer, but Billy had entered into a number of disreputable enterprises, such as working on ships, selling second-hand cars and trading in government-surplus goods. I saw nothing wrong with this at all, but for some reason it was considered dubious by my mother.

One day, Uncle William turned up at our house, and at once my life was vested with excitement. Billy was tall and sunburnt, had a big curly moustache and drove an open-top car with an old-fashioned horn. He spoke with a lazy, exciting drawl, and he picked me up and carried me around the garden upside-down and screeching. His big hands had dark calluses on them, and he smoked a dirty pipe. His eyes saw distance. Later, he took me for a breathtaking drive in his car, whizzing through country lanes at great speed, and honking his horn at a policeman on a bicycle. He bought me a toy machine gun, one which could fire wooden bullets right across the room, and showed me how to build a den in a tree.

Then he was gone, as suddenly as he arrived, and I was sent to bed. I lay in my room, listening to my parents arguing together. I could not hear what they were saying, but my father was shouting and a door slammed. Then my mother started crying.

I never saw Uncle William again, and neither of my parents mentioned him. Once or twice I asked about him, but the subject was changed with the sort of parental adroitness children can never overcome. About a year later my father told me that Billy was now working abroad ('somewhere in the East'), and that I was unlikely to see him again. There was something about the way my father said this that made me doubt him, but I was not a subtle child and infinitely preferred to believe what I was told. For a long time after that, Billy's adventures abroad were a familiar imaginative companion: with a little help from the comics I read, I saw him mountain-climbing and game-hunting and building railroads. It was all in keeping with what I knew of him.

When I grew up, and was thinking for myself, I knew that what I had been told was probably untrue, that Billy's disappearance was almost certainly explicable to the real world, but even so the glamorous image of him remained.

It was only after my father died, and I was having to go through his papers, that I came across the truth. I found a letter from the Governor of Durham Prison, saying that Uncle William had been admitted to the hospital wing; a second letter, dated a few weeks later, reported that he had died. I made some inquiries through the Home Office, and discovered that William had been serving a twelve-year sentence for armed robbery. The crime for which he had been convicted was committed within a few days of that crazy, thrilling afternoon in summer.

Even as I wrote about him, though, there was still a powerful part of my imagination that had Uncle Billy away in some exotic place, grappling with man-eaters or skiing down mountain-sides.

Both versions of him were true, but in different qualities of truth. One was sordid, disagreeable and final. The other had imaginative plausibility, in my personal terms, and furthermore had the distinctly attractive bonus that it allowed for Billy to return one day.

To discuss matters like this in my writing I had to be at a stage removed from myself. There was a duplication of myself involved, perhaps even a triplication.

There was I who was writing. There was I whom I could remember. And there was I of whom I wrote, the protagonist of the story.

The difference between factual truth and imaginative truth was constantly on my mind.

Memory was still fundamental, and I had daily reminders of its fallibility. I learnt, for instance, that memory itself did not present a narrative. Important events were remembered in a sequence ordered by the subconscious, and it was a constant effort to reassemble them into my story.

I broke my arm when I was a small child, and there were photographs to remind me in the albums Felicity had sent. But was this accident before or after I started school, before or after the death of my maternal grandmother? All three events had had a profound effect on me at the time, all three had been early lessons in the unfriendly, random nature of the world. As I wrote, I tried to recall the order in which they had occurred, but this was not possible; memory failed me. I was forced to re-invent the incidents, working them into a continuous but false order so that I could convey why they had influenced me.

Even aids to memory were unreliable, and my broken arm was a surprising example of this.

It was my left arm that was fractured. This I know beyond doubt, as one does not misremember such things, and to this day I am slightly weaker in that arm than in the other. Such memory must be beyond question. And yet, the only objective record of the injury was in a short sequence of black-and-white photographs taken during a family holiday. There, in several pictures taken in sunlit countryside, was a mournful-

22

looking infant whom I recognized as myself, his *right* arm carried in a white sling.

I came across these photographs at about the same time as I was writing about the incident, and the discovery came as something of a shock. For a few moments I was confused and confounded by the revelation, as it seemed to be, and I was forced to question every other assumption I had been making about memories. Of course, I soon realized what must have happened: the processor had apparently printed the entire spool of film from the wrong side of the negative. As soon as I examined the prints more closely – at first, all I had looked at was myself – I saw a number of background details which confirmed this: car registration numbers printed in reverse, traffic driving on the right, clothes buttoned the wrong way round, and so on.

It was all perfectly explicable, but it taught me two more things about myself: that I was becoming obsessed with checking and authenticating what hitherto I had taken for granted, and that I could rely on nothing from the past.

I came to a second pause in my work. Although I was satisfied with my new way of working, each new discovery was a setback. I was becoming aware of the deceptiveness of prose. Every sentence contained a lie.

I began a process of revision, going back through my completed pages and rewriting certain passages numerous times. Each successive version subtly improved on life. Every time I rewrote a *part* of the truth I came nearer to a whole truth.

When I was at last able to continue where I had left off, I soon came across a new difficulty.

As my story progressed from childhood to adolescence, then to young adulthood, other people entered the narrative. These were not family, but outsiders, people who came into my life and who, in some cases, were still a part of it. In particular, there was a group of friends I had known since university, and a number of women with whom I had had affairs. One of these, a girl named Alice, was someone I had been engaged to for several months. We had seriously intended to marry, but in the end it went wrong and we parted. Alice was now married to someone else, had two children, but was still a good and trusted friend. Then there was Gracia, whose effect on my life in recent years had been profound.

If I was to serve my obsessive need for truth then I had to deal with these relationships in some way. Every new friendship marked a moving on from the immediate past, and every lover had changed my outlook for better or worse in some way. Even though there was very little chance anyone mentioned in my manuscript would ever read it, I nevertheless felt inhibited by the fact that I still knew them.

Some of what I intended to say would be unpalatable, and I wanted to be free to describe my sexual experiences in detail, if not in intimate detail.

The simplest method would have been to change names, and fudge around the details of time and place in an attempt to make the people unrecognizable. But this was not the sort of truth I was seeking to tell. Nor could it be done by simply leaving them out; these experiences had been important to me.

I discovered the solution at last by use of indirection. I invented new friends and lovers, giving them fictitious backgrounds and identities. One or two of them I brought forward from childhood, so to speak, implying that they had been lifelong friends, whereas in my real life I had lost contact with the other children I had grown up with. It made the narrative more of a piece, with a greater consistency in the story. Everything seemed to have coherence and significance.

Virtually nothing was wasted; every described event or character had some form of correlative elsewhere in the story.

So I worked, learning about myself as I went. Truth was being served at the expense of literal fact, but it was a higher, *better* form of truth.

As my manuscript proceeded I entered a state of mental excitation. I was sleeping only five or six hours a night, and when I woke up I always went directly to my desk to re-read what I had written the day before. I subordinated everything to the writing. I ate only when I absolutely had to, I slept only when I was exhausted. Everything else was neglected; Edwin and Marge's redecoration was postponed indefinitely.

Outside, the long summer was tirelessly hot. The garden was overgrown, but now the soil was parched and cracked, and the grass was yellow. Trees were dying, and the stream at the end of the garden dried up. On the few occasions I went into Weobley I overheard conversations about the weather. The heatwave had become a drought; livestock was being slaughtered, water was being rationed.

Day after day I sat in my white room, feeling the warm draught from the windows. I worked shirtless and unshaven, cool and comfortable in my squalor.

Then, quite unexpectedly, I came to the end of my story. It ceased abruptly, with no more events to describe.

I could hardly believe it. I had anticipated the experience of finishing as being a sudden release, a new awareness of myself, an end to a quest. But the narrative merely came to a halt, with no conclusions, no revelations.

I was disappointed and disturbed, feeling that all my work had been to no avail. I sifted through the pages, wondering where I had gone wrong. Everything in the narrative proceeded towards a conclusion, but it ended where I had no more to say. I was in my life in Kilburn, before I split with Gracia, before my father died, before I lost my job. I could take it no further, because there was only here, Edwin's house. Where was the end?

It occurred to me that the only ending that would be right would be a false one. In other words, because I had reassembled my memories to make a story, then the story's conclusion must also be imaginary.

But to do that I should first have to acknowledge that I really had become two people: myself, and the protagonist of the story.

At this point, conscience struck me about the neglect in the house. I was disillusioned by my writing, and by my inability to cope with it, and I took the opportunity to take a break. I spent a few days in the garden, during the last hot days of September, cutting back the overgrown shrubbery and plucking what fruit I could find still on the trees. I cut the lawn, dug over what remained of the dehydrated vegetable patch.

Afterwards, I painted another of the upstairs rooms.

Because I was away from my failed manuscript, I started to think about it again. I knew I needed to make one last effort to get it right. I had to bring shape to it, but to do so I had to straighten out my daily life.

The key to a purposeful life, I decided, lay in the organization of the day. I created a pattern of domestic habit: an hour a day to cleaning, two hours to Edwin's redecoration and the garden, eight hours for sleep. I would bathe regularly, eat by the clock, shave, wash my clothes, and for everything I did there would be an hour in the day and a day in the week. My need to write was obsessive but it was dominating my life, probably to the detriment of the writing itself.

Now, paradoxically liberated by having constrained myself, I began to write a third version, more smoothly and more effectively than ever before.

I knew at last exactly how my story must be told. If the deeper truth could only be told by falsehood – in other words, through metaphor – then to achieve total truth I must create total falsehood. My manuscript had to become a metaphor for myself.

I created an imaginary place and an imaginary life.

My first two attempts had been muted and claustrophobic. I described myself in terms of inwardness and emotion. External events had a shadowy, almost wraith-like presence beyond the edge of vision. This was because I found the real world imaginatively sterile; it was too anecdotal, too lacking in story. To create an imagined landscape enabled me to shape it to my own needs, to make it stand for certain personal symbols in my life. I had already made a fundamental step away from pure autobiographical narrative; now I took the process one stage further and placed the protagonist, my metaphorical self, in a wide and stimulating landscape.

I invented a city and I called it 'Jethra', intending it to stand for a composite of London, where I had been born, and the suburbs of Manchester, where I had spent most of my childhood. Jethra was in a country called 'Faiandland', which was a moderate and slightly old-fashioned place, rich in tradition and culture, proud of its history but having difficulty in a modern and competitive world. I gave Faiandland a geography and laws and constitution. Jethra was its capital and principal port, situated on the southern coast. Later, I sketched in details of some of the other countries which made up this world; I even drew a rough map, but quickly threw it away because it codified the imagination.

As I wrote, this environment became almost as important as the experiences of my protagonist. I discovered, as before, that by invention of details the larger truths emerged.

I soon found my stride. The fictions of my earlier attempts now seemed awkward and contrived, but as soon as I transferred them to this imaginary world they took on plausibility and conviction. Before, I had changed the order of events merely to clarify them, but now I discovered that all this had had a purpose that only my subconscious had understood. The change to an invented background made sense of what I was doing.

Details accumulated. Soon I saw that in the sea to the south of Faiandland there would be islands, a vast archipelago of small, independent countries. For the people of Jethra, and for my protagonist in particular, these islands represented a form of wish, or of escape. To travel in these islands was to achieve some kind of purpose. At first I was not sure what this would be, but as I wrote I began to understand.

Against this background, the story I wanted to tell of my life emerged. My protagonist had my own name, but all the people I had known were given false identities. My sister

Felicity became 'Kalia', Gracia became 'Seri', my parents were concealed.

Because it was all strange to me I responded imaginatively to what I was writing, but because everything was in another sense totally familiar to me, the world of the other Peter Sinclair became one which I could recognize, and inhabit mentally.

I worked hard and regularly, and the pages of the new manuscript began to pile up. Every evening I would finish work at the time I had predetermined on my daily chart, and then I would go over the finished pages, making minor corrections to the text. Sometimes I would sit on my chair in my white room, with the manuscript on my lap, and I would feel the weight of it and know that I was holding in my hands everything about me that was worth telling or that could be told.

It was a separate identity, an identical self, yet it was outside me and was fixed. It would not age as I would age, nor could it ever be destroyed. It had a life beyond the paper on which it was typewritten; if I burned it, or someone took it away from me, it would still exist on some higher plane. Pure truth had an unageing quality; it would outlive me.

This final version could not have been more different from those first tentative pages I had written a few months before. It was a mature, outward account of a life, truthfully told. Everything about it was invention, apart from the use of my own name, yet everything it contained, every word and sentence, was as true in the high sense of the word as truth could attain. This I knew beyond doubt or question.

I had found myself, explained myself, and in a very personal sense of the word I had *defined* myself.

At last I could feel the end of my story approaching. It was no longer a problem. As I worked I had felt it take shape in my mind, as earlier the story itself had taken form. It was merely a question of setting it down, of typing the pages. I only sensed what the ending would be; I would not know the actual words until the moment came to write them. With that would come my release, my fulfilment, my rehabilitation into the world.

But then, when I had less than ten pages to go, everything was disrupted beyond any hope of retrieval.

CHAPTER 4

The drought had at last broken, and it had been raining continuously for the past week. The lane leading to the house was an almost impassable morass of deep puddles and squelching mud. I heard the car before I saw it: the revving engine and the tyres sucking out of the sticky mud. I hunched over the typewriter, dreading an interruption, and I stared down at the last words I had written, holding them there with my eyes lest they should slip.

The car halted outside the house, beyond the hedge and just out of sight. I could hear the engine running slowly and the wiper-blades thwacking to and fro across the windscreen. Then the engine was turned off, and a car door slammed.

'Hello? Peter, are you there?' The voice came from outside, and I recognized it as Felicity's.

I continued to stare at my unfinished page, hoping that by silence I could fend her off. I was so nearly finished. I wanted to see no one.

'Peter, let me in! It's pouring with rain!'

She came to the window and tapped on the glass. I turned to look at her because she had dimmed the daylight.

'Open the door. I'm getting soaked through.'

'What do you want?' I said, staring at my unfinished page and seeing the words recede.

'I've come to see you. You haven't answered my letters. Look, don't just sit there. I'm getting wet!'

'There's no lock,' I said, and waved my hand in the general direction of the front door.

In a moment I heard the handle turn and the door scraped open. I knelt on the floor, scooping up my neatly typed pages, sorting them into a pile. I did not want Felicity to read what I had written, I wanted no one to see it. I seized the last page from the typewriter, and placed it at the bottom of the pile. I was trying to sort the pages into my carefully devised sequence when Felicity came into the room.

'There's a heap of mail out there,' she said. 'No wonder you haven't replied. Don't you ever look at your post?'

'I've been busy,' I said. I was checking through the numbered pages, fearing that some might have gone out of order. I was wishing I had taken a carbon copy of my work, and kept it in some secret place.

Felicity had come right into the room, and was standing over me.

'I had to come, Peter. You sounded so strange on the phone, and James and I both felt something must be wrong. When you didn't answer the letters, I telephoned Edwin. What are you doing?'

'Leave me alone,' I said. 'I'm busy. I don't want you interrupting me.'

I had numbered each page carefully, but 72 was missing. I searched around for it, and some of the others slipped to the side.

'God, this place is a mess!'

For the first time I looked straight at her. I felt an odd sensation of recognizing her, as if she were somebody I had created. I remembered her from the manuscript: she was there and her name was Kalia. My sister Kalia, two years older than me, married to a man named Yallow.

'Felicity, what do you want?'

'I was worried about you. And I was right to be worried. Look at the state of this room! Do you ever clean it?'

I stood up, holding my manuscript pages. Felicity turned away to go into the kitchen. I was trying to think of somewhere I could hide the manuscript until Felicity left. She had seen it but she could have no idea of what I had been writing, nor how important it was.

There was a clattering of metal and crockery, and I heard a

31

gasp from Felicity. I went to the kitchen door and watched what she was doing. She was standing by the sink, moving the plates and pans to one side.

'Have Edwin and Marge seen the mess you're making of their house?' she said. 'You never could look after yourself, but this is the limit. The whole place stinks!'

She forced open the window and the room filled with the sound of rain.

'Would you like a cup of coffee?' I said, but Felicity just glared at me.

She rinsed her hands under the tap and looked around for a towel. In the end she wiped her hands on her coat; I had lost my towel somewhere. Felicity and James lived in a modern detached house in what had once been a field out-side Sheffield. Now it was an estate, with thirty-six identical houses placed in a neat circular avenue. I had been to the house a few times, once with Gracia, and there was a whole chapter of my manuscript describing the weekend I spent there after they had their first child. I had an impulse to show Felicity the relevant pages, but then I thought she might not appreciate them.

I held the manuscript tight against my chest.

'Peter, what's been happening to you? Your clothes are filthy, the house is a tip, you look as if you haven't eaten a proper meal in weeks. And your fingers!'

'What's wrong with them?'

'You never used to bite your nails.'

I turned away. 'Leave me alone, Felicity. I'm working hard and I want to finish what I'm doing.'

'I'm not going to leave you alone! I had to sort out all Father's business, I had to sell the house, I had to wet-nurse you all through all that legal business you wanted to know nothing about . . . *and* run my own home and look after my family. You did nothing! And what about Gracia?'

'What about her?'

'I've had her to worry about too.'

'Gracia? How have you seen her?'

32

'She got in touch with me when you left her. She wanted to know where you were.'

'But I wrote to her. She didn't answer.'

Felicity said nothing, but there was anger in her eyes.

'How is Gracia?' I said. 'Where is she living?'

'You selfish bastard! You know she nearly died!'

'No she didn't.'

'She overdosed herself. You must have known!'

'Oh yes,' I said. 'Her flatmate told me.'

I remembered then: the girl's pale lips, her shaking hands, telling me to go, not to bother Gracia.

'You know Gracia's got no family. I had to take a week in London, because of you.'

'You should have told me. I was looking for her.'

'Peter, don't lie to yourself! You know you ran away.'

I was thinking about my manuscript, and suddenly I recalled what had happened to page 72. When I was numbering the pages one evening I had made a mistake. I had been meaning to re-number the other pages ever since. I felt relieved that the page was not lost.

'Are you listening to me?'

'Yes, of course.'

Felicity pushed past me and returned to my white room. Here she opened both windows, admitting a cold draught, then went noisily up the wooden stairs. I followed her, feeling a stir of alarm.

'I thought you were supposed to be decorating the place,' Felicity said. 'You've done nothing. Edwin will be furious. He thinks you've nearly finished.'

'I don't care,' I said. I went to the door of the room I had been sleeping in, and closed it. I did not want her to look inside because my magazines were all over the place. I leant against the door to stop her entering. 'Go away, Felicity. Go away, go away.'

'My God, what have you been doing?' She had opened the door of the lavatory, but immediately closed it again.

'It's blocked,' I said. 'I've been meaning to clear it.'

'You're living like an animal.'

'It doesn't matter. No one's here.'

'Let me see the other rooms.'

Felicity advanced on me and tried to grab my manuscript. I clutched it tighter against me, but she had been feinting. She seized the door handle and had the door open before I could stop her.

She stared past me into the room for several seconds. Then she looked at me with contempt.

'Open the window,' she said. 'It stinks in there.' She walked across the landing to inspect the other rooms.

I went into my bedroom to clear up what she had seen. I closed the magazines and shoved them guiltily beneath my sleeping-bag, and kicked my soiled clothes into a heap in one corner.

Downstairs, Felicity was in my white room, standing by my desk and looking down at it. As I walked in she glanced in a pointed way at my manuscript.

'Can I see those papers, please?'

I shook my head, and clutched them to me.

'All right. You don't have to hold them like that.'

'I can't show them to you, Felicity. I just want you to go away. Leave me alone.'

'OK, just hold on.' She pulled the chair away from the desk, and placed it in the middle of the floor. The room looked suddenly lopsided. 'Sit down, Peter. I've got to think.'

'I don't know what you're doing here. I'm all right. I'm fine. I need to be alone. I'm working.'

But Felicity was no longer listening. She went through into the kitchen and ran some water into the kettle. I sat on the chair and held the manuscript against my chest. I watched her through the door to the kitchen as she held two cups under the tap, and looked around for where I kept the tea. She found my instant coffee instead, and spooned some of it into each cup. While the kettle sat on the gas she started clearing my unwashed pots and pans to one side and filled the sink with water, holding her fingers in the flow.

'Is there no hot water?'

'Yes . . . it's hot.' I could see the steam cascading around her arms.

Felicity turned off the tap. 'Edwin said an immersion heater had been installed. Where is it?'

I shrugged. Felicity found the switch and clicked it on. Then she stood by the sink, her head bowed. She seemed to be shivering.

I had never seen Felicity like this before; it was the first time we had been alone together in years. Perhaps the last time was when we had been living at home, during one of my vacs from university, when she was engaged. Since then James had always been with her, or James and the children. It gave me a new insight into her, and I recalled the difficulty with which I had written of Kalia in my manuscript. The scenes of childhood with her had been amongst the most difficult of all, and those for which the greatest amount of background invention had been necessary.

I watched Felicity as she stood there in the kitchen, waiting for the kettle to boil, and I silently urged her to leave. Her interruption made my need to write even greater than before. Perhaps this had been her unintended role in coming to the house: to disturb me to help me. I wanted her to leave so I could finish what I was doing. I even saw the possibility of yet another draft, one driven deeper into the realms of invention in my quest for a higher truth.

Felicity was staring through the window towards the garden, and some of the tension in the room had faded. I put the manuscript on the floor by my feet.

Felicity said: 'Peter, I think you need help. Will you come and stay with James and me?'

'I can't. I've got to work, I haven't finished what I'm doing.'

'What *are* you doing?' She was looking at me now, leaning back against the window sill.

I tried to think of an answer. I could not tell her everything. 'I'm telling the truth about myself.'

Something moved in her eyes, and with a precognitive insight I sensed what she was going to say.

Chapter Four in my manuscript: my sister Kalia, two years older than me. We were close enough in age to be treated as a twosome by our parents, but far enough apart for real differences between us to be felt. She was always that little bit ahead of me, in school, in staying up late, in going to parties. Yet I caught her up because I was clever at school while she was just pretty, and she never forgave me. As we went through our teens, as we became people, a dividing rift became apparent. Neither of us tried to bridge it, but took up positions within striking distance of each other, the ground falling away between us. Her attitude was usually an assumed knowingness about what I was doing or thinking. Everything was said to be inevitable, nothing I could do would ever surprise her, because either I was completely predictable in her terms or else she had been there before me. I grew up loathing Kalia's knowing smile and experienced laugh, as she tried to place me forever two years behind. And as I told Felicity what I had been writing in my manuscript, I anticipated the same smile, the same dismissive click of the tongue.

I was wrong. Felicity merely nodded and looked away.

'I've got to get you out of this place,' she said. 'Is there nowhere you can go in London?'

'I'm all right, Felicity. Don't worry about me.'

'And what about Gracia?'

'What about her?'

Felicity looked exasperated. 'I can't interfere any more. You ought to see her. She needs you, and she's got no one else.'

'But she left me.'

Chapter Seven in my manuscript, and several chapters that followed: Gracia was Seri, a girl on an island. I had met Gracia on the Greek island of Kos one summer. I had gone to Greece in an attempt to understand why it represented an obscure threat in my life. Greece seemed to me the place other people went to, and fell in love. It was somewhere that was like a sexual rival. Friends returned from package-tour holidays and they had become enraptured, their dreams charged with the thrall of Greece. So I went at last to confront this rival, and there I met Gracia. We travelled around the Aegean islands for a time, sleeping together, then returned to London, where we lost touch with each other. A few months later we met again by chance, as one does in London. We were both haunted by the islands, the pervasive distant rapture. In London we fell in love, and slowly the islands faded. We became ordinary. Now she had become Seri and would be alone in Jethra at the end of the manuscript. Jethra was London, the islands were behind us, but Gracia had overdosed on sleeping tablets and we had split up. It was all in the manuscript, translated to its higher truth. I was tired.

The kettle boiled and Felicity went to make the coffee. There was no sugar, no milk, and nowhere for her to sit. I moved the manuscript pages to the side and gave her the chair. She said nothing for a few minutes, holding the cup of black coffee in her hands and sipping at it.

'I can't keep driving down to see you,' she said.

'I'm not asking you to. I can look after myself.'

'With blocked-up plumbing, no food, all this filth?'

'I don't want the same things as you.' She said nothing, but glanced around at my white room. 'What are you going to tell Edwin and Marge?' I said.

'Nothing.'

'I don't want them here either.'

'It's their house, Peter.'

'I'll clean it up. I'm doing it all the time.'

'You haven't touched the place since you've been here. I'm surprised you haven't caught diphtheria or something, in this mess. What was it like in the hot weather? The place must have stunk to high heaven.'

'I didn't notice. I've been working.'

'So you say. Look, where were you ringing me from? Is there a call-box?'

'Why do you want to know?'

'I'm going to telephone James. I want him to know what's going on here.'

'*Nothing*'s going on here! I just need to be left alone long enough to finish what I'm doing.'

'And then you'll clean up and paint the house and clear the garden?'

'I've been doing bits of it all summer.'

'You haven't, Peter, you know you haven't. It hasn't been touched. Edwin told me what you agreed with him. He was trusting you to get the place cleaned up for them, and it's worse now than it was before you moved in.'

'What about this room?' I said.

'This is the worst slum in the place!'

I was shocked. My white room was the focus of my life in the house. Because it had become what I imagined, it was central to everything I was doing. The sun dazzled against the newly painted walls, the rush matting was pleasantly abrasive against my naked feet, and every morning when I came down from sleeping I could smell the freshness of paint. I always felt renewed and recharged by my white room, because it was a haven of sanity in a life become muddled. Felicity threw this in doubt. If I looked at the room in the way she obviously did . . . yes, I had not yet actually got around to painting it. The boards were bare, the plaster was cracked and bulging with fungus, and mildew clung around the window frames.

But this was Felicity's failure, not mine. She was perceiving it wrongly. I had learnt how to write my manuscript by observing my white room. Felicity saw only narrow or actual truth. She was unreceptive to higher truth, to imaginative coherence, and she would certainly fail to understand the kinds of truth I told in my manuscript.

'Where's the call-box, Peter? Is it in the village?'

'Yes. What are you going to say to James?'

'I just want to tell him I got here safely. He's looking after the children this weekend, in case you were wondering.'

'Is it a weekend?'

'Today's Saturday. Do you mean you don't know?'

'I hadn't thought about it.'

Felicity finished her coffee and took the cup to the kitchen. She collected her handbag, then went through my white room towards the front door. I heard her open it, but then she came back.

'I'll get some lunch. What would you like?'

'Anything at all.'

Then she was gone, and at once I picked up my manuscript. I found the page I had been working on when Felicity arrived; I had written only two and a half lines, and the white space beneath seemed recriminatory of me. I read the lines but they made no sense to me. The longer I worked I had found that my typing-speed increased to the point where I could write almost as fast as I could think. My style was therefore loose and spontaneous, depending for its development on the whim of the moment. In the time Felicity had been at the house I had lost my train of thought.

I read back over the two or three pages before my enforced abandonment of it, and at once I felt more confident. Writing something was rather like the cutting of a groove on a gramophone record: my thoughts were placed on the page, and to read back over them was like playing the record to hear my thoughts. After a few paragraphs I discovered the momentum of my ideas.

Felicity and her intrusion were forgotten. It was like finding my real self again. Once I was submerged in my work it was as if I became whole again. Felicity had made me feel mad, irrational, unstable.

I put the unfinished page to one side and inserted a clean sheet in the typewriter. I quickly copy-typed the two and a half lines, and I was poised ready to continue.

But I stopped, and it was in the same place as before: 'For a moment I thought I knew where I was, but when I looked back—'

When I looked back at what?

I read back over the preceding page, trying to hear the recording of my thoughts. The scene was the build-up to my climactic row with Gracia, but through Seri and Jethra it had become distanced. The layers of my realities momentarily confused me. In the manuscript it was not an argument at all, more an impasse between the way two people interpreted the world. What had I been trying to say?

I thought back to the real row. We were in Marylebone Road, on the corner with Baker Street. It was raining. The argument blew up from nowhere, ostensibly some trivial disagreement about whether to see a film or spend the evening at my flat, but in reality the tensions had been there for days. I was cold and feeling angry, and disproportionately conscious of the cars and lorries accelerating away from the lights, their tyres noisy on the wet road. The pub by Baker Street Station had just opened, but to get there meant we had to cross the road by the pedestrian underpass. Gracia was a claustrophobe; it was raining; we started shouting. I left her there and never saw her again.

How had I been intending to deal with this? I would have known that before Felicity arrived; everything about the text spoke of an anticipated continuity.

Felicity's arrival had been doubly intrusive. Apart from interrupting me, she had imposed different ideas about perceived truth.

For instance, she had brought new information about Gracia. I knew that Gracia had taken an overdose after our row, but it had not been important. Once before in our relationship, Gracia had taken a small overdose after an argument; even she had said later that it was a way of drawing attention to herself. Then during that chilling doorstep argument with her flatmate, the importance of it had been diminished by the girl. Through her dislike of me, through her evident contempt, the bitter information had been passed, but minimized somehow; it was not for me to worry about it. I took it at face value. Perhaps even then Gracia had been in hospital. Felicity told me she had nearly died.

But the truth, the higher truth, was that I had evaded it. I had not wanted to know. Felicity made me know. Gracia had made what was probably a serious attempt on her life.

I could, in my manuscript, describe a Gracia who drew attention to herself; I did not know a Gracia who would make a serious effort to kill herself.

Because Felicity had revealed a side of Gracia's character I had never detected before, did it also mean that there were other parts of my life where I made similar failures of judgement? How much truth was I capable of telling?

Then there was the source, Felicity herself. In my life she was not an impartial figure. It was part of her tactic to me, as it always had been, to present herself as maturer, wiser, more sensible, more practised in life. From the time we had played together as children she had always sought dominance over me, whether it was the temporary advantage of being slightly bigger than me, or the knowingness, assumed or otherwise, of being in adulthood that little bit more experienced. Felicity arrogated to herself a normality that was deemed superior to mine. While I remained unmarried and lived in rented rooms, she had a family, a house, a bourgeois respectability. Her way of life was not mine, yet she assumed I aspired to it, and because I had not yet achieved it she gave herself the right to be critical.

Her manner since her arrival was entirely consistent with her normal attitude to me: a curious mixture of concern and criticism, misunderstanding not only me but what I was trying to do with my life.

It was all there in Chapter Four, and I thought I had at last dealt with it by writing of it. Yet she had done her damage, and the manuscript had been halted a few pages from the end.

She threw into question everything I had tried to do, and there, at the actual interface, the last words I had written, was the evidence. The sentence lay unfinished on the page: '. . . but when I looked back—'

But what? I typed in, 'Seri was waiting', then promptly crossed it out. It was not what I had intended to say, even if, ironically, those actual words were what I had been going to write. The motivating impulse had died with the sentence.

I glanced back through the bulk of the manuscript. It made a satisfactorily heavy pile: well over two hundred pages of typewritten script. It felt solid in my hand, a proof of my existence.

Now, though, I had to question what I had done. I sought the truth, but Felicity reminded me of its tenuous nature. She could not see my white room.

Suppose someone *disagreed* with my version of the truth?

Felicity certainly would, even assuming I allowed her to read it. And Gracia too, from what Felicity said, would probably remember a different version of the same events. My parents, were they still around, would probably be shocked by some of the things I had said about childhood.

So truth was subjective, but I had never pretended otherwise. The manuscript aspired to be nothing more than an account of my own life, honestly told. I even made no claim for the quality or originality of my life. It was not unusual in any way, except to me. It was all I knew of myself, all I had in the world. No one could disagree with it because events were portrayed in the way I alone had perceived them.

I read the last completed page again, and scanned the two and a half lines once more. I began to sense what I was about to say. Gracia, in her guise as Seri, was at the street corner because—

The outside door banged, as if a shoulder was being rammed against it. I heard the handle rattle, and sounds from outside poured in. Felicity came into the room, laden with a rain-sodden paper carrier bag which she cradled in her arms.

'I'll cook lunch, but after that you'd better pack. James says it's best if we go back to Sheffield tonight.'

I stared at her incredulously, not because of what she said but in amazement at her timing. It beggared belief that she should twice interrupt me at precisely the same place.

I looked down at the retyped page. It was in every way identical to the one it had replaced.

Slowly, I wound it out of the typewriter carriage, and put it in its place at the bottom of the manuscript.

I sat silently while Felicity moved about the kitchen. She had bought an apron in the village. She washed the dirty dishes, put some chops on to cook.

When we had eaten I sat quietly at the table, retreating from Felicity with her plans and opinions and concern. Her normality was an infusion of madness into my life.

I would be fed and bathed and brought back to health. It was Father's death that had done it. I had flipped. Not much, according to Felicity, but I had nevertheless flipped. I was not able to care for myself, so she would take over. I would see by her example what I was denying myself. We would make weekend forays to Edwin's cottage, she and I and James, and the children too, and we would bustle about with brooms and paint brushes, and James and I would clear the overgrown garden, and in no time at all we would make the house habitable, and then Edwin and Marge would come and see it. When I was better we would all visit London, she and I and James, but perhaps not the children this time, and we would see Gracia, and the two of us would be left together to do whatever the two of us needed to do. I would not be allowed to flip again. I would visit Sheffield every two or three weeks, and we would go for long walks on the moors, and perhaps I should even travel abroad. I liked Greece, didn't I? James could get me a job in Sheffield, or in London if I really wanted it, and Gracia and I would be happy together and get married and have—

I said: 'What are you talking about, Felicity?'

'Were you listening to what I said?'

'Look, it's stopped raining.'

'Oh God! You're impossible!'

She was smoking a cigarette. I imagined the smoke drifting about my white room, settling on the new paintwork, yellowing it. It would reach the pages of my manuscript, discolouring those too, setting down a layer of Felicity's influence.

The manuscript was like an unfinished piece of music. The fact of its incompleteness was bigger than its existence. Like a dominant seventh chord it sought resolution, a final tonic harmony.

Felicity started to clear away the plates, clattering them in the kitchen sink, so I picked up my manuscript and headed for the stairs.

'Are you going to pack?'

'I'm not coming with you,' I said. 'I want to finish what I'm doing.'

She appeared from the kitchen, suds of washing-up liquid dripping from her hands.

'Peter, it's all been decided. You're coming back with me.'

'I've got work to do.'

'What *is* it you've been writing?'

'I told you once.'

'Let me see.' Her soapy hand extended, and I clutched the manuscript tightly.

'No one is ever to see this.'

Then she reacted the way I had expected before. She clicked her tongue, tilted her head quickly back; whatever it was I had done had not been worth doing.

I sat alone on the shambles of my sleeping-bag, holding the manuscript to me. I was near to tears. Downstairs, Felicity had discovered my empty whisky bottles, and was shouting up at me, accusing me of something.

No one would ever read my manuscript. It was the most private thing in the world, a definition of myself. I had told a story, and had crafted it to make it readable, but my intended audience was myself alone.

At last I went downstairs, to discover that Felicity had lined up my empty bottles in the small hallway at the bottom of the stairs. There were so many I had to step over them to get into my white room. Felicity was waiting there.

'Why did you bring in the bottles?' I said.

'You can't leave them in the garden. What have you been trying to do, Peter, drink yourself to death?'

'I've been here for several months.'

'We'll have to get someone to take them away. Next time we come here.'

'I'm not leaving with you,' I said.

'You can have the spare room. The children are out all day, and I'll leave you alone.'

'You never have yet. Why should you start now?'

She had already taken some of my stuff and put it in the back of her car. Now she was closing windows, turning off taps, checking the plugs. I watched her mutely, holding the manuscript to my chest. It was spoiled now forever. The words would have to stay unwritten, the thought remain unfinished. I heard imaginary music in my head: the dominant seventh rang out, forever seeking its cadence. It began to fade, like the run-off track on a gramophone record, music replaced by unplanned crackle. Soon the stylus in my mind would settle in the final, central groove, indefinitely stuck but clicking with apparent meaning, thirty-three times a minute. Eventually someone would have to lift the pick-up arm away, and silence would fall.

CHAPTER 5

Suddenly the ship came into sunlight, and it was as if I had broken with what lay behind me.

I narrowed my eyes against the brilliant sky, and saw that the cloud was some effect of the land, for it ran in a clearly defined east–west line. Ahead, all was clear and blue, promising warmth and calm seas. We headed south, as if propelled by the cold wind blustering from astern.

I felt my senses extend, and awareness spread around me like delicate nerve-cells reaching for sensation. I became aware. I opened.

There was a smell of diesel oil, of salt, of fish. The cold wind reached me, even though I was protected by the ship's superstructure; my city clothes felt thin and inadequate. I breathed in deeply, holding the air for several seconds, as if it might contain cleansing agents that would scrub out my system, refresh my mind, rejuvenate and re-inspire me. Beneath my feet, the deck was vibrating with the grind of engines. I felt the pitching movement of the ship in the swell, but my body was balanced and in tune with it.

I went forward to the prow of the ship, and here I turned to look back at what was behind me.

On the ship itself, a few other passengers huddled on the foredeck. Many of them were elderly couples, sitting or standing together, and most of them wore windcheaters or plastic rainproofs. They seemed to look neither forward nor back, but within. I stared past them, and beyond the ship's superstructure and funnel, where silent sea-birds glided effortlessly, to the coast we had left. The ship had turned slightly since leaving the harbour, and much of Jethra was visible. It seemed to spread along the coast, sheltering behind its quayside cranes and warehouses, filling its broad, estuarine valley. I tried to imagine its daily life continuing without me there to see it, as if everything might cease in my absence. Already, Jethra had become an idea.

Ahead was our first port of call: Seevl, the offshore island I had never visited. It was the island of the Dream Archipelago closest to Jethra, and for all my life had merely been a part of the scenery. Dark, treeless Seevl dominated and blocked the view to the south of Jethra, yet to all but a few people with family connections, Seevl was prohibited to Jethrans. Politically it was part of the Archipelago, and while the war continued neutral territories were inaccessible. Seevl was the first, the nearest; there were ten thousand neutral islands beyond.

I wanted the ship to go faster, because while Jethra lay behind I felt I had not truly started, but the sea at the mouth of the estuary was shallow, and the ship changed course a number of times. We were approaching Stromb Head, the great broken cliffs at the eastern end of Seevl, and once we had rounded this all that lay ahead would be unknown.

I paced the deck, impatient for the journey, cold in the wind and frustrated by my fellow passengers. Before boarding I had imagined that I would be travelling with many people of my own age, but it seemed that almost everyone who was not crew was at retirement age. They appeared to be self-absorbed, heading for their new homes; one of the few methods of legal entry to the islands was by buying a house or apartment on one of a dozen or so listed islands.

At last we rounded the Head and sailed into the bay outside Seevl Town. Jethra disappeared from view.

I was eager for my first sight of an Archipelagan town, for a glimpse of what other islands might be like, but Seevl Town was a disappointment. Grey stone houses rose in uneven tiers on the hillsides surrounding the harbour, looking untidy and drab. It was easy to imagine the place in winter, with the doors and shutters closed, the rain slicking the roofs and streets, people bent against the sea wind, few lights showing. I wondered if they had electricity on Seevl, or running water, or cars. There was no traffic that I could see in the narrow streets surrounding the harbour, but the roads were paved. Seevl Town was quite similar to some of the remote hill villages in the north of Faiandland. The only obvious difference was that smoke was pouring from most of the chimneys; this was a novelty to me, because there were strict anti-pollution laws in Jethra and the rest of Faiandland.

None of the passengers disembarked at Seevl, and our arrival caused little stir in the town. A few minutes after we had tied up at the end of the quay, two uniformed men walked slowly down and boarded the ship. They were Archipelagan immigration officers, a fact which became clear when all passengers were instructed to assemble to Number One deck. To see the other passengers together gave me the opportunity to confirm that there were very few young people aboard. While we were queuing up to have our visas checked I was thinking that the nine days it would take to reach Muriseay, where I was leaving the ship, might turn out to be lonely. There was a youngish woman in the queue behind me – I guessed her age to be in the early thirties – but she was reading a book and seemed incurious about anyone else.

I had seen my voyage to the Dream Archipelago as a break with the past, a new beginning, but already it seemed as if the first few days, at least, would have to be spent in the same sort of half-hearted isolation I had grown used to in Jethra.

I had been lucky. Everyone I knew said it about me, and I even believed it myself. At first there had been parties, but as we all began to appreciate what had happened to me, I found myself more and more cut off from them. When finally the time had come to leave Jethra, to travel to the Dream Archipelago to collect my prize, I was glad to go. I was eager for travel, for the heat of the tropics, for the sound of different languages and a sight of different customs. Yet now it had started I knew that it would be more enjoyable in company.

I said something to the woman behind me, but she merely replied, smiled politely and returned to her book.

I reached the head of the queue and handed over my passport. I had already opened it at the page where the Archipelagan High Commission in Jethra had stamped the visa, but the officer closed it and examined it from the front. The other sat beside him, staring at my face.

The officer looked at my photograph and personal details.

'Robert Peter Sinclair,' he said, looking up at me for the first time.

I confirmed this, but was distracted by the fact that his was the first authentic island accent I had ever heard. He pronounced the name I usually used with a lengthened vowel: 'Peyter'. The only time I had heard the accent before was when actors used it in films; hearing it used naturally gave me the odd feeling that he was putting on the accent to amuse me.

'Where are you travelling to, Mr Sinclair?'

'Muriseay, at first.'

'And where are you going after that?'

'Collago,' I said, and waited for his reaction.

He gave no obvious sign that he had heard. 'May I see your ticket, Mr Sinclair?'

I reached into an inner pocket and produced the sheaf of flimsy dockets issued by the shipping company, but he waved them away.

'Not those. The lottery ticket.'

'Of course,' I said, feeling embarrassed that I had misunderstood, although it was a natural error. I put the shipping tickets away and found my wallet. 'The number has been printed on the visa.'

'I want to see the ticket itself.'

I had sealed it up inside an envelope which was folded into the deepest pocket of my wallet, and it took a few seconds of fumbling to retrieve it. I had been keeping it as a souvenir, and no one had warned me it would be inspected.

I passed it over, and the two immigration officers looked

closely at it, painstakingly comparing the serial number with the one inked into my passport. After what seemed like an over-zealous inspection they passed back the ticket and I returned it to the safety of my wallet.

'What are your intentions after leaving Collago?'

'I don't know yet. I understand there is a long convalescence. I thought I'd make my plans then.'

'Are you intending to return to Jethra?'

'I don't know.'

'All right, Mr Sinclair.' He pressed a rubber date-stamp in the space beneath the visa, closed the passport and slid it back across the desk to me. 'You're a lucky man.'

'I know,' I said conventionally, although I did have my doubts.

The woman behind me stepped forward to the desk, and I walked through to the bar on the same deck. Many of the passengers I had seen in the queue in front of me were already there. I bought myself a large whisky, and stood with the others. I soon struck up a tentative conversation with two people who were heading for a retirement home on Muriseay. Their names were Thorrin and Dellidua Sineham. They came from the university town of Old Haydl in the north of Faiandland. They had bought a luxury apartment overlooking the sea in a village just outside Muriseay Town, and they promised to show me a picture of it when they next came back from their cabin.

They seemed pleasant, ordinary people, who were at pains to explain that a luxury flat in the Archipelago cost no more to buy than a small house at home.

I had been speaking to them for a few minutes when the woman behind me in the queue came into the bar. She glanced briefly in my direction, then went and bought herself a drink. She came to stand near me, and as soon as the Sinehams said they were going down to their cabin, she turned and spoke to me.

'I hope you don't mind,' she said. 'I couldn't help overhearing. Have you really won the lottery?'

I felt myself going on the defensive. 'Yes.'

'I've never known anyone who's won before.'

'Neither have I,' I said.

'I didn't believe it was genuine. I've been buying the tickets for years, but the winning numbers are always so different from mine that I thought it must be crooked.'

'I've only ever bought one ticket. I won straight away. I can still hardly believe it.'

'Could I see the ticket?'

In the weeks since the news that I had won the big prize, innumerable people had asked to see the ticket, as if by looking at it or touching it some of my luck might rub off on them. It was now well thumbed and slightly frayed, but I took it out of my wallet again and showed it to her.

'And you bought this in the ordinary way?'

'Just one of those booths in the park.'

A fine day in late summer: I had been waiting to meet a friend in Seigniory Park, and while I walked up and down I noticed one of the Lotterie-Collago booths. These little make-shift franchise stands were a common sight in Jethra and the other big cities, and presumably also in other parts of the world. The franchises were normally granted to the disabled, or to wounded ex-servicemen. Hundreds of thousands of lottery tickets were sold every month, yet the odd thing was that you rarely saw anyone ever go to the stands and buy one. Nor did people talk openly about buying the tickets, although almost everyone I knew had bought a few tickets at one time or another, and the day the winners were announced you always saw people standing in the streets checking the list in the newspapers.

Like most people I was tempted by the prize, even though the odds against winning were so long that I had never seriously thought about taking part. But on that particular day, idling in the park, I had noticed one of the vendors. He was a soldier, probably ten years younger than me, sitting stiffly and proudly in his wooden booth, wearing a dress uniform. He was badly disfigured by wounds: he was lacking an eye and an arm, and his neck was in a brace. Taken by compassion – the guilty, helpless compassion of a civilian who managed to avoid the draft – I went across and bought one of his tickets. The transaction was conducted quickly and, for my part, furtively, as if it were pornography I was buying, or illegal drugs.

Two weeks later I discovered I had won the major prize. I would receive the athanasia treatment, and afterwards live forever. Shock and surprise, disbelief, extreme jubilation . . . these were a part of my reactions, and even now, a few weeks after the news, I had still not entirely adjusted to the prospect.

It was part of the lore of the Lotterie that winners, even those who won the subsidiary cash prizes, returned to the place where they had bought the winning ticket and gave a present or tribute to the vendor. I did this at once, even before going to register my claim, but the little stall in the park had gone and the other vendors knew nothing about him. Later, I was able to make inquiries through the Lotterie, and discovered that he had died a few days after my purchase; the missing eye, the arm, the broken neck, were just the wounds that showed.

The Lotterie claimed that twenty major prizes were awarded every month, yet one heard remarkably little about the winners. I discovered part of the reason when I registered my claim. The Lotterie counselled utmost discretion in what I said about the prize, and warned me not to talk to the media. Although Lotterie-Collago welcomed the publicity, experience had shown that it put the winners in danger. They told me several cases of publicized winners who had been attacked in the streets; three of them had been killed.

Another reason was that because the lottery was international, only a small proportion of winners came from Faiandland. The tickets were on sale in every country of the northern continent, and throughout the Dream Archipelago.

The Lotterie staff plied me with documents and information sheets, urging me to sign over my affairs to them. I considered for a few days the mountain of business I should have to undertake on my own, then did as they suggested. From that time I had been completely in their hands. They helped me wind up my affairs in Jethra, my job, my flat, the few investments I had, they obtained the visa for me and they booked the passage on the ship. They would continue to manage my affairs until I returned. I had become a helpless functionary for their organization, swept irresistibly towards the athanasia clinic on the island of Collago.

The young woman passed me back my ticket, and I folded it away again inside its envelope, inside my wallet.

'So when will you start the treatment?' she said.

'I don't know. Presumably as soon as I arrive on Collago. But I haven't made up my mind yet.'

'But surely . . . there's no question?'

'No, but I'm just not sure yet.'

I was beginning to feel self-conscious, talking about this in a crowded bar with someone I hardly knew. In the last few weeks I had grown tired of other people's assumptions about the prize, and because I was not as sure about it as they were I had grown equally tired of being defensive.

I had imagined that the long slow voyage through the islands would be time for contemplation, and I was looking forward to having enough solitude to think. The islands would give me space. Yet the ship was still tied up in Seevl Town, and Jethra was just an hour away.

Perhaps the woman sensed my reservedness, because she introduced herself to me. Her name was Mathilde Englen, and she had a doctorate in biochemistry. She had secured a two-year attachment to the agricultural research station on the island of Semell, and she talked for some time about the problems in the islands. Because of the war, food was in short supply in some parts of the Archipelago. Now, though, several previously uninhabited islands were being cleared, and farms established. They were short of many commodities: seed-stock, implements, manpower. Her own speciality was in hybrid cereals, and several were being developed for use in the islands. She was doubtful whether two years would be long enough for the research she had to do, but under the terms of her attachment it could be renewed for a second two-year period.

The bar was filling up as more people were cleared by the immigration officers, and as we had both finished our drinks I suggested that we go for lunch. We were the first to arrive in the dining saloon, but the service was slow and the food was indifferent. The main dish was paqua-leaves stuffed with a spiced mince; hot in flavour it was only lukewarm in temperature. I had eaten in Archipelagan-style restaurants in Jethra, so I was used to the food, but in the city the restaurants had to offer competitive service. On the ship there was no competition. At first disappointed, we saw no point in ruining the day by complaining, and concentrated instead on talking to each other.

By the time we had finished the ship was under way. I went up to the afterdeck and stood by the rail in the sunshine, watching dark Seevl and the distant mainland slipping away behind us.

That night I had a vivid dream about Mathilde, and when I met her in the morning my perception of her had undergone a subtle change.

CHAPTER 6

As the ship sailed further south, and the weather became endlessly warm and sunny, there was no time for contemplating the pros and cons of my prize. I was distracted by the scenery, the unfolding panorama of the islands, and Mathilde was constantly on my mind.

I had not really expected to meet someone on the ship, but from the second day I thought of almost nothing else. Mathilde, I think, was glad of my company, and flattered by my interest in her, but that is as far as it went. I found that I was pursuing her with such single-minded intent that even I became self-conscious about it. I soon ran out of excuses for being with her, because she was the sort of woman who made excuses necessary. Every time I approached her I had to think of some new device: a drink in the bar?, a stroll around the deck?, a few minutes ashore? After these minor excursions she always slipped away with an excuse of her own: a short nap, hair to be washed, a letter to write. I knew she was not interested in me in the way I was interested in her, but that was no deterrent.

In some ways it was inevitable we should spend time together. We were the same age group – she was thirty-one, two years older than myself – and we came from the same sort of Jethran background. She, like me, felt outnumbered by the retirement couples on board with us, but unlike me made friends with several of them. I found her intelligent and shrewd, and, after a few drinks, possessed of an unexpectedly bawdy sense of humour. She was slim and fair-haired, read a lot of books, had been politically active in Jethra (we found we had a friend of a friend in common) and on the one or two occasions we were able to leave the ship briefly, she revealed herself knowledgeable about island customs.

The dream that started it all was one of those rare lucid dreams that are still comprehensible after waking. It was extremely simple. In a mildly erotic way I was on an island with a young woman, readily identified as Mathilde, and we were in love.

When I saw Mathilde in the morning I felt such a surge of spontaneous warmth that I acted as if we had known each other for years, rather than just met briefly the day before. Probably out of surprise, Mathilde responded with almost equal warmth, and before either of us realized it a pattern had been set. From then I pursued her, and she, with tact, firmness and a generous amusement, eluded me.

My other main preoccupation on the ship was my discovery of the islands. I never tired of standing at the rail of the ship to watch the view, and our frequent calls at ports on the way were all rich visual experiences.

The shipping line had fixed an immense, stylized chart on the wall of the main saloon, and this showed the entire Midway Sea and all the principal islands and shipping routes. A first reaction to the chart was the complexity of the Archipelago and the sheer quantity of islands, and amazement that ships' crews could navigate safely. The sea carried a lot of shipping: in a typical day on deck I would see twenty or thirty cargo ships, at least one or two steamers like the one I was on, and innumerable small inter-island ferries. Around some of the larger islands there was traffic of privately owned pleasure boats, and fleets of fishing boats were common sights.

It was generally said that the islands of the Archipelago were impossible to count, although upwards of ten thousand had been named. The whole of the Midway Sea had been surveyed and charted, but quite apart from the inhabited islands, and the larger uninhabited ones, there was a multitude of tiny islets, crags and rocks, many of which appeared and disappeared with the tides.

From the chart I learned that the islands which lay

immediately to the south of Jethra were known as the Torqui Group; the main island, Derril, was one we called at on the third day. Beyond these to the south lay the Lesser Serques. The islands were grouped for administrative and geographical reasons, but each island was, in theory at least, politically and economically independent.

In simple terms, the Midway Sea girdled the world at the equator, but it was larger by far than either of the two continental land masses lying to the north and south of it. In one part of the world, the sea extended to within a few degrees of the South Pole, and in the northern hemisphere the country called Koillin, one of those with which we were presently at war, actually had part of its territory crossing the equator; in general, though, the continents were cool and the islands were tropical.

One of the anecdotal facts taught in schools about the Dream Archipelago, and one which I heard the other passengers repeat many times, was that the islands were so numerous and so close together that from every single island at least another seven could be seen. I never doubted this, except to think it was probably an understatement; even from the relatively low eminence of the ship's deck I could frequently see more than twelve separate islands.

It was extraordinary to reflect that I had spent my life in Jethra without awareness of this totally strange place. Two days' sailing from Jethra and I felt I had travelled to another world, yet I was still closer to home than, say, the mountain passes in the north of Faiandland.

And if I continued to travel, south or west or east through the Archipelago, I could sail for months and still see the same unfolding diversity, impossible to describe, impossible even to absorb when seeing it. Large, small, rocky, fertile, mountainous and flat; these simple variations could be seen in an afternoon, to just one side of the ship. The senses became dulled to the scenic variety, and the imagination took over. I began to see the islands as designs on a painted cyclorama, one hauled smoothly past the ship, endlessly inventive, meticulously fabricated.

But then came our ports of call, confounding the fancy.

Our brief visits to islands were the real regulators of the ship's day. Ports disrupted everything. I soon learned this, and gave up trying to eat or sleep by the clock. The best time to sleep was mid-voyage, because then the ship had a steady rhythm to it, and the food in the restaurant was also better, because then the crew was eating.

The ship was always expected, whether we docked at noon or midnight, and its arrival was obviously an event of some importance. Crowds were generally waiting on the quay, and behind them stood rows of trucks and carts to take away the cargo and mail we brought. Then there was the chaotic exchange of deck passengers, and as they came or left there were always arguments, greetings or farewells, suddenly re-membered last messages shouted to the shore, disrupting our otherwise placid existence. In the ports we were reminded that we were a ship: something that called, something that carried, something from outside.

I always left the ship when I could, and made brief explora-tions of the little towns. My impressions were superficial: I felt like a tourist, unable to see beyond the war memorials and palm trees to the people beyond. Yet the Archipelago was not meant for tourists, and the towns had no guides or currency exchanges, no museums of local culture. On several islands I tried to buy picture postcards to send home, but when at last I found some I discovered that mail to the north could only be sent by special permit. By trial and error I worked out a few things for myself: the usage of the archaic non-decimal currency, the difference between the various kinds of bread and meat on sale, and a rule-of-thumb guide to how prices compared with home.

Mathilde sometimes accompanied me on these expedi-tions, and her presence was enough to blind me to surround-ings. All the time I was with her I knew I was making a mistake, yet she continued to attract me. I think we were both relieved, although in my case it was a perverse kind of relief, when on the fourth day we came to Semell Town and she disembarked. We went through the motions of making an arrangement to meet again, even though her voice was glib with insincerity. When she was ashore I stood by the ship's rail and watched her walk along the concrete wharf, her pale hair shining in the sunlight. A car was waiting to meet her. I saw a man load her bags into the back, and before she climbed in she turned towards the ship. She waved briefly to me, then she was gone.

Semell was a dry island, with olive trees growing on the rocky hills. Old men sat in the shade; I heard a donkey braying somewhere behind the town.

After Semell I began to tire of the ship and its slow, devious voyage through the islands. I was bored with the noises and routines of the ship: the rattle of chains, the constant sound from the engine and the pumps, the voluble dialect conversations of the deck passengers. I had given up eating on the ship, and now bought fresh bread, cooked meat and fruit whenever we stopped at an island. I drank too much. I found the few conversations I had with other passengers repetitive and predictable.

I had boarded the ship in a state of extreme receptivity, open to the new experience of travel, to the discovery of the Archipelago. Now, though, I began to miss my friends at home, and my family. I remembered the last conversation I had had with my father, the night before I left Jethra: he was against the prize and feared that as a result of it I would choose to stay on in the islands.

I was abandoning much for the sake of a lottery ticket, and I still questioned what I was doing.

Part of the answer lay in the manuscript I had written a couple of summers before. I had brought it with me, stuffed into my leather holdall, but I had packed it without re-reading it, just as I had never re-read it since leaving the cottage. The writing of my life, of telling myself the truth, had been an end in itself.

Since that long summer in the Murinan Hills overlooking Jethra I had entered a muted phase of life. There had been no upsets, few passions. I had had lovers, but they had been superficial relationships, and I had made a number of new acquaintances but no new friends. The country had recovered from the recession that put me out of a job, and I had gone back to work.

But writing the manuscript had not been a wasted effort. The words still held the truth. It had become a kind of prophecy, in the pure sense of being a teaching. I therefore had a feeling that somewhere in those pages would be some kind of internal guidance about the lottery prize. It was this I needed, because there was no logical reason for refusing it. My doubts came from within.

But as the ship moved into hotter latitudes, my mental and physical sloth increased. I left my manuscript in my cabin, I postponed any thoughts about the prize.

On the eighth day we came to open sea, with the next group of islands a faint darkening on the southern horizon. Here was one of the geographical boundaries and beyond it lay the Lesser Serques, with Muriseay at their heart.

We made only one islandfall in the Serques before Muriseay, and by the early afternoon of the next day the island was in sight.

After the confusion of islands behind us, arriving off Muriseay was like once again approaching the coast of a continent. It seemed to stretch forever into the distance beyond the coast. Blue-green hills ran back from the coastline, dotted with white-painted villas and divided up by winding, curving highways that strode across the valleys on great viaducts. Beyond the hills, almost on the horizon as it seemed, I could see brown-purple mountains, crowned with cloud.

At the very edge of the sea, following the coastline, was a ribbon development of apartments and hotels, modern, tall, balconied. The beaches below were crowded with people, and brightly coloured by huge sunshades and cafeterias. I borrowed a pair of binoculars and stared at the beaches as we passed. Muriseay, seen thus, was like the stereotype of the Archipelago depicted in films, or described in pulp fiction. In the Faiandland culture the Dream Archipelago was synonymous with a leisured class of sun-loving émigrés, or the indigenous islanders. Depictions of the sort of small islands I had been passing were rare; there was more plot material in a heavily populated place like Muriseay. Romantic novels and adventure films were frequently set in a never-never world of Archipelagan exotica, complete with casinos, speed-boats and jungle hide-outs. The natives were villainous, corruptible or simple; the visiting class either wealthy and self-indulgent, or scheming madmen. Of course, I recognized the fiction in this fiction, but it was nevertheless potent and memorable.

So in seeing at last an island of real economic substance I viewed it with a kind of double vision. One part of me was still receptive and involved, trying to see and understand everything in objective terms. But another part, deeper and more irrational, could not help but see this concrete-slab coastline of Muriseay with the received glamour of popular culture.

The beaches were therefore crowded with the indulgent rich, tanning themselves in the golden sunshine of Muriseay's legendary heat. Everyone was a tax-exile, philanderer or remittance man; the modern yachts moored a short distance offshore were the scenes of nightly gambling and murder, a place for playboys and high-class whores, corrupt and fascinating. Behind the modern apartment blocks I visualized the squalid hovels of the peasant islanders, parasitic on the visitors, contemptuous of them, yet servile. Just like the films, just like the cheap paperbacks that filled the bookstalls of Jethra.

Thorrin and Dellidua Sineham were on deck, standing beside the rail further down the ship. They too were gazing interestedly across at the shore, pointing at the coastal buildings, talking together. The tattily romantic version of Muriseay faded, and I walked down and lent them the glasses.

Those villas and apartments would be mostly occupied by decent, ordinary people like the Sinehams. I stayed with them for a while, listening to them talk excitedly of their new home and life. Thorrin's brother and his wife were already here, and they were in the same village, and they had been getting the apartment ready.

Later, I went back to my place alone and watched the terrain change as we moved further south. Here the hills came down to the sea, breaking as cliffs, and the blocks of flats were hidden from view; soon we were passing shores as wild as any I had seen in the islands. The ship was close inshore, and through the glasses I could see the flash of birds in the trees that grew to the edge of the cliffs.

We reached what I first assumed was the mouth of a river, and the ship turned and headed upstream. Here the water was deep and calm, a stupendous bottle green, the sun shafting down through it. On either bank was dense jungle of monstrous aroids, unmoving in the humid silence.

After a few minutes in this airless channel it became clear that we had turned inland between an offshore island and the mainland, because it opened out into a vast, placid lagoon, on the far side of which was the sprawl of Muriseay Town.

Now, with the end of the long voyage imminent, I felt a strange sense of insecurity. The ship had become a symbol of safety, the object that had fed me and carried me, that I returned to after venturing ashore. I had grown used to the boat, and knew my way about it like I knew the apartment I had left in Jethra. To leave it would be to take a second step into strangeness. We impose familiarity on our surroundings; from the deck of the ship the scenery merely passed, but now I had to disembark, set foot in the islands.

It was a return to the inner-directed self I had temporarily lost when I boarded the ship. Unaccountably I felt nervous of Muriseay, yet there was no logical reason for this. It was just a transit, a place to change ships. Also, I was expected in Muriseay. There was an office of the Lotterie-Collago here, and the next leg of the journey was one they would arrange.

I stood in the prow of the ship until it had docked, then went back to find the Sinehams. I wished them luck, said goodbye, then went down to my cabin to collect my holdall.

A few minutes later I was heading up the quay, looking for a taxi to take me into town.

CHAPTER 7

The offices of Lotterie-Collago were in a shaded side street about five minutes' drive from the harbour. I paid off the taxi driver and he drove quickly away, the dusty old saloon car bouncing noisily on the cobbles. At the far end of the street the car turned into the harsh brilliance of sunlight, joining the chaos of traffic that roared past.

The offices were like a large showroom, fronting the street with two plate glass windows. Behind, there were no lights on but at the far end, away from the doors and behind a small forest of potted plants, there was a desk and some cabinets. A young woman sat there, looking through a magazine.

I tried the doors, but they were locked. The young woman heard me, looked up and acknowledged me. I saw her take down some keys.

I was still only a few minutes away from the lulling, lazy routines of shipboard life, but already Muriseay Town had instilled in me an acute sense of culture shock. Nothing I had seen in any of the small islands had prepared me for this busy, hot and noisy city, nor was it like anywhere I knew at home.

Muriseay, experienced raw, seemed like a chaos of cars, people and buildings. Everyone moved with astonishing yet mysterious purpose. Cars were driven faster than anyone would have dared in Jethra, accompanied by heavy braking, sharp cornering and constant use of the horn. Street signs, in two languages, obeyed no apparent overall system, nor even consistency in their use. Shops in the streets were open to the world, quite unlike the prim emporia of Jethra's main boulevards, and their goods spilled out in a colourful mess across the pavements. Discarded boxes and bottles were all over the place. People lounged around in the sun, lying in the grassy squares, leaning against the walls of buildings or sitting under the bright canopies of the open-air bars and restaurants. One street had been completely blocked by what appeared to be an impromptu football match, causing my driver to swear at me and reverse violently and dangerously into the main street. Further complicating the city were the buses, which hurtled down the centres of the carriageways, passengers bulging from windows and doorways, and claiming right of way by sheer nerve alone. The layout of the city seemed to have no overall design, being a warren of criss-crossing narrow streets between the ramshackle brick buildings; I was used to the stately avenues of Jethra, built, according to tradition, suffi- ciently wide for a full company of Seigniorial troops to march abreast.

All this was glimpsed and absorbed in the few minutes I was in the taxi, whirled through the streets in a sort of car I had only ever before seen in movies. It was a huge, battered old saloon, spattered with dust and dried mud, the wind- screen plastered with dead insects. Inside, the seats were covered with synthetic fur, and were far too soft for comfort; one sank into them with a feeling of excessive and cloying luxury. The fascia of the car was tarnished chrome and peel- ing wood veneer; the inside of the windscreen was stuck all over with photographs of women and children. A dog lay asleep on the back seat, and shrilling, distorted pop music was blasting from the radio. The driver steered with only one hand on the wheel, the other out of the window and clasp- ing the roof, slapping in time with the music. The car swooped through corners, setting up a banging noise from the suspension and a rocking motion inside.

The whole city was a new kind of sensation: a feeling of careless indifference to many things I took for granted – quiet, safety, laws, consideration towards others. Muriseay Town seemed to be a city in eternal conflict with itself. Noise, heat, dust, white light; a teeming, shouting and colliding city, uneven and untidy, yet charged with life.

But I did not feel unsafe, and neither was I excited, except in a way best described as cerebral. The taxi driver's careering progress through the milling traffic was something that took the breath away, but it was in a larger context of confusion and disorder. A car driven like that in Jethra would certainly crash within a few moments, if not stopped by the police, but in Muriseay Town everything was at the same level of chaos. It was as if I had somehow crossed over into another universe, one where the degree of activity had been perceptibly increased: reality's tuner had been adjusted, so noises were louder, colours were brighter, crowds were more dense, heat was greater, time moved faster. I felt a curious sense of diminished responsibility, as if I were in a dream. I could not be hurt or endangered in Muriseay, because I was protected by the dangerous chaos of normality. The car would not crash, those ancient leaning buildings would never fall, the crowds would always skip out of the way of the traffic, because we were in a place of higher response, a place where mundane disasters simply never occurred.

It was an exhilarating, dizzying feeling, one that told me that to survive here I had to adjust to the local *ad hoc* rules. Here I could do things I never dared at home. Sober responsibilities were behind me.

So as I stood by the Lotterie-Collago office, waiting for the doors to be unlocked, I was still in the early throes of this new awareness. On the ship, receptive to the new though I had thought myself to be, in fact I had been moving in a protective bubble of my own life. I had brought attitudes and expectations with me. After just a few minutes in Muriseay the bubble had been popped, and sensations were still pouring in on me.

The lock rattled and one of the two doors swung open.

The young woman said nothing, but stared at me.

'I'm Peter Sinclair,' I said. 'I was told to come here as soon as I landed.'

'Come in.' She held the door open, and I walked in to the shock of air conditioning. The office was dry, refrigerated, and the chill of it made me cough. I followed the girl to her desk.

'I've got you down as Robert Sinclair. Is that you?'

'Yes. I don't use my first name.'

My eyes too had needed to adjust to the relative dimness of the office, because when she got to her desk and faced me, I noticed the young woman's appearance for the first time. She bore a remarkable physical similarity to Mathilde Englen.

'Won't you sit down?' She indicated the visitors' chair.

I did as she said, making a small production of putting my holdall to one side. I needed a few moments to collect myself. The resemblance between her and Mathilde was extraordinary! Not in detail, but in colouring, hair, body shape. I supposed that if the two women could be seen together it would not be so obvious, but for the last few days I had been holding a mental image of Mathilde and suddenly to meet this girl came as a distinct surprise. The generalities of my memory image were fulfilled exactly.

She was saying: 'My name is Seri Fulten, and I am your Lotterie representative here. Any help I can give you while you're here, or—'

It was the company speech, and it drifted over and past me. She was shaped in the company mould: she was wearing the same bright red uniform of skirt and jacket I had seen on the staff in the Jethran Lotterie office, the sort of clothes that are worn in hotel receptions, car rental firms, shipping offices. It was attractive in a bland way, but sexless and multinational. Her one gesture to individuality was a small badge pinned to her lapel: it had the face of a well-known pop singer.

I did find her attractive, but then the company image supposed I would. Beyond that, the coincidence with Mathilde was setting up distracting resonances.

I said, when she had finished her patter: 'Have you been waiting here just for me?'

'Somebody had to. You're two days late.'

'I'd no idea.'

'It's all right. We contacted the shipping line. I haven't been sitting here for two days.'

I judged her to be in her late twenties, and either married or living with someone. No ring, but that meant nothing anymore.

She opened a drawer in the desk and brought out a neatly packaged folder of papers.

'You can have this,' she said. 'It tells you everything you need to know about the treatment.'

'Well, I haven't quite decided yet—'

'Then read this.'

I took the file from her and glanced through the contents. There were several glossily printed pages of photographs, presumably of the athanasia clinic, and further on a series of questions and answers printed out. Going through the sheets gave me the chance to look away from her. What had happened? Was I seeing Mathilde in her? Unsuccessful with one woman, I find another who happens to look rather like her, and so transfer my attention?

With Mathilde I had always felt I was making a mistake, yet I went on with the pursuit; she, nobody's fool, had deflected me. But suppose I *had* been making a mistake, that I had mistaken Mathilde for someone else? In a reversal of causality, I had thought Mathilde was this girl, the Lotterie rep?

While I had been ostensibly going through the photographs, Seri Fulten had opened what I presumed was the Lotterie file on me.

She said: 'I see you're from Faiandland. Jethra.'

'Yes.'

'My family came from there originally. What's it like?'

'Parts of it are very beautiful. The centre, round the Seignior's Palace. But they've built a lot of factories in the last few years, and they're ugly.' I had no idea what to say. Until I left Jethra I had never really thought about it, except as the place I lived in and took for granted. I said, after a pause: 'I've already forgotten it. For the last few days all I've been aware of is the islands. I'd no idea there were so many.'

'You'll never leave the islands.'

She said it in the same colourless way she had recited the company speech, but I sensed that this was a different kind of slogan.

'Why do you say that?'

'It's just a saying. There's always somewhere new to go, another island.'

The short fair hair, the skin that showed pale through the superficiality of tan. I suddenly remembered finding Mathilde on the boat deck, sunbathing with her chin turned up to avoid a shadow on her neck.

'Can I get you a drink?' Seri said.

'Yes, please. What have you got?'

'I'll have to look. The cabinet's usually locked.' She opened another drawer, looking for a key. 'Or we could check you into your hotel, and have a drink there.'

'I'd prefer that,' I said. I had been travelling too long; I wanted to dump my luggage.

'I'll have to check the reservation. We were expecting you two days ago.'

She picked up the phone, listened to the receiver then worked the rest up and down a few times. She frowned, and drew in her breath sharply. After a few seconds I heard the line click, and she started dialling.

The number at the other end was a long time answering, and she sat with the receiver against her ear, staring across the desk at me.

I said: 'Do you work here alone?'

'There's usually the manager and two other girls. We're supposed to be closed today. It's a public holiday – Hello!' I heard a voice at the other end, sounding tinnily across the quiet showroom. 'Lotterie-Collago. I'm checking the reservation for Robert Sinclair. Do you still have it?'

She grimaced at me, and stared out of the window with that vacant expression worn by people waiting on the phone.

I got up and sauntered about the office. Hanging on the walls were a number of colour photographs of the Lotterie's clinic on Collago; I recognized some of the pictures from my glance through the brochure. I saw clean modern buildings, a number of white-painted chalets set out on a lawn, flower-beds, jagged mountains in the distance behind. Everyone seemed to be smiling. Several photographs were of lottery winners arriving at or leaving the island, handshakes and smiles, arms around shoulders. Shots of the interiors revealed the antiseptic cleanliness of a hospital with the luxurious appointments of an hotel.

I was reminded of the sort of photographs you sometimes saw in brochures for holidays. One I remembered in particular: a ski-resort in the mountains of northern Faiandland. It had exactly the same overstated atmosphere of jollity and friendship, the same garish colours from a salesman's samples book.

At the far end of the office was a waiting area, with several comfortable chairs surrounding a low, glass-topped table. On this there was a package of lottery tickets, placed there to be found and looked at. I picked them up and flicked through them. Each one had been neatly defaced with an overprinted legend (SAMPLE, NOT FOR SALE), but in every other respect they were the same as the one that had won the prize for me.

At that moment I managed to identify at last the vague feeling of unease I had had ever since winning.

The lottery was something that existed for other people. I was the wrong person to have won.

Lotterie-Collago gave athanasia treatment as its principal prize: genuine immortality, medically guaranteed. The clinic claimed a success rate of 100 per cent; no one who ever received the treatment had yet died. The oldest recipient was said to be one hundred and sixty-nine years old, had the physical appearance of a woman in her mid-forties, and, it was claimed, was in full possession of all her faculties. She was often featured in the Lotterie's television advertising: playing tennis, dancing, solving crosswords.

Before all this I had sometimes made the sardonic

comment that if eternal life meant a century and a half of crossword puzzles, I was content to die of natural causes.

There was also a feeling I had never entirely thrown off, that the award always went to the wrong kind of person: in short, it went to people who entered lotteries, who were deserving only of luck.

In spite of what I now knew was the Lotterie's advice, prize-winners were sometimes given a great deal of publicity. More often than not, under media examination these winners turned out to be dull, ordinary people from narrow backgrounds, who lacked ambition or inspiration, and who were patently incapable of envisaging themselves living forever. In interviews they would usually come out with homilies about devoting their new lives to good or public works, but the sameness of these sentiments seemed to indicate that they had been prompted by the Lotterie. This aside, their main ambition was generally to see their grandchildren grow up, or take a long holiday or retire from work and settle down in a nice house somewhere.

Although I had derided the prosaic aspirations of such innocent winners, now that I had become one myself I found I had not much more to offer. All I had done to deserve the prize was to take temporary, and ultimately meaningless, pity on a crippled soldier in a park. I was no less dull or ordinary than any of the other prize-winners. I had no use for a prolonged life. Before the lottery I had lived a safe, uncontroversial life in Jethra, and after the athanasia treatment I should probably continue it. According to the publicity, I could expect to do so for at least another century and a half, and possibly as much as four or five hundred years.

Athanasia increased the quantity of life, but offered nothing for the quality.

Even so, who would turn down a chance of it? I feared death rather less now than I had done when I was an adolescent; if death was a loss of consciousness then it held no horrors. But I had always been lucky with my health, and like many people who escape illness I dreaded pain and disability, and the prospect of actually dying, of going through a helpless decline, suffering pain and immobility, was something I could not think about without shrinking away. The athanasia clinic gave treatment that totally cleansed the system, that controlled cell regeneration indefinitely. It gave immunity from the degenerative diseases like cancer and thrombosis, it protected against viral diseases and it ensured the retention of all muscular and mental abilities. After the treatment, I should remain forever at my present physical age of twenty-nine.

I wanted that; I could not deny it. Yet I knew the unfairness of the Lotterie system, both from my own short experience of it and from the many passionate criticisms that had been voiced in public. It was unfair; I knew I was unworthy of it.

But who was worthy? The treatment effectively provided a cure for cancer, but hundreds of thousands of people still died of the disease every year. The Lotterie said that cancer could not be cured, except as a by-product of their treatment. The same was true of heart disease, of blindness, of senility, of ulcers, of a dozen serious ailments that marred or shortened the lives of millions of people. The Lotterie said the treatment, expensive and difficult, could not be given to everyone. The only fair way, the only unquestionably democratic and undiscriminating way, was by lottery.

Hardly a month passed without the Lotterie being criticized. Were there not, for instance, genuinely deserving cases? People who had devoted their lives to the care of others? Artists, musicians, scientists, whose work would be curtailed by the inevitable decline? Religious leaders, peacemakers, inventors? Names were frequently put forward by the media, by politicians, all intending to further the apparent quality of the world.

Under such pressure, the Lotterie had several years before proposed a scheme designed to counter the criticism. A panel of international judges was appointed to sit annually, and every year they nominated a small number of people who, in their opinion, were worthy of the elixir of life. The Lotterie then undertook to provide the treatment.

To the surprise of most ordinary people, almost all of these laureates declined the treatment. Notable amongst them was an eminent author named Visker Deloinne.

As a result of his nomination, Deloinne later wrote an impassioned book called *Renunciation*. In this he argued that to accept athanasia was to deny death, and as life and death were inextricably linked it was a denial of life too. All his novels, he said, had been written in the knowledge of his inevitable death, and none could or would have been written without it. He expressed his life through literature, but this was in essence no different from the way other people expressed their own lives. To aspire to live forever would be to acquire living at the expense of life.

Deloinne died of cancer two years after *Renunciation* was published. It was now recognized as his greatest work, his highest literary achievement. I had read it while still at school. It had had a profoundly moving effect on me, yet here I was, halfway to Collago, halfway to eternal living.

At the other end of the office I heard Seri put down the telephone receiver, and I turned towards her.

'They had to let your reservation go,' she said. 'But they've booked you into another hotel.'

'Can you tell me how to find it?'

She picked up a raffia basket from the floor, and placed it on the desk in front of her. She took off her red jacket, and laid it down between the handles.

'I'm leaving now. I'll show you where it is.'

She locked the desk drawers, checked that an inner door was closed, and we went out into the road. Heat assaulted me, and I looked around and above me in a reflexive gesture, thinking stupidly that some hot-air vent must be blowing out from above. It was just the climate, the tropical humidity. I was wearing only light slacks and a short-sleeved shirt, but with my holdall I felt totally unadapted to this place.

We walked to the main street and headed through the

crowds. The shops and doorways were open, lights were blazing, and the traffic rushed past in a bedlam of noise and speed. It was all vested with a *purpose* I had never noticed at home; everyone seemed to know where they were going, and obeying the chaotic rules of this unreal place.

Seri led the way along the densely crowded pavements, passing restaurants, coffee shops, strip clubs, bookstalls, cinemas. Everyone seemed to be jostling or shouting, no one moved slowly or silently. On several corners, open-air kitchens were selling skewered meat on rice, served in flimsy paper wrappers. Meat, bread and vegetables lay bare to the hot air in the open-fronted shops, attracting hundreds of flies. Transistor radios, strapped to the wooden uprights of stalls, gave crackling, distorted pop music to the uproar. A water truck roared down the road, sluicing the street and pavement with total disregard for anyone there; afterwards, vegetable peelings collected in the gutters. Through it all, a sickly, pervasive scent, far too sweet and unwholesome: perhaps it was rancid meat, or incense burned to smother the smell of dung. It had an intangible 'hot' quality, as if the climate brought the perfume seeping from the walls and streets themselves.

Within a few moments I was drenched with sweat, and it was almost as if the humid air were condensing on me. I paused once or twice to switch hands on my holdall. When we reached the hotel we went straight inside, into the welcome cold of air conditioning.

Checking in was a brief formality, but before giving me the room key, the clerk asked to see my passport. I handed it over to him. He placed it, without looking at it, behind the counter.

I waited for a few moments, but there was no sign it would reappear.

'What do you want the passport for?' I said.

'It has to be registered with the police. You may collect it on your departure.'

Something made me suspicious, so I moved over to where Seri was waiting.

I said to her: 'What's going on?'

'Have you got a ten-credit note?'

'I think so.'

'Give it to him. Ancient local custom.'

'Extortion, you mean.'

'No . . . it's just cheaper than the police. They'll charge you twenty-five.'

I returned to the desk, passed over the bill and got my key and passport in exchange; no regrets, no explanations, no apology. The clerk impressed a rubber stamp beside the Archipelago visa.

'Are you going to stay and have a drink with me?' I said to Seri.

'Yes, but don't you want to unpack?'

'I'd like a shower. That'll take about a quarter of an hour. Shall we meet in the bar?'

She said: 'I think I'll go home and change my clothes. I live just a short way from here.'

I went up to the room, lay on the bed for a few minutes, then stripped off my clothes and showered. The water was pale brown and felt very hard; the soap barely lathered. Some twenty minutes later, refreshed and wearing clean clothes, I went down to the bar at street level. This was actually outside the hotel, opening on to a side road, but there was a glass canopy and a number of high-pressure fans kept the air cool around the tables. Darkness had fallen while I was inside. I ordered a large beer, and Seri arrived shortly afterwards. She had changed into a flared, loose-fitting skirt and semi-transparent cheesecloth blouse, looking less like a company stereotype and more like a woman. She ordered a glass of iced wine, sitting across the table from me, looking relaxed and very young.

She asked me a number of questions about myself: how I had come to buy the lottery ticket, what I did for a living, where my family came from, and various other questions that people ask each other when they have just met. I was having difficulty making her out. I was unable to tell whether these harmless personal questions were prompted by polite, genuine or professional interest. I had to keep reminding myself that she was my Lotterie-Collago contact here, that she was just doing her job. After the celibacy of the ship, aggravated by Mathilde's evasions, it was disconcerting to be sitting casually with such an attractive and friendly woman. I could not help looking at her appraisingly: she had a small, neat figure, and a pretty face. She was obviously intelligent, but holding something back, keeping a distance, and I found it very enticing. She made conversation with apparent interest, leaning slightly towards me, smiling a lot, but there was also a sense of withdrawal in her. Perhaps she was on overtime, hosting a company client; perhaps she was merely being cautious with a man she had only just met.

She told me she had been born on Seevl, the sombre island that lay offshore from Jethra. Her parents were Jethrans but they had moved to Seevl just before the war broke out. Her father had been an administrator at a theological college there, but she had left home in her early teens. Since then, she had been moving about the islands, drifting from one job to another. Both parents were now dead. She said little, changed the subject quickly.

We had two more drinks each, and I was starting to feel hungry. The prospect of spending the rest of the evening with Seri was appealing, so I asked her where we could find a good restaurant.

But she said: 'I'm sorry, I've got a date this evening. You can eat at the hotel. It's all on the Lotterie. Or any of the Salayan restaurants around here. They're all excellent. Have you tried Salay food?'

'In Jethra.' It was probably not the same, but then eating alone would not be the same, either.

I regretted suggesting the meal because it had obviously reminded her of what she was doing for the rest of the evening. She drank the remainder of her wine, then stood up.

'I'm sorry I have to leave. It was nice to get to know you.'

'Same here,' I said.

'Tomorrow morning, meet me at the office. I'll try to book you a passage to Collago. A ship leaves about once a week, but you've just missed one. There are a number of different routes. I'll see what's available.'

For a moment I glimpsed the other Seri, the one who wore the uniform.

I confirmed I would be there, and we said goodnight. She walked off into the perfumed night and did not look back.

I ate alone in a crowded, noisy Salay restaurant. The table was set for two, and I felt more isolated than I had done since leaving home. It was weak and stupid of me to fix on the first two women I met, but I had done so and there was nothing I could reverse. Seri's company had successfully rid me of thoughts of Mathilde, but she seemed set to become a second Mathilde. Was her date tonight just the first evasion of me?

After the meal, I walked through the rowdy narrow streets of Muriseay, lost my way, found where I was, then returned to the hotel. My room was air-conditioned to the point of refrigeration, so I threw open the windows and lay awake for hours, listening to arguments, music and motorbikes.

CHAPTER 8

I overslept, so it was late morning by the time I walked around to the Lotterie office. I had awoken to a feeling of indifference about Seri, determined not to start another pursuit. I would accept her for what she was, a Lotterie employee doing her job. When I went inside the office Seri was not there, and I felt a quite distinct pang of disappointment, making a fraud of my new determination.

Two other young women, both wearing the smart company outfit, were working behind desks: one was speaking on the telephone, the other was typing.

I said to the one at the typewriter: 'Is Seri Fulten here, please?'

'Seri isn't coming in today. May I help you?'

'I was supposed to be meeting her here.'

'Are you Peter Sinclair?'

'Yes.'

The girl's expression changed; that subtle shift from formality to recognition. 'Seri left a message for you.' She tore a sheet from a notepad. 'She asked you to call at this address.'

I looked at it but of course it meant nothing to me. 'How do I find this?'

'It's just off the Plaza. Behind the bus station.'

I had crossed the Plaza during my late-night walk, but no longer had any idea how to find it.

'I'll have to go by cab,' I said.

'Would you like me to call one for you?' she said, and lifted the telephone.

While we were waiting for the car to arrive, the girl said: 'Are you a lottery winner?'

'Yes, of course.'

'Seri didn't say.' The girl smiled, hinting at intrigue, then looked down at her work. I went to sit at the glass-topped table.

A man appeared from the inner office, glanced briefly in my direction, then went to the desk Seri had been using the day before. There was something about the office-life quality to the Lotterie that made me uneasy, and I remembered how my doubts had been focused when I was here before. The bright and reassuringly confident image projected by the staff and their surroundings made me think of cabin crew on aircraft, who attempt to calm nervous passengers with professional blandness. But the Lotterie's product surely did not need to be backed up with reassurances? It was paramount that the treatment was safe, or so it was claimed.

At last the taxi arrived, and I was taken the short distance across the centre of town to the address Seri had left.

Another side street, bleached by sunlight: shops were shuttered, a van waited by the kerb with its engine running, children squatted in shadowed doorways. As the taxi drove away I noticed fresh water was running in the gutters on both sides of the street; a dog limped forward and licked at it, glancing to the side between gulps.

The address was a stout wooden door, leading through a cool corridor to a courtyard. Unclaimed mail was scattered on the floor and large containers of household waste spilled out across the uncut grass. On the far side of the courtyard, in another corridor, was an elevator, and I rode up in this to the third floor. Directly opposite was the numbered door I was looking for.

Seri opened the door within a few seconds of my ring.

'Oh, you're here,' she said. 'I was just about to telephone the office.'

'I slept late,' I said. 'I didn't realize there was anything urgent.'

'There isn't . . . come in for a moment.'

I followed her in, any remaining intention of seeing her as a mere employee confounded by this new insight into her. How many lottery winners did she normally invite round to her flat? Today she was wearing a revealing open-neck shirt and a denim skirt, buttoned down the front. She looked as she had done the night before: youthful, attractive, divorced from the image the job gave her. I remembered that feeling of resentment when she left me to meet someone else, and while she closed the door I realized I was hoping the apartment would show no signs of some other man in her life. Inside it was very small: to one side there was a tiny bathroom – through the half-open door I glimpsed antique plumbing and clothes hanging up to dry – and to the other was a cramped living-cum-bedroom, cluttered with books, records and furniture. The bed, a single, was neatly made. The apartment backed on to a main street, and because the windows were open the room was warm and noisy.

'Would you like a drink?' Seri said.

'Yes please.' I had drunk a whole bottle of wine the evening before, and was feeling the worse for it. Another would clear my head . . . but Seri opened a bottle of mineral water and poured two glasses.

'I can't get you a passage,' she said, sitting on the edge of her bed. 'I tried one shipping line, but they won't confirm reservations yet. The earliest I can get you on is next week.'

'Whatever is available,' I said.

There the business side of our meeting came to an end, as far as I knew. She could have told me this in the office, or left the message with one of the other staff, but clearly that was not all.

I had drunk my mineral water quickly; I liked it. 'Why aren't you at work today?'

'I've taken a couple of days off, and I need the break. I'm thinking of going up into the hills for the day. Would you like to come with me?'

'Is it far?'

'An hour or two, depending on whether the bus breaks

down or not. Just a trip. I want to get out of town for a few hours.'

'All right,' I said. 'I'd like that.'

'I know it's a bit of a rush, but there's a bus in a few minutes' time. I was hoping you would get here earlier, so we could talk about it more. Do you need to collect anything from the hotel?'

'I don't think so. You say we'll be back by this evening?'

'Yes.'

Seri finished her drink, picked up her shoulder bag, and we went down the road. The bus station was a short walk away: a dark, cavernous building with two ancient motor buses parked in the centre. Seri led the way to one of them. It was already more than half full, and the aisle between the two double rows of seats was blocked by other passengers standing up to talk to their friends. We squeezed past, and found a pair of seats near the back.

'Where are we going?' I said.

'A village I found last year. A few visitors go there, but it's usually quiet. You can get a good meal, and there's a river where you can swim.'

A few minutes later the driver climbed aboard, and moved down the bus taking the fares. When he reached us I offered to pay, but Seri already had a note in her hand.

'This is on the Lotterie,' she said.

The bus was soon out of the centre of the city and moving through broader streets lined with elderly and crumbling apartment buildings. The drabness of the area was emphasized by the pure white light of the midday sun, and relieved only by a horizontal forest of brightly coloured washing, hanging on lines suspended between the buildings. Many of the windows were broken or boarded up, and children scattered in the road as the bus clanked through. Whenever we slowed children jumped on the running board and clung to the side, while the driver snarled at them.

The last of the children dropped away, tumbling in the roadside dust, when we reached a steel bridge thrown high over the gorge of the river. As we crossed I could see on the clean water below the other face of Muriseay Town: the white-painted yachts of visitors, the riverside cafés and bars, the chandlers' shops, the boutiques.

On the other side of the gorge the road turned sharply inland, following the course of the river to our right. I watched this view for some minutes, until Seri touched my arm to point out what could be seen through the other windows. Here a vast shanty town existed. Hundreds or thousands of makeshift dwellings had been thrown together out of every conceivable piece of waste material: corrugated iron, crates, auto tyres, beer barrels. Many of these mean houses were open to the sky, or sheltered beneath worn-out tarpaulins or plastic sheeting. None of the houses had windows, only crude holes, and very few of them had any kind of door. Adults and children squatted by the side of the road, watching with dull eyes as the bus went by. Rusty cars and old oil drums littered every flat space. Dogs ran wild everywhere.

I watched this sordid township with a feeling of vague but painful guilt, aware that Seri and I were the only two people on the bus dressed in new or clean clothes, that the other passengers probably recognized this as the 'real' Muriseay, that they had no economic access either to my hotel or Seri's apartment. I recalled the ribbon development of luxury homes I had seen from the ship, and my thoughts about the glamorized image of the islands portrayed in the media.

I looked away, to my side of the bus, but now the road had wandered away from the river and the shanty town extended here too. I watched the tumbledown shacks as we passed and tried to imagine what it must be like to live there. Would I even consider the Lotterie treatment, I wondered, if I lived in a place like that?

At last the bus left the township and entered open country-side. Far ahead the mountains rose. Some of the parched land was being cultivated, but much of it lay empty.

We passed an airport on the right, surprising me. Air travel was supposed to be prohibited within the Archipelago, the airspace regulated by the Covenant of Neutrality. But to judge by the pylons of electronic sensors, and the ground-radar dishes, Muriseay Airport was as modern as any equivalent in the north. Approaching the terminal buildings I saw several large aircraft parked in the distance, but they were too far away for me to distinguish the markings.

'Is this a passenger airport?' I said quietly to Seri.

'No, purely military. Muriseay receives most of the troops from the north, but there are no camps here. The men are taken straight to ships, on the southern coast.'

Some friends of mine in Jethra were associated with a civil rights group, concerned with monitoring the Covenant. According to them, many of the larger islands were the sites of military transit- and rest-camps. These were not strictly in breach of the Covenant, but represented one of its odder aspects. Such camps were used by both sides, and sometimes by both armies at once. However, I had seen no sign of them, and assumed they must be situated a long way from the roads or regular shipping lanes.

The bus halted outside the airport, and most of the passengers climbed out, clutching their bundles and parcels. Seri said they would be the civilian staff: caterers, cleaners, and so on. Soon after we set off again, the well-paved road we had been following gave out, and became a dusty, pot-holed track instead. From here, the rest of the journey was marked by the constant lurching of the bus, the roaring of the engine in low gear and occasional bangs from the suspension. And dust: the tyres threw up clouds of dust and grit which flew in the open windows, griming our clothes, marking the tiny lines of the face and gritting between the teeth.

Seri became talkative, and as the track rose into the foot-hills and the countryside became greener, she told me about some of the islands she had visited and things she had seen. I discovered a few more facts about her: she had worked on ships for some time, she had learned how to weave, she had been married for a brief period.

Now that we were in rising agricultural country, the bus

made frequent stops to take on or let off passengers. At each of these stops people clustered around the bus, offering things for sale. Seri and I, marked out by our clothes, were the obvious focus of attention. Sometimes we bought fruit, and once we were served lukewarm black coffee from a chipped enamel bucket; by then I was so thirsty from the heat and dust that I easily overcame fastidiousness and drank from the one cup shared by everyone.

A few minutes later the bus broke down. The driver investigated, and steam burst forth from the radiator.

Seri was smiling.

'I take it this always happens?' I said.

'Yes, but not as soon as this. It normally boils when we start climbing.'

After loud discussion with the passengers at the front, the driver set off back down the road towards the last village, accompanied by two of the men.

Unexpectedly, Seri slipped her hand into mine and leaned against me slightly. She squeezed my fingers.

'How much further are we going?' I said.

'We're nearly there. The next village.'

'Couldn't we walk? I'd like to stretch my legs.'

'Let's wait. He's only gone to get water. It doesn't look steep, but it's uphill all the way.'

She closed her eyes, resting her head on my shoulder. I stared ahead, looking at the bulk of the mountains now rising directly before us. Although we had climbed a long way since leaving the town, the air was still warm and there was hardly any wind. Vineyards stretched on either side of the road. I could see tall cypresses in the distance, black against the sky. Seri dozed for a while, but I was getting stiff so I roused her. I climbed down from the bus and walked a distance up the road, relishing the exercise and the sunshine. It was not as humid here, the air smelt different. I walked as far as the crest of the rise the bus had been climbing when it broke down, and here I stopped and looked back. The plain stretched out before me, wavering in the thermals, a fusion of greys and greens and ochrous yellows. In the distance, on the horizon, was the sea, but there was a haze and I could not see any other islands.

I sat down, and after a few minutes I saw Seri walking up the road to join me. As she sat down beside me she said: 'The bus has broken down every time I've been on it.'

'It doesn't matter. We're not in a hurry.'

Again she slipped her hand into mine. 'Why did you leave me there?'

I thought of excuses – fresh air, exercise, see the view – but changed my mind.

'I suppose I'm a bit shy of you,' I said. 'Last night, when you left me in the bar, I thought I'd made a mistake.'

'I just had to see someone. A friend. I'd rather have been with you.' She was looking away, but she was holding my hand tightly.

Later, we saw the group of men returning to the bus with a can of water, so we walked down and took our seats again. In a few minutes the journey resumed, as dusty and lurching as before. Soon the road was rising through trees, turning into a pass in the mountains invisible from where we had halted. Tall eucalypts grew on each side of the track, the white bark peeling. Above, a ceiling of blueish-green leaves, glimpses of sky; below, a twisting shallow river, seen fleetingly through the trees. The pass curved, and the road with it, and for a minute I saw a superb mountainscape, rocks and trees and broad shoulders of scree. Water tumbled down the face of the rocks, bouncing and spuming through the gum trees to the river below. The dusty plain around Muriseay Town was lost to sight.

Seri was staring through the open window as if it was the first time she too had been along this road. I began to sense the scale of these mountains; by Faiandland standards they were low and unspectacular, because the High Massif in the north of the country contained the grandest mountain scenery in the world. Here on Muriseay, scale and expectations were smaller, the effect more compact yet more startling. One could relate emotionally to this scenery: it was human-sized without being domestic.

'Do you like it?' Seri said.

'Yes, of course.'

'We're almost there.'

I looked ahead but could see only the track climbing through the trees into green penumbra.

Seri shouldered her bag and made her way up the aisle to the front of the bus. She spoke briefly to the driver. In a few moments we came to a part of the road where it opened out, and where two wooden benches had been built at the side. The bus halted, and we climbed down.

CHAPTER 9

A path led down from the road, worn from the undergrowth to expose the soil. Stripped tree-branches had been laid in the ground at intervals to provide crude steps, and in the steepest places there was a handrail. We descended rapidly because the soil was dry and firm, and almost before the sound of the bus's engine had faded into the distance we saw the roofs of a village below us.

The path opened out on to a levelled area, where several cars were parked, and from here we came straight into the centre of the village. This was a pleasing double row of well-preserved old buildings. One or two had been converted to shops: there was a souvenir shop, a small restaurant and a garage. Because we were both hungry we went straight to the restaurant, and sat at one of the tables under the trees at the back.

It was good to sit down without the intrusive racket of the bus, or the flying grit; we were in the shade, the river flowed at the end of the garden and high in the trees overhead were birds invisible to us, making a strange and abrupt bell-like call. The meal was a dish called valti. Native to Muriseay it was a colourful mixture of rice, beans, tomatoes and meat, served in a spicy saffron-coloured sauce. Seri and I spoke little, but we had become detectably closer to each other.

Afterwards, we walked through the village until we came to the river. Here, a broad lawn had been laid and a number of people were sitting around, relaxing in the shade of the trees. It was a peaceful place, made oddly more silent by the river sounds and the birdsong. A wooden bridge, rustic but solid, led across to the other side where another path climbed erratically through the trees. There was a great stillness to the air, and the smell of the eucalypts, reminding me obscurely of childhood medicines, hung thick in the warm day. Below, we could hear the river on the stones.

We had not climbed far when we came to a single-bar gate across the path. Seri slipped two coins into a box, and we went through. Beyond the gate the path went more steeply up the hillside, leading to a narrow cleft in the rock. We clambered through, and I saw that the corners and angles of the rock had been worn smooth by feet. Now the path went down, while the walls of rock steepened above us. A few small trees and bushes grew on the ground beside us, but the rock was bare, crowned with foliage, darkening the vale.

Three people were walking back along the path towards us, but they passed without saying anything. It was oppressively quiet in the tiny valley, and the few things Seri and I said to each other were in hushed voices. It was the same sort of quietude adopted by non-believers who visit a church; here in the mountains the same serene stasis existed.

I heard the sound of water, and as the path turned towards the tallest face of rock I saw the pool.

There was a spring in the rock, flowing across a flat surface, and trickling out over the edge were a number of tiny water-falls. They poured down into the dark pool below, making a sonorous dripping noise, amplified into a hollow echoing by the concave wall of rock behind. The pool itself was black, with an illusion of greenness from the overhanging shrubbery. Its surface trembled continuously, while the unceasing water fell from above.

Although the air in the valley was as warm as elsewhere, there was a chill quality given by the sound of the water. Unaccountably, I felt myself shiver, the nervous tic that brings an unexplained shudder, the feeling that is said to be like someone walking over your grave. The pool was beautiful in a simple way, but it had a presence I could not like. It was cluttered with incongruity.

Hanging from the lip of the water shelf was a bizarre array

of household items. There, in the flow of water, someone had dangled an old shoe. Next to it swung a child's knitted jacket, bobbing as the water turned it. Then there was a pair of sandals, a wooden matchbox, a ball of string, a raffia basket, a necktie, a glove. They had a faint sheen of greyness, unclearly seen as the water poured over and through them.

This juxtaposition had an eerie, unexplained quality to it, like a sheep's heart nailed to a door, a token of ritual magic.

Seri said, 'They're petrifying, turning to stone.'

'Not literally.'

'No . . . but there's something in the water. Silica, I think. Anything hung in the water builds up a coating.'

'But why should anyone want a stone shoe?'

'That's the people who run the souvenir shop. They put most of the stuff here, although anyone can leave something. The people in the shop say it will bring you luck. It's just a novelty, really.'

'Is this what you brought me to see?' I said.

'Yes.'

'Why, Seri?'

'I'm not sure. I thought you'd like it here.'

We sat down together on the grass, regarding the petrifying pool and its motley of domestic fetishes. While we were there, more people walked through the vale and visited the pool. They were in a group of about ten, with children running around and making a noise. They made much of the objects dangling in the falls, and one of the men was photographed leaning out over the pool with his hand in the trickling water. Afterwards, as they walked away, he was still pretending his hand had been turned to stone, as he wielded it like a rigid claw.

I wondered what would happen if something living really was laid out beneath the falling water. Would it too acquire a veneer of stone, or would skin reject it? Obviously a human being or an animal would simply not keep still or stay long enough. A corpse, though, could probably turn to stone; organic death to inorganic permanence.

With such distracting macabre thoughts I sat silently with Seri while the birds made their strange noise overhead. It was still warm, but I noticed a gradual reduction in the intensity of sunlight on the trees above us. I was unused to being so far south as this, and the sudden twilights still surprised me.

'What time does it get dark?' I said.

Seri glanced at her wristwatch. 'Not long. We ought to get back up to the road. There's a bus in about half an hour.'

'If it hasn't broken down again.'

'That's if it has,' she said with a wry smile. We walked up through the little valley, then along the path to the bridge over the river. Lights were coming on in the village as we passed through, and by the time we had clambered up to the road it was almost dark. We sat down on one of the benches and listened to the evening sounds. Cicadas scraped for a while, but then there was a brief and lovely burst of birdsong, like the dawn chorus in the Faiandland countryside, transformed in the tropics. Below us, we heard music from the village, and the shallow river.

As the dark became absolute, the physical tension we had both been suppressing suddenly was released. Without either of us initiating it, or so it seemed, we were kissing passionately, leaving no doubts. But in a while, Seri drew back from me and said: 'The bus won't be coming now. It's too late. Nothing's allowed on the road past the airport after dark.'

I said: 'You knew that before we came here.'

'Well, yes.' She kissed me.

'Can we stay somewhere in the village?'

'I think I know a place.'

We went slowly down the wooded path, stumbling on the steps, heading down to the village lights we could just see through the trees. Seri led me to a house set back slightly from the road, and spoke in patois to the woman who came to the door. Money changed hands, and we were taken up to a room tucked under the roof: black-painted wooden rafters sloped over the bed. We had said nothing on the way, suspending it all, but as soon as we were alone, Seri slipped out of her clothes and lay on the bed. I quickly joined her.

An hour or two later, drained of the tension but still not really knowing each other, we dressed and went across to the restaurant. There were no other visitors in the village, and the owner had closed for the night. Again, Seri spoke persuasively in patois, and gave the man some money. After a delay we were brought a simple meal of bacon and beans, served in rice.

I said, while we were eating: 'I must give you some money.'

'Why? I can get all this back from the Lotterie.'

Under the table our knees were touching, hers slightly gripping mine. I said: 'Do I have to give you back to the Lotterie?'

She shook her head. 'I'm thinking of quitting the job. It's time I changed islands.'

'Why?'

'I've been on Muriseay long enough. I want to find somewhere quieter.'

'Is that the only reason?'

'Part of it. I don't get on too well with the manager in the office. And the job's not quite what I expected.'

'What do you mean?'

'It doesn't matter. I'll tell you sometime.'

We did not want to return to the room immediately, so we walked up and down the village street, our arms around each other. It was getting cool.

We stopped by the souvenir shop and looked in at the lighted window display. It was full of petrified objects, bizarre and mundane at once.

Walking again, I said: 'Tell me why you want to quit the job.'

'I thought I did.'

'You said it wasn't what you expected.'

Seri said nothing at first. We crossed the wide lawn by the river, and stood on the bridge. We could hear the myrtaceous trees moving in the breeze. At last Seri said: 'I can't make up my mind about the prize. I'm full of contradictions about it. In the job I've got to help people, and encourage them to go on to the clinic and receive the treatment.'

'Do many of them need encouragement?' I said, thinking of course of my own doubts.

'No. A few are worried in case it's dangerous. They just need someone to tell them it isn't. But you see, everything I do is based on the assumption that the Lotterie is a good thing. I'm just not sure any more that it is.'

'Why?'

'Well, for one thing, you're the youngest winner I've ever seen. Everyone else is at least forty or fifty, and some of them are extremely old. What it seems to mean is that the majority of people who buy the tickets are the same age. If you think about it, it means the Lotterie is just exploiting people's fear of dying.'

'That's understandable,' I said. 'And surely athanasia itself was developed because of the same fear?'

'Yes . . . but the lottery system seems so indiscriminate. When I first started the job I thought the treatment should only go to people who are ill. Then I saw some of the mail we get. Every day, the office receives hundreds of letters from people in hospital, pleading for the treatment. The clinic simply couldn't cope with even a fraction of them.'

'What do you do about the letters?'

'You'll hate the answer.'

'Go on.'

'We send them a form letter, and a complimentary ticket for the next draw. And we only send a ticket if they write from a hospital for incurable diseases.'

'That must bring them comfort,' I said.

'I don't like it any more than you do. No one at the office likes it. Eventually, I began to understand why it was necessary. Suppose we gave the treatment to anyone with cancer. Why is someone deserving of athanasia just because they're ill? Thieves and swindlers and rapists get cancer just like anyone else.'

'But it would be humanitarian,' I said, thinking that thieves and rapists can also win lotteries.

'It's unworkable, Peter. There's a booklet in the office. I'll let you read it if you want to. It's the Lotterie's argument against treating the sick. There are thousands, perhaps millions, of people suffering from cancer. The clinic can't treat them all. The treatment's too expensive, and it's too slow. So they would have to be selective. They would have to go through case histories, look for people they consider deserving, narrow it down to a few hundred a year. And *who* sits in judgement? Who can decide that one person deserves to live while another deserves to die? It might conceivably work for a short time . . . but then there would be someone denied the treatment, someone in power or someone in the media. Perhaps they'd be given the treatment to keep them quiet, and at once the system is corrupted.'

I felt the skin on Seri's arm as she pressed a hand on mine. She was cold, like me, so we started walking back towards the house. The mountains loomed black around us; everything was silent.

'You've talked me out of going to the clinic,' I said. 'I don't want anything more to do with this.'

'I think you should.'

'But why?'

'I told you I was full of contradictions.' She was shivering. 'Let's go inside and I'll tell you.'

In the house the upstairs room felt as if it had been heated, after the unexpected freshness of the night mountain air. I touched one of the overhead beams, and it was still warm from the day's sun.

We sat down on the edge of the bed, side by side, very chaste. Seri took my hand, teasing the palm with her fingers.

She said: 'You've got to have the treatment because the lottery is run fairly, and the lottery is the only defence against corruption. Before I got the job I used to hear the stories. You know, the ones we've all heard, about people buying their way in. The first thing they tell you when you start the job is that this isn't true. They show you what they call the proof . . . the total amount of drugs they can synthesize in a year, the maximum capacity of the equipment. It tallies exactly with the number of prize-winners every year. They're very defensive about it, to the point where you suspect they're covering something up.'

'Are they?'

'They *must* be, Peter. What about Mankinova?'

Yosep Mankinova was the former prime minister of Bagonne, a country in the north with supposed non-aligned status. Because of its strategic importance – oil reserves, plus a geographical location commanding crucial sea-lanes – Bagonne exercised political and economic influence out of all proportion to its size. Mankinova, an extreme right-wing politician, had governed Bagonne in the years leading up to the war, but about twenty-five years ago had been forced to resign when evidence was found that he had corruptly received the athanasia treatment. No final proof was established. Lotterie-Collago had emphatically denied it, but shortly afterwards two of the investigating journalists died in mysterious circumstances. Events moved on, the scandal faded and Mankinova went into obscurity. But recently, a few months before I left Jethra, the story had been revived. A number of photographs appeared in newspapers, alleged to be of Mankinova. If this was so, they revealed that he looked no older than he had been at the time of his resignation. He was a man in his eighties who looked like a man in his fifties.

I said: 'It would be naïve to think that that sort of thing doesn't happen.'

'I'm not naïve. But the number of people they can treat *is* limited, and anyone who wins the prize and then turns it down simply makes it possible.'

'Now you're supposing that I deserve to live, and someone else doesn't.'

'No . . . that's already been decided by the computer. You're just a random winner. That's why you must go on.'

I stared at the threadbare carpet, thinking that everything

she said only deepened my doubts. I was of course tempted by the idea of living a long and healthy life, and the notion of refusing it was one which would require a strength I had never before possessed. I was not a Deloinne, highly principled, austerely moralistic. I was greedy for life, greedy even for living, as Deloinne had put it, and a part of me could never deny this. But it continued to feel wrong, in a way I understood only vaguely. It was not for me.

And I thought of Seri. So far we were casual lovers, two people who had recently met, who had already made love and who probably would again, yet who had no emotional commitment to each other. It was possible the relationship would develop, that we would continue to know each other, perhaps fall in love in the conventional sense. I tried to imagine what would happen if I took the treatment while she did not. She, or anyone I might become involved with, would grow steadily older and I would not. My friends, my family, would move on into biological future, while I would be fixed, or petrified.

Seri left the bed, stripped off her shirt and ran water for washing into the basin. I watched her curved back as she leaned down to wash her face and arms. She had a slim, ordinary body, very compact and supple. Bending down she looked at me around her shoulder, smiling invertedly.

'You're staring,' she said.

'Why not?'

But I was only looking abstractedly. I was thinking about what decision, if any, I should make. I supposed that it was conflict between mind and heart. If I followed my instincts, my selfish greed, I should abandon my doubts and travel to Collago and become an athanasian; if I listened to my thoughts, I should not.

When we were in bed we made love again, less urgently than the first time but with an affection that had not been there before. I was wide awake afterwards, and I lay back in the crumpled sheets staring at the ceiling. Seri lay curled in my arm, her head against my neck, a hand lying on my chest.

'Are you going to go to Collago?' she said.

'I don't know yet.'

'If you do, I'll go with you.'

'Why?'

'I want to be with you. I told you, I'm quitting my job.'

'I'd like that,' I said.

'I want to be sure—'

'That I'll go through with it?'

'No . . . that if you do, then afterwards you'll be all right. I can't say why.' She moved suddenly, resting on an elbow and looking down at me. 'Peter, there's something about the treatment I don't like. It frightens me.'

'Is it dangerous?'

'No, not dangerous. There's no risk. It's what happens afterwards. I'm not supposed to tell you.'

'But you will,' I said.

'Yes.' She kissed me briefly. 'When you get to the clinic there are a few preliminaries. One of them is a complete medical check-over. Another is, you have to answer a questionnaire. It's one of the conditions. In the office we call it the longest form in the world. It asks you everything about yourself.'

'I have to write my autobiography.'

'That's what it amounts to, yes.'

'They told me this in Jethra,' I said. 'They didn't say it was a questionnaire, but that before the treatment I would have to write a complete account of myself.'

'Did they tell you why?'

'No. I just assumed it was part of the treatment.'

'It's nothing to do with the treatment itself. It's used in the rehabilitation afterwards. What they do to you, to make you athanasian, is clean out your system. They renew your body, but they wipe your mind. You'll be amnesiac afterwards.'

I said nothing, looking back into her earnest eyes.

She said: 'The questionnaire becomes the basis for your new life. You become what you wrote. Doesn't that scare you?'

I remembered the long months in Colan's villa in the hills

near Jethra, my quest to tell the truth, the various devices I had used to discover that truth, the certainty that I had succeeded, and, finally, the sense of renewal I had felt when I finished. That manuscript, presently lying in my hotel room in Muriseay Town, contained my life as surely as words contained meaning. I had already become what I had written. I was *defined* by my work.

I said: 'No, it doesn't scare me.'

'It does me. That's why I want to be there with you. I don't believe what they claim, that the patients recover their identities.'

I hugged her, and although she resisted at first she soon relaxed and lay down beside me again.

'I haven't made up my mind yet. But I think I'll go to the island, and decide when I'm there.'

Seri said nothing, holding herself against me.

'I've got to find out for myself,' I said.

Her face buried in my side, Seri said: 'Can I come with you?'

'Yes, of course.'

'Talk to me, Peter. While we travel, tell me who you are. I want to know you.'

We drifted off into sleep soon after that. During the night I dreamed I was hanging on a rope beneath a waterfall, spinning and bobbing in the relentless torrent. Gradually my limbs became stiffer and my mind became frozen, until I shifted in my sleep and the dream died.

CHAPTER 10

It was raining in Sheffield. I had been given the small front bedroom in Felicity's house, and when I was there I could be alone. I would sometimes stand for hours at the window looking across the roofs at the industrial scenery beyond. Sheffield was an ugly, functional city, fallen from its great days of steelworking, now an untidy urban mess that flowed up to the Pennine Hills in the west and blended under the arches of the motorway viaduct with the smaller town of Rotherham to the east. It was on this side of Sheffield that Felicity and James had their house.

Greenway Park was an island of clean middle-class houses and gardens, surrounded by the older and gloomier suburbs of the city. In the centre of the estate the planners had left an open space of about half an acre, in which young saplings had been planted, and into which the residents took their dogs to defecate. Felicity and James had a dog, and his name was Jasper or Jasper-boy, depending.

From the moment I arrived at the house, I entered a complicated, withdrawn state of mind. I acknowledged that Felicity was doing me a favour, that I had made a mess of my life in Edwin's cottage, that the time had come for a form of recuperation, and so I became submissive and compliant. I knew that my obsessive interest in my manuscript was responsible for my errors, so I tried to put it out of my mind. At the same time, I continued in the belief that the work I had been doing was crucial to my sense of identity, and that Felicity had dragged me away from it. I was therefore deeply resentful and angry, and I withdrew from her.

I became detached from life in her house, and was obsessed

with trivia. I could not help but notice everything. I was critical of the house, their habits, their attitudes. I disliked their friends. I felt suffocated by their closeness, their normality. I watched the way James ate, the fact that he had a little paunch, that he went jogging. I noted the television programmes they watched, the sort of food Felicity cooked, the things they said to their children. These two, Alan and Tamsin, were for a time allies, because I too was treated like a child.

I suppressed my feelings. I tried to join in with their life, to show the gratitude that I knew I ought to feel, but Felicity and I had simply grown apart. Everything about her life grated on me.

Many weeks went by. Autumn passed and winter came; Christmas was a brief respite because the children became more important than me. But in general we were irritants for each other.

On alternate weekends all five of us would drive down in James's Volvo to the house in Herefordshire. These were expeditions I dreaded, although Felicity and James seemed to look forward to them. It gave the children a taste for the countryside, Felicity said, and Jasper-boy enjoyed the exercise.

The house was shaping up well, James said, and often telephoned Edwin and Marge to give them what he called progress reports. I was always made to work in the garden, clearing the tangle of overgrown shrubs and making them into compost. James and Felicity and the children concentrated on the decorating. My white room, still intact until these visits, was the first to be done: magnolia emulsion made a tasteful background for the curtain material Marge had described on the phone to Felicity. James hired local electricians and plasterers, and soon the simple cottage was turned into just what Edwin and Marge wanted.

Felicity helped me in the garden one weekend, and while I was on the other side of the house she uprooted the honeysuckle and dumped it on the huge new heap that would one day decay into garden compost.

I said: 'That was a honeysuckle.'

'It was dead, whatever it was.'

'Plants lose their leaves in winter,' I said. 'It's called nature.'

'Then that proves it wasn't a honeysuckle, because they're evergreen.'

I rescued the plant from the heap, and stuck its roots back in the soil, but when we returned two weeks later it had mysteriously vanished. I was extremely saddened by this vandalism, because the honeysuckle was something I had loved. I remembered those evening scents while I was writing in my white room, and it was this incident that at last returned me to my manuscript. As soon as we were back in Greenway Park I took it from my holdall where I kept it hidden, and started to read through it.

I had difficulty with it at first, because I was disappointed with what I found. It was as if, during the weeks I had been away from it, the words had decayed or diminished. What I found seemed like a synopsis for the real thing. Later pages were better, but I was unhappy.

I knew I ought to go through the manuscript yet again, but something held me back. I shrank away from the prospect of renewing Felicity's interest in what I had been writing; while the manuscript was hidden in my bag I could forget it, and so could Felicity. Everyone said how well I was doing.

The manuscript was a reminder of my past, what I might have been. It was dangerous to me; it excited me and seduced me, charged me with imagination, but the reality of it was a disappointment.

So I stared at the unsatisfactory pages spread on the table in my room, and for a while I stood at the window and looked across the city at the distant Pennines, and then at last I bulked the pages and squared them off and returned them to the holdall. Afterwards, I stood by the window for the rest of the afternoon, playing idly with the macramé plant holder that hung from the ceiling, and watched the city lights come on as the Pennines receded into the mist.

With the coming of the New Year the weather deteriorated,

and so too did the atmosphere in the house. The children no longer wanted to play with me, and although James remained superficially friendly to me, Felicity became almost overtly hostile. She served my food at mealtimes in a glaring silence, and if I offered to help around the house I was told to keep out of the way. I spent more and more time in my room, standing by the window and looking at the snow on the distant hills.

The Pennine Chain had always been an important part of my mental environment. Childhood in the Manchester suburb: safe houses and streets with neighbours and gardens, school close at hand, but always a few miles to the east, dark and undulating and wild, the Pennine Hills. Now I was to the other side of them but the hills were the same: a barren wilderness bisecting England. It seemed to me they were a symbol of neutrality, a balance, dividing my past life from my present. Perhaps there, in the steep curving valleys between the limestone moors, was some more abstract clue to where I had failed in my life. Living on a small island like Britain, modern and civilized, one felt the elements less. There were just the sea and the hills, and in Sheffield the hills were nearer. I needed something elemental to clarify me.

One day, following an idea, I asked the children if they had ever been to the caves in Castleton, deep in the Pennines. Before long they were pestering their parents to take them to see the Bottomless Pit, the Blue John Caves, the pool which could turn things to stone.

Felicity said to me: 'Have you put them up to this, Peter?'

'It would be nice to go up in the hills.'

'James won't drive up there in the snow.'

Fortunately, the weather changed soon after this, and a spell of warm wind and rain melted the snow and once again sharpened the dark silhouette of the Pennines. For a few days it looked as if the children had forgotten my idea, but then, entirely without my prompting, Alan brought up the subject again. Felicity said she would see, frowned at me and changed the subject.

I turned again to my manuscript, feeling that something was beginning to move in me.

I made a resolution that this time I would read it through to the end, suppressing criticism. I wanted to discover *what* I had written, not how I had written. Only then would I decide whether another draft should be undertaken.

Stylistically, the early pages were the worst, but as soon as I was past them I found it easy to read. My strongest impression was an odd one: that I was not so much reading as recalling. I was still virtually word-perfect, and I felt that all I had to do was hold the pages in my hand and turn them one by one, and the story would spring spontaneously to mind.

I had always believed that I had put the essence of myself into the pages, and now that I was again in touch with the preoccupation of the long summer I experienced the most extraordinary feeling of security and reassurance. It was as if I had wandered away from myself, but now I was returning. I felt confident, sane, outward-looking and energetic.

Downstairs, while I read, James was putting up some bookshelves, even though the house was almost devoid of books. Felicity had some pot plants and ornaments that needed a place. The sound of the electric drill interrupted the reading, like incorrect punctuation.

I had taken my work for granted. During the weeks I had been languishing in Felicity's house I had neglected my identity. Here, in the pages, was all I had missed. I was in contact with myself again.

Certain passages were astonishingly acute in their observation. There was a roundness to the ideas, a consistency to the whole. With each revelation I felt my confidence return. I started to live again, as once before I had lived vicariously through my writing. I recognized the truths, as once I had created them. Above all, I identified strongly with the fictions I had devised and the landscape in which they were set.

Felicity, in real life changed beyond recognition by her children, her husband, her attitudes, became explicable to me as 'Kalia'. James featured, in shadow, as 'Yellow'. Gracia was

'Seri'. I lived again in the city of Jethra, by the sea, over-looking islands. I sat at my table by the window in Felicity's house, staring across Sheffield at the bleak moors beyond, as in the closing passages of the manuscript I stood on a rise in Jethra's Seigniory Park, staring across the roofs at the sea.

Those islands of the Archipelago were as the Pennine Hills: neutral territory, a place to wander, a division between past and present, a way of escape.

I read the manuscript through to the end, to that last unfinished sentence, then went downstairs to help James with his carpentry. My mood was good and we all responded. Later, before the children went to bed, Felicity suggested we could all visit Castleton at the weekend; it would make a nice day out.

I remained in high spirits until the day. Felicity packed a picnic lunch in the morning, saying that if it rained we could eat in the car, but there was a picnic area just outside the village. I anticipated freedom, a lack of direction, a wander-ing. James drove the Volvo through the crowded centre of Sheffield, then headed up into the Pennines, following the road to Chapel-en-le-Frith, climbing past sodden green hill pasture and by scree slopes of fallen limestone. The wind buffeted the car, exhilarating me. These were the horizon hills, the distant shapes that had always been on the margin of my life. I sat in the centre of the back seat, between Alan and Tamsin, listening to Felicity. The dog was crouched in the baggage space behind.

We parked in a small open space on the edge of Castleton village, and we all climbed out. The wind blustered around us, spotting us with rain. The children burrowed deeper into their weatherproof anoraks, and Tamsin said she wanted to go to the lavatory. James locked the car, and tested the handles.

I said: 'I think I'll go for a walk by myself.'

'Don't forget lunch. We're going to look at the caves.'

They headed off, content to be without me. James had a walking stick, and Jasper bounded around him.

Alone, I stood with my hands deep in my pockets, looking around for a walk to take. There was only one other car in the park: a green Triumph Herald, spotted with rust. The woman sitting behind the wheel had been regarding me, and now she opened the door and stood where I could see her.

'Hello, Peter,' she said, and at last I recognized her.

Chapter 11

Dark hair, dark eyes; these I noticed at once. The wind took her hair back from her face, exposing the rather wide forehead, the eyes sunk beneath. Gracia had always been too thin, and the wind was not flattering her. She had her old fur coat on, the one we had bought from a stall in Camden Lock one Saturday afternoon in summer, the one with the torn lining and the rents beneath the sleeves. This had never buttoned, and she held it closed in front of her by keeping her hands in the pockets. Yet she stood erect, letting me see her, letting the wind knock her. She was as she had ever been: tall, angular of face, untidy and casual, unsuited to open air or countryside, more at home in London flats and streets, the basements of cities. There she blended, here she was incongruous. Gypsy blood, she once had told me, but she rarely left London, she had never known the road.

I went across to her, surprised as much by how familiar she looked as by the fact she was there. I was not thinking, only noticing. There was an awkward moment, when we stood facing each other by her car, neither of us saying anything, then spontaneously we moved quickly and put our arms around one another. We held tight, pressing our faces together without kissing; her cheeks were cold, and the fur of the coat was damp. I felt a surge of relief and happiness, a marvelling that she was safe and we were together again. I held on and held on, unwilling to let the reality of her frail body go, and soon I was crying with her. Gracia had never made me cry, nor I her. We had been sophisticates in London, whatever that meant, although at the end, in the months before we parted, there had been a tautness in us that was just a suppression of emotion. Our coolness to each other had become a habit, a mannerism that became self-generating. We had known each other too long to break out of patterns.

Suddenly, I knew that Seri, by whom I tried to understand Gracia, had never existed. Gracia, holding me as tightly as I held her, defied definition. Gracia was Gracia: fickle, sweet-smelling, moody, unpredictable, funny. I could define Gracia only by being with her, so that through her I defined myself. I held her more tightly still, pressing my lips against her white neck, tasting her. The fur coat had opened as she raised her arms to take me, and I could feel her thin body through her blouse and skirt; she had been wearing the same clothes when I last saw her, at the end of the previous winter.

At last I stepped back from her, but held her hands. Gracia stood looking down at the ground, then let go of my hands, blew her nose on a tissue. She reached into the car for her shoulder bag, then slammed the door. I held her again, arms around her back, but not pressing her to me. She kissed me, and we laughed.

'I didn't think I'd see you again,' I said.

'Neither did I. I didn't want to, for a long time.'

'Where have you been living?'

'I moved in with a friend.' She had looked away, briefly. 'What about you?'

'I was down in the country for a time. I had to sort things out. Since then I've been with Felicity.'

'I know. She told me.'

'Is that why you—?'

She glanced at James's Volvo, then said: 'Felicity told me you'd be here. I wanted to see you again.'

Felicity had arranged the meeting, of course. After the weekend I had spent in Sheffield with Gracia, Felicity had gone out of her way to befriend her. But the two women were not friends, in the usual sense. Felicity's gestures towards Gracia had been political, significant to me. She saw Gracia as a victim of my shortcomings, and helping Gracia was her way of expressing disapproval of me, and something more general: responsibility, and sisterhood between women. It was revealing that Felicity had not arranged the meeting at Greenway Park. She probably despised Gracia without knowing it. Gracia was just a wounded bird, someone to be helped with a splint and a spoon of warm milk. That I had done the wounding was where her concern began, naturally enough.

We started walking into the village, holding hands and pressing shoulders, heedless of the cold and the wind. I had become alive in my mind, sensing a further move forward. I had not felt like this since before my father died. I had been obsessed with the past too long, too concerned with myself. All that I had been damming up in me now flowed towards an outlet: Gracia, part of my past yet returning.

The main street of the village was narrow and winding, pressed in by the grey houses. Traffic went through noisily, throwing up fine spray with the tyres.

'Can we find somewhere for coffee?' Gracia said. She had always drunk a lot of cheap instant coffee, made too weakly and with white sugar. I squeezed her hand, remembering a stupid argument.

In a tiny side street we found a café, the front room of a terraced house, converted with a large pane of plate glass and metal-topped tables. Little glass ashtrays rested exactly in the centre of each one. It was so quiet as we went in that I assumed the place was closed, but after we had been seated for a minute or two, a woman in a blue gingham kitchen overall came to take our order. Gracia ordered two poached eggs, as well as coffee; she had been driving since half-past seven, she said.

'Are you still staying with your friend?' I said.

'At the moment. That's one of the things I want to talk to you about. I've got to move out soon, but there's a place coming up. I want to know whether to take it or not.'

'How much is it?'

'Twelve pounds a week. Controlled rent. But it's a basement, and not a very good area.'

'Take it,' I said, thinking of London rents.

'That's all I wanted to know,' Gracia said, and stood up. 'I'll go now.'

'What?'

I watched her in amazement as she turned towards the door. But I had forgotten Gracia's odd sense of humour. She leaned forward against the condensation-covered window, made a squiggle with her fingertip, then came back to the table. She ruffled my hair as she passed. Before sitting down again she shrugged off the fur coat and let it fall over the back of the chair.

'Why didn't you write to me, Peter?'

'I did . . . but you never answered.'

'That came too soon. Why didn't you write again?'

'I didn't know where you were. And I wasn't sure your flatmate was forwarding mail.'

'You could have found me. Your sister did.'

'I know. The real reason is . . . I didn't think you wanted to hear from me.'

'Oh, I did.' She had the ashtray in her fingers, turning it around. She was smiling slightly. 'I think I wanted the chance to throw you out again. At least, I did at first.'

'I really didn't know how upset you were,' I said, and the devil of conscience reminded me of those hot summer days, obsessively writing about myself. I had had to put Gracia from my mind, I needed to find myself. Was this the truth?

The woman came back then, and put down two cups of coffee. Gracia heaped in the sugar, stirred the liquid slowly.

'Look, Peter, it's all passed now.' She took my hand across the top of the table, gripping it firmly. 'I got over it. I had a lot of problems, and it was difficult for a while. I needed a break, that's all. I saw some other people, talked a lot. But I'm over it all now. What about you?'

'I think so,' I said.

The fact was that Gracia exerted an irresistible sexual influence over me. When we split up, one of the worst things about it was the thought of her in bed with someone else. She had often used that as an unstated threat, one used to hold us together yet one which eventually drove us apart. When I had finally convinced myself that we had reached the end, the only way I knew of coping was to close my mind to her. My possessiveness was irrational, because in spite of the sexual magnetism we had not often been good lovers for each other, but nonetheless my awareness of her sexuality pervaded everything I did with her and every thought I had of her. I was aware of it now, sitting there in the bleak café with her: the unbrushed hair, her loose and careless clothes, colourless skin, vagueness behind the eyes, tension within. Above all, perhaps, the fact that Gracia had always cared for me, even when I did not deserve it, or when her neuroses came like radio interference to our attempts to communicate.

'Felicity said you weren't well, that you've been acting strangely.'

'That's just Felicity,' I said.

'Are you sure?'

'Felicity and I don't get on too well,' I said. 'We've grown apart. She wants me to be like her. We've got different standards.'

Gracia was frowning, looking down at her cup of coffee.

'She told me frightening things about you. I wanted to see you.'

'Is that why you're here?'

'No . . . just a part of it.'

'What sort of things was she telling you?'

Still avoiding my eyes, she said: 'That you were hitting the bottle again, and not eating properly.'

A sense of relief that that was all. 'Does that seem as if it's true?'

'I don't know.'

'Look at me and tell me.'

'No, it doesn't.'

She had glanced at me, but now she kept her eyes averted as she drained her cup. The woman arrived with Gracia's eggs.

'Felicity's materialistic,' I said. 'She's full of wrong ideas about me. All I wanted to do after we split up was get away somewhere on my own, and try to work things out.'

I stopped talking because I had suddenly been distracted by the kind of stray thought that had come so often in the last few weeks. I knew that I was not telling Gracia the whole story; somehow that kind of wholeness had been sucked out of me by my manuscript. Only there lay the truth. Would I one day have to show it to her?

I waited while Gracia finished her meal – she ate the first egg quickly, then picked at the second; she had never had a long attention span for food – and then I ordered two more coffees. Gracia lit a cigarette. I had been waiting for that, wondering if she still smoked.

I said then: 'Why couldn't you have seen me last year? After the row?'

'Because I couldn't, that's all. I'd had enough and it was still too soon. I wanted to see you but you were always so critical of me. I was just demoralized. I needed time to put things right.'

'I'm sorry,' I said. 'I shouldn't have said those things.'

Gracia shook her head. 'They don't mean anything now.'

'Is that why you're here?'

'I've sorted things out. I told you, I'm feeling a lot better.'

'Have you been with another guy?'

'Why?'

'Because it matters. I mean, it would have mattered.' I sensed myself heading into danger, disrupting everything.

'I was with someone for a while. It was all last year.'

Last year: the words made it sound as if it was a long time ago, but last year was still only three weeks ago. Now it was I who looked away. She knew the irrationality of my possessiveness.

'He was just a friend, Peter. A good friend. Someone I met who's been looking after me.'

'Is that who you're still living with?'

'Yes, but I'm moving out. Don't be jealous, please don't be jealous. I was on my own, and I had to go into hospital, and when I came out you weren't there, and Steve came along just when I needed him.'

I wanted to ask her about him, but at the same time I knew I wanted to ask to stake territory, not to hear answers. It was stupid and unfair, but I resented this Steve for being who he was, for being a friend. I resented him more for arousing in me an emotion, jealousy, that I had tried to rid myself of. Leaving Gracia had purged me of that, I thought, because only with her had it been so acute. Steve became in my mind everything I was not, everything that I could never be.

Gracia must have seen it in my eyes. She said: 'You're being unreasonable about this.'

'I know, but I can't help it.'

She put down her cigarette and took my hand again.

'Look, this isn't about Steve,' she said. 'Why do you think I've come here today? I want *you*, Peter, because I still love you in spite of everything. I want to try again.'

'I do too,' I said. 'But would it go wrong again?'

'No. I'll do anything to make it work. When we split up, I realized that we had to go through all that to be sure. It was me that was wrong before. You made all that effort, trying to repair things, and all I did was destroy. I knew what was happening, I could feel it inside me, but I was obsessed with myself, so miserable. I started to loathe you because you were trying so hard, because you couldn't see how awful I was being. I hated you because you wouldn't hate me.'

'I never hated you,' I said. 'It just went wrong, again and again.'

'And now I know why. All those things that caused tension before, they're gone. I've got a job, somewhere to live, I'm back in touch with my own friends. I was dependent on you for everything before. Now it really is different.'

More different than she knew, because I had changed too. It seemed she possessed all the things that once were mine. My only possession now was self-knowledge, and that was on paper.

'Let me think,' I said. 'I want to try again, but . . .'

111

But I had lived for so long with uncertainty that I had grown used to it; I rejected Felicity's normality, James's security. I welcomed the unreliability of the next meal, the morbid fascinations of solitude, the introspective life. Uncertainty and loneliness drove me inwards, revealed me to myself. There would be an imbalance between Gracia and myself again, of the same type but weighted the opposite way. Would I cope with it any better than she had?

I loved Gracia; I knew it as I sat with her. I loved her more than I had ever loved anyone, including myself. Especially myself, because I was explicable only on paper, only by fictionalization and faulty memory. There was a perfection to myself as shaped by the manuscript, but it was the product of artifice. I had needed to re-invent myself, but I could never have invented Gracia. I remembered my faltering attempts to describe her through the girl, Seri. I had left out so much, and in making up for the omissions I had made her merely convenient. Such a word could never be applied to Gracia, and no other would describe her exactly. Gracia resisted description, whereas I had defined myself with ease.

Even so, making the attempt had served its purpose. In creating Seri I had failed, but then I had discovered something else. Gracia was affirmed.

Minutes passed in silence, and I stared at the table-top as I felt my complicated emotions and feelings turn within me. I experienced again the same sort of instincts that had driven me to my first attempt at the manuscript: the wish to straighten out my ideas, to rationalize what perhaps would be better left unclear.

Just as from now I should always be a product of what I had written, so too would Gracia be understood through Seri. Her other identity, the convenient Seri of my imagination, would be the key to her reality. I had never been fully able to understand Gracia, but from now Seri would be there to make me recognize what I *did* comprehend of her.

The islands of the Dream Archipelago would always be with me; Seri would always haunt my relationship with Gracia.

I needed to simplify, to let the turbulence subside. I knew too much, I understood too little.

At the heart of it all was an absolute, that I had discovered I still loved Gracia. I said to her: 'I'm really sorry everything went wrong before. It wasn't your fault.'

'Well, it was.'

'I don't care about that. It was my fault too. It's all in the past.' Distractingly, the thought came that it too, the split-up, had been somehow defined by my writing. Could it all have been as easy as that? 'What are we going to do now?'

'Whatever you like. That's why I'm here.'

'I've got to get away from Felicity,' I said. 'I'm only staying with her because I've nowhere else to go.'

'I told you I'm moving. This week, if I can manage it. Do you want to try living with me?'

As I realized what she had said I felt a thrill of sexual excitement; I imagined lovemaking again.

'What do you think about that?' I said.

Gracia smiled briefly. We had never actually lived together, although at the height of the relationship we would often spend several consecutive nights together. She had always had somewhere of her own to stay, and I had mine. In the past we had resisted the idea of moving in together, perhaps because both of us feared we might tire of each other. In the end it had taken less than that to split us up.

I said: 'If I lived with you because I had nowhere else to go, it would fail. You know that.'

'Don't think of it like that. It invites failure.' She was leaning towards me across the table, and our hands were still clenched. 'I've worked this out on my own. I came up here today because of what I decided. It was stupid before. It *was* my fault, whatever you say. But I've changed, and I think you've grown too. It was only selfishness that made me react away from you before.'

'I was very happy,' I said, and suddenly we were kissing, reaching awkwardly towards each other across the table-top. We upset Gracia's coffee cup, and it fell on the floor, breaking into pieces. We started trying to mop up the spilled coffee with paper serviettes, and the woman came with a cloth. Later, we walked through the cold streets of Castleton, then followed a path that led up one of the hills. When we had climbed for about a quarter of an hour we came to a place above the tree line where we could see down over the village. In the car park the back door of the Volvo was open. A few more cars had driven in since we were there, and these were parked in a line beside it. Amongst them was Gracia's; she had told me she could drive, but in all the time I had known her she had never owned a car.

We stared down at Felicity's little family group huddled around their car.

Gracia said: 'I don't really want to meet Felicity today. I owe her too much.'

'So do I,' I said, knowing it was true, yet nevertheless continuing to resent her. I would as soon never see Felicity again, so troubled were my feelings about her. I remembered James being smug, Felicity being patronizing. Even as I took advantage of them, and sponged off Felicity, I resented everything they stood for and rejected anything they offered me.

It was cold on the hillside, with the wind curling down from the moors above, and Gracia held close to me.

'Shall we go somewhere?' she said.

'I'd like to spend the night with you.'

'So would I . . . but I haven't any money.'

'I've got enough,' I said. 'My father left me some, and I've been living off it all year. Let's find a hotel.'

By the time we had walked down to the village, Felicity and the others had gone off again. We wrote a note and left it under the windscreen wipers, then drove to Buxton in Gracia's car.

The following Monday I went with Gracia to Greenway Park, collected my stuff, thanked Felicity effusively for everything she had done for me, and left the house as quickly as I could. Gracia waited in the car and Felicity did not go out to see her. The atmosphere in the house remained tense all the time I was there. Resentments and accusations were suppressed. I had a sudden, eerie feeling that this would be the last time I should ever see my sister, and that she knew it too. I was unmoved by the idea, yet as we drove down the crowded motorway to London my thoughts were not of Gracia and what we were about to start, but of my ungracious and inexplicable resentment of my sister. I had my manuscript safe in my holdall, and I resolved that as soon as I had the time in London I would read through the sections dealing with Kalia, and try to understand. As we drove along it seemed to me that all my weaknesses and failings were explained to me in the manuscript, but that in addition there were clues to a new beginning.

I had created it by the force of imagination; now I could release that imagination and channel it into a perception of my life.

Thus, it seemed to me now that I was moving from one island to another. Beside me was Seri, behind me were Kalia and Yallow. Through them I could discover myself in the glowing landscape of the mind. I felt that at last I saw a way to free myself from the confinements of the page. There were now two realities, and each explained the other.

CHAPTER 12

The ship was called *Mulligayn*, a name which we could trace to neither geography, personality nor reason. Registered in Tumo, she was an elderly, coal-burning steamer, given to rolling in the mildest swell. Unpainted, uncleaned and lacking at least one of her lifeboats, the *Mulligayn* was typical of the hundreds of small passenger ships that linked the populous southern islands of the Archipelago. For fifteen days Seri and I sweltered in her airless cabins and companionways, grumbling at the crew because it was expected of us, although privately neither of us felt we had much to complain about.

Like my earlier voyage to Muriseay, this second leg of the journey was in part a discovery of myself. I found that I had already absorbed some island attitudes: an acceptance of crowding, and of general uncleanliness, and of late ships and unreliable telephones and corruptible officials.

I frequently remembered the saying I had heard from Seri, the first time we met: that I would never leave the islands. The longer I stayed in the Archipelago the more I understood it. I still had every intention of going back to Jethra, regardless of whether or not I took the Lotterie treatment, but with every day that passed I felt the rapture of islands grow within me.

Because I had lived all my life in Jethra I accepted its values as the norm. I never saw the city as prim, old-fashioned, conservative, over-legislated, cautious and inward-looking. I had simply grown up in it, and although I was aware of its faults as well as its virtues, its standards had become my own. Now that I had left, now that the happy-go-lucky outlook of many islanders was becoming something I liked, I wanted to experience more of the culture, become a small part of it.

As my perceptions changed, the thought of returning to Jethra became less and less attractive. I was enthralled by the Archipelago. On one level, travelling around the islands was undoubtedly a bore, but the constant knowledge that there was going to be another island, somewhere else to visit and explore, opened broad internal vistas in me.

During the long voyage to Collago, Seri told me about the effect the Covenant of Neutrality had had within the Archipelago. The Covenant was the invention of governments in the north, imposed on the islands from without. It enabled both warring factions to use the Archipelago as an economic, geographic and strategic buffer against the other side, distancing the war from their own territories by adventurism and in the great empty continent to the south.

Once the Covenant had been signed, a sense of timelessness and apathy had descended on the Archipelago, sapping cultural energy. The islanders had always been racially and culturally distinct from the people in the north, although trading and political links went back as far as could be remembered. But now the islands were isolated. It affected Archipelagan life on every level. Suddenly there were no new films from the north, no books, no cars, virtually no visitors, no steel or grain or fertilizer, no oil or coal, no newspapers or academics or expertise or industrial equipment. The same sanctions closed the islands' only export markets. All the dairy produce of the Torqui Group, the fishing, the timber, the minerals, the hundreds of different types of arts and crafts, no longer had the mass consumer markets of the north open to them. Obsessed with its local squabble, the northern continent closed its doors to the rest of the world, and it did so because it considered itself to *be* the world.

The worst effects of the Covenant had been felt in the years immediately following it. Both it and the war had by now become a part of everyday life and the Archipelago was beginning to recover, both economically and socially. Seri told me there had been a noticeable change of mood in recent years, a reaction against the north.

A kind of pan-islandic nationalism was growing in the Archipelago. There had been a renewal of religious faith, for one thing, a sweeping evangelism that was taking worship to the Orthodox cathedrals as never before in the last thousand years. In step with this there had been a secular revival: a dozen new universities had been built or were in the process of construction, and more were planned. Tax revenue was being put into the new industries appearing to replace the imported goods. Major discoveries of oil and coal had been made, and counter-Covenant offers of assistance or investment from the north had been pointedly turned down. Arising with this was a new emphasis on the arts and agriculture and the sciences: investment and grant money was obtainable with a minimum of bureaucratic delay. Seri said she knew of dozens of new settlements on previously uninhabited islands, each pursuing a way of life centred on their own interpretation of what cultural independence really meant. For some it was an artists' colony; for others, subsistence farming; others, an opportunity to experiment with lifestyles, educational programmes or social structures. All were united, though, by the renaissance spirit, and by a common instinct to prove to themselves, and to anyone else who cared to inquire, that the old hegemony of the north was at an end.

Seri and I intended to become two of those who would inquire. Our plan, after Collago, was to go island-hopping for a long time.

Before all this, standing in the way, was Collago. The island where living was bestowed, where life was denied. I had still not decided what to do.

We were following one of the main sea-lanes between Muriseay and Collago, and so it was inevitable that other lottery winners would be aboard. I was unaware of the others at first, preoccupied with Seri, watching the islands, but after a couple of days it was obvious who they were.

They had formed a clique, the five of them. There were two men and three women, all of an age; I judged the youngest, one of the men, to be in his late fifties. They were invulnerable in their conviviality, eating and drinking, filling the first-class lounge with jollity, often drunk but always tiresomely polite. Once I started watching them, fascinated in a rather morbid way, I kept willing them to break out, perhaps to swing a punch at one of the stewards or to eat to such excess that they would be sick in public; already, though, they were superior beings, above such venality, humble in their imminent role of demi-gods.

Seri had recognized them from the office, but she said nothing to me until I had worked it out for myself. Then she confirmed it. 'I can't remember all their names. The woman with the silver hair, she's called Treeca. I quite liked her. One of the men is called Kerrin, I think. They're all from Glaund.'

Glaund: the enemy country. There was enough of the north still in me to think of them as foes, but enough of the islands to recognize the instinct as irrelevant. Even so, the war had been going on for most of my life, and I had never before left Faiandland. We sometimes saw propaganda films in Jethran cinemas about the Glaundians, but I had never given them much credence. Factually, the Glaundians were a fairer-skinned race than mine, their country was more industrialized and they had a history of being territorially ambitious; less authentically, they were supposed to be ruthless businessmen, indifferent sportsmen and incompetent lovers. Their political system was different from ours. While we lived under the benevolent feudalism of the Seignior, and the whole impenetrable apparatus of the Tithe Laws, the Glaundians operated a system of state socialism, and were supposed to be socialized equals.

These five appeared not to recognize me as being one of them, which suited me. I was disguised from them by my youth, and by the fact I was with Seri. To them we must have seemed to be mere drifters, island-hoppers, young and irresponsible. None of them seemed to recognize Seri without her uniform. They were wrapped up in themselves, united in their impending athanasia.

As the days passed I went through a number of different states of mind about them. For a time I simply disliked them for the vulgarity of the way they displayed their luck. Then I began to pity them: two of the women were obese, and I tried to imagine what an eternity of waddling breathlessness would be like. Then I felt sorry for them all, seeing them as plain people to whom great fortune had come late in life, and celebrating it in the only way they knew how. Soon afterwards I underwent a period of self-dislike, knowing that I was patronizing them and that I was no better than them, just younger and healthier.

Because of the link between us, because I was just like them, I several times was tempted to approach them and find out what they thought about the prize. Perhaps they had the same doubts about it as I had; I only assumed they were hurrying to salvation, and did not know for sure. But the thought of being drawn into their card-playing, good-natured drinking circle deterred me. They would be, inevitably, as interested in me as I could not help being interested in them.

I tried to understand this stand-offishness and explain it to myself. Because I was unsure of my own intentions I did not wish to have to explain myself, either to them or to me. I frequently overheard snatches of their conversations: rambling and imprecise, they often spoke of what they were going to do 'afterwards'. One of the men was convinced that great wealth and influence would be his after he left Collago. The other kept repeating that he would be 'set up for life', as if he only needed enough athanasia to see him through the rest of his retirement, a nice little nest egg to tell his grandchildren about.

I knew, though, that if someone asked me what use I should put my own long life to, my answer would be equally vague. I too would utter homilies about embarking on good works in the community, or returning to university, or joining the Peace Movement. Each of these would be untrue, but they were the only things I could think of as worthwhile, as sufficient moral excuse for accepting the treatment.

The best use to which I could put a long life would be the selfish one of living for a long time, of avoiding death, of being perpetually twenty-nine years old. My only ambition for 'afterwards' was to travel around the islands with Seri.

As the voyage progressed I therefore slipped into a more introspective mood than ever before, feeling unaccountably sad about what I had become involved in. I concentrated on Seri, I watched the ever-changing islands. The names slipped by – Tumo, Lanna, Winho, Salay, Ia, Lillen-cay, Paneron, Junno – some of them names I had heard, some of them not. We were a long way south now, and for a time we could see the distant coast of the wild southern continent: here the Qataari Peninsula reached northwards into the islands, stacked high behind rocky cliffs, but beyond this the land receded southwards and the illusion of endless sea returned, more temperate in this latitude. After the barren appearance of some of the islands in the tropics, the scenery here was soothing to the eye: it was green and more forested, with tidy towns rising up the hills from the sea, and domestic farm animals grazing, and cultivated crops and orchards. The cargoes we loaded and unloaded also revealed the gradual southwards progress: we carried bulk food and oils and machinery in the equatorial seas, later we carried grapes and pomegranates and beer, later still it was cheese and apples and books.

Once I said to Seri: 'Let's get off. I want to see this place.'

The island was Ia, a large, wooded island with sawmills and shipyards. Watching from the deck I liked the way Ia Town was laid out, and I admired the unhurried efficiency of the docks. Ia was an island I wanted to walk in, and sit on grass and smell the earth. From the look of the place you could visualize cold springs and wild flowers and whitewashed farmhouses.

Seri, suntanned from her long idle hours on deck, was beside me as I leaned on the rail.

'We'll never get to Collago if we do.'

'No more ships?'

'No more resolution. We can always come back here.'

Seri had the will to get me to Collago. She remained something of a mystery to me, however much time we spent together. We never talked together very much, and so we argued rarely; by the same token, though, we reached a level of intimacy beyond which it seemed we would never proceed. The plans for island-hopping were hers. I was included in them, and included to the extent that when once I revealed a hesitancy about them she was prepared to abandon them, but I felt I was incidental to them. Her interest in lovemaking was disconcertingly sporadic. Sometimes we would crawl into our tiny bunk in the cramped cabin, and she would say she was too tired or too hot, and that would be the end of it; at other times she would exhaust me with her passions. She was sometimes intensely caring and affectionate, and I liked that. When we talked she asked me all sorts of questions about myself and my past life, yet about herself she was uncommunicative.

Throughout the long voyage, as my doubts about the athanasia treatment remained, the relationship with Seri was dogged by a growing feeling of my own inadequacy. When I was apart from her – when she sunbathed alone, or I was in the bar or was speculating about my fellow would-be immortals – I could not help but wonder what she saw in me. I obviously fulfilled some need in her, but it seemed an unselective need. I sometimes had a suspicion that if someone else came along she would leave me for him. But no one else appeared, and in general I judged it better not to question what was in many ways an ideal, casual friendship.

Towards the end I unpacked my long-neglected manuscript, and took it to the bar, intending to read it through.

It was now two years since I had finished work on it, and it was strange to hold the loose pages again and remember the period I had been writing them. I wondered if I had left it too long, if I had grown away from the person who had tried to resolve a temporary crisis by committing himself to the permanence of the written word. As we grow we do not see ourselves changing – there is the apparent continuity of the mirror, the daily awareness of immediate past – and it takes the reminders of old photographs or old friends to point out the differences. Two years was a substantial period, yet for all that time I had been in a sort of stasis.

In that sense, my attempt to define myself had been a success. By describing my past I had intended to shape my future. If I believed that my true identity was contained in the pages, then I had never left them.

The manuscript was yellowing and the corners of the pages were curled. I slipped off the elastic band that held them all together, and started to read.

The first thing I noticed came as a surprise. In the first two or three lines I had written that I was twenty-nine years old, noting it as one of the few certainties in my life.

Yet this must have been a conceit, a falsification. I had written the manuscript two years ago.

At first this confused me, and I tried to remember what I had had in mind. Then I saw that it was perhaps a clue to understanding the rest of the text. In a sense, it helped account for the two years of stagnation that had followed: my writing had already taken *itself* into account, disallowing further progress.

I read on, trying to identify with the mind that had produced the manuscript and finding, against initial expectations, that I could do so with ease. After I had read only a few chapters, much of which dealt with my relationship with my sister, I felt I needed to read no more. The manuscript confirmed what I had known all along, that my attempt to reach a higher, better truth had been successful. The metaphors lived, and my identity was defined amongst them.

I was alone in the bar; Seri had gone early to our cabin. I sat by myself for another hour, thinking over my uncertainties and reflecting on the irony that the only thing in the world I knew for sure was a rather tattered stack of typewritten pages. Then, exhausted with myself and tired of my endless inner concerns, I went below to sleep.

The next morning, at last, we came to Collago.

CHAPTER 13

When I first won the lottery, and realized that athanasia was mine for the taking, I had tried to imagine what the clinic on Collago would be like. I visualized a gleaming glass-and-steel skyscraper, filled with modern medical equipment, and doctors and nurses moving about the shining corridors and wards with purpose and expertise. Relaxing in the landscaped gardens would be the new immortals, perhaps reclining in bath chairs with blankets over their legs and cushions behind their heads, while orderlies wheeled them to admire the profusion of flowerbeds. Somewhere there would be a gymnasium, where rejuvenated muscles would be exercised; perhaps there would even be a university, where newly acquired wisdom could be disseminated.

The photographs I saw in the office in Muriseay made literal whatever imaginings I might have had. These I had reacted against: the smiling faces, the saturated colours, the blatant attempt to sell me something I had already unwittingly purchased. The clinic, as depicted in the brochure, looked as if it would be somewhere between a health farm and a ski-resort, with physical well-being, exercise and social intercourse predominating.

The ways of the Archipelago were always surprising me, though, for I found none of this. The brochure was a lie, but only in the way all brochures are lies. Everything in the pictures was there to be seen, although the faces were different and now there was no photographer to be smiling for, but when I saw the place for myself everything seemed subtly different. Brochures, by omission, encourage you to bring your own wishes to what you do not see. I had assumed, for instance, that the clinic was in open countryside, but this was the product of careful choice of photographic angle, because it was on the very edge of Collago Town itself. Then I had thought that the gardens and chalets and antiseptic corridors were all there was of the place, but the pictures had not shown the central administrative building. This, an incongruous, dark-brick mansion, loomed over the tastefully spaced wooden chalets. That the interior of the place had been gutted, modernized and equipped with advanced medical facilities I discovered later, but the first sight of the old house gave one an oddly sinister feeling; it had the quality of moor and wind to it, as if it had been transplanted from some romantic melodrama of the past.

We had been met from the ship by a modern minibus operated by the clinic. A driver had stacked our baggage in the back of the vehicle, while a young woman, wearing the Lotterie uniform, took a note of our names. As I guessed, my five fellow passengers had not realized I was one of them. While we drove up the hilly streets of Collago Town, there was an almost palpable sense that Seri and I were interlopers in a private party.

Then we came to the clinic grounds, and our first sight of the place. The incongruities registered themselves, but what I noticed most was how small it was.

'Is this all there is?' I said quietly to Seri.

'What do you want, a whole town?'

'But it seems so small. No wonder they can only treat a few people at a time.'

'The capacity's nothing to do with size. It's the manufacture of the drugs which is the problem.'

'Even so, where's the computer, where do they keep all the files?'

'It's all done here, as far as I know.'

'But the clerical work alone . . .'

It was a minor distraction, but my weeks of self-questioning had given me the habit of doubt. Unless there were more premises elsewhere, the Lotterie-Collago could not operate on its pan-national scale from this place. And the tickets would have to be printed somewhere; the Lotterie would hardly subcontract the work, with all the risk of fraud.

I wanted to ask Seri, but I suddenly felt I should be careful what I said. The bus we were in was tiny, the seats crammed close together. The uniformed young woman, standing at the front beside the driver, was not showing much interest in us but she would be in easy hearing of me if I spoke in normal tones.

The bus drove around to the far side of the house; on this side there were apparently no more outbuildings. The gardens stretched away for some distance, blending imperceptibly with wild ground beyond.

We alighted with the other people and went in through a doorway. We passed through a bare hall and went into a large reception area at the side. Unlike the other people I was carrying my luggage: the holdall, which I slung over my shoulder. My five fellow passengers were now subdued, for the first time since I had noticed them, apparently overawed by the fact that they had finally entered the very building where they would be made to live forever. Seri and I hung back from the rest, near the door.

The young woman who had met us at the harbour went behind a desk placed to one side.

'I need to verify your identities,' she said. 'Your local Lotterie office has given you a coded admission form, and if you would now give this to me I will assign you your chalets. Your personal counsellor will meet you there.'

A minor upheaval followed, as the other passengers had left their forms in their baggage, and had to retrieve them. I wondered why the girl had not said anything on the bus; and I noticed the bored, sour expression she wore.

I took the opportunity to go forward first and identify myself. My admission form was in one of the pouches on the side of my bag, and I laid it on the desk in front of her.

'I'm Peter Sinclair,' I said.

She said nothing, but ticked my name off the list she had

compiled on the bus, then punched the code number on my form into a keyboard in front of her. Silently, and invisibly to me, a readout must have appeared on the screen facing her. There were some thin metal bracelets on the desk, and she passed one of them through a recessed channel in the surface of the desk, presumably encoding it magnetically, then held it towards me.

'Attach this to your right wrist, Mr Sinclair. You will be in Chalet 24, and one of the attendants will show you how to find it. Your treatment will commence tomorrow morning.'

I said: 'I haven't finally decided yet. Whether or not to take the treatment, I mean.'

She glanced up at me then, but her expression remained cold.

'Have you read the information in our brochure?'

'Yes, but I'm still not sure. I'd like to find out more about it.'

'Your counsellor will visit you. It's quite usual for people to be nervous.'

'It's not that I'm—' I was aware of Seri standing close behind me, listening to this. 'I just want to ask a few questions.'

'Your counsellor will tell you anything you wish to know.'

I took the bracelet, feeling my antipathy harden. I could feel the momentum of my win, my travels, my arrival and induction here, taking me ineluctably on towards the treatment, my reservations cast aside. I still lacked the strength to back out, to reject this chance of living. I had an irrational fear of this counsellor, visiting me in the morning, uttering soothing platitudes and propelling me on towards the operating table and the knife, saving my life against my will.

Some of the other people were now returning, their admission forms clasped like passports.

'But if I decide against it,' I said. 'If I change my mind . . . is there any reason why I shouldn't?'

'You are committed to nothing, Mr Sinclair. Your being

here does not imply consent. Until you sign the release form, you may leave at any time.'

'All right,' I said, conscious of the small group of elderly optimists assembling behind me. 'But there's something else. I've got my girlfriend with me. I want her to stay with me in the chalet.'

Her eyes turned briefly towards Seri. 'Does she understand that the treatment is for you alone?'

Seri exhaled breath sharply. I said: 'She's not a child.'

'I'll wait outside, Peter,' Seri said, and went out into the sunlight.

'We can't allow misunderstandings,' the girl said. 'She can stay tonight, but tomorrow she will have to find accommodation in the town. You will only be in the chalet for one or two nights.'

'That suits me fine,' I said, wondering if there was still a chance *Mulligayn* was in the harbour. I turned my back on her and went outside to find Seri.

An hour later Seri had calmed me down, and we were installed in Chalet 24. That evening, before going to bed, Seri and I walked in the darkness through the gardens. Lights were on in the main building, but most of the chalets were dark. We walked as far as the main gate, where we found that two men with dogs were on guard.

As we walked back, I said: 'It's like a prison camp. They've overlooked the barbed wire and watchtowers. Perhaps someone should remind them.'

'I had no idea it was like this,' Seri said.

'I had to go into hospital when I was a child. What I didn't like about that, even then, was the way they treated me. It was as if I didn't exist, except as a body with symptoms. And this place is the same. I really resent that bracelet.'

'Are you wearing it?'

'Not at the moment.' We were following a path through the flowerbeds, but the further we moved from the lights of the main building the more difficult it was to see. A patch of open ground was on our right, so we sat down, discovering that it was a lawn. 'I'm going to leave. First thing in the morning. Will you understand if I do?'

Seri was silent for a while, then said: 'I still think you should go through with it.'

'In spite of all this?'

'It's just a sort of hospital. They've got the institutionalized mind, that's all.'

'It's most of what's putting me off at the moment. I just feel I'm here for something I don't need. As if I volunteered for open-heart surgery or something. I need someone to give me a good reason to go on with it.'

Seri said nothing.

'Well, if it was you, would you take the treatment?'

'It doesn't apply. I haven't won the lottery.'

'You're avoiding the question,' I said. 'I wish I'd never bought that damned ticket. Everything about this place is wrong. I can feel it, but I can't say why.'

'I just think you've been given a chance to have something that very few people have, and that a lot would like. You shouldn't turn your back on it until you're sure. It will stop you dying, Peter. Doesn't that mean anything to you?'

'We all have to die in the end,' I said defensively. 'Even with the treatment. All it does is delay it a bit.'

'No one's died yet.'

'How can you be sure of that?'

'I can't be completely, of course. But in the office we were sent annual reports on all the people who have been treated. The records go back to the beginning, and the list always got longer. There were people on Muriseay. When they came in for their check-ups, they always said how well they felt.'

I said: 'What check-ups?'

In the darkness I could see Seri was facing me, but I could not make out her expression.

'There's an option. You can monitor your health afterwards.'

'So they're not even sure the treatment works!'

'The Lotterie is, but sometimes the patients aren't sure. I

suppose it's a form of psychological reassurance, that the Lotterie does not abandon them once they leave here.'

'They cure everything except hypochondria,' I said, remembering a friend of mine who had become a doctor. She used to say that at least half her patients came to the surgery for the company. Illness was a habit.

Seri had taken my hand. 'It's got to be your decision, Peter. If I was in your position, perhaps I'd feel the same. But I wouldn't want to regret turning down the chance.'

'It just doesn't feel real,' I said. 'I've never worried about death because I've never had to face it. Do other people feel that?'

'I don't know.' Seri was looking away now, staring at the dark trees.

'Seri, I realize I'm going to die one day . . . but I don't *believe* that, except cerebrally. Because I'm alive now I feel I always will be. It's as if there's a sort of life force in me, something strong enough to fend off death.'

'The classic illusion.'

'I know it's not logical,' I said. 'But it means something.'

'Are your parents still alive?'

'My father is. My mother died several years ago. Why?'

'It's not important. Go on.'

I said: 'A couple of years ago I wrote my autobiography. I didn't really know why I was doing it at the time. I was going through something, a kind of identity crisis. Once I started writing I began to discover things about myself, and one of them was the fact that memory has continuity. It became one of the main reasons for writing. As long as I could *remember* myself, then I existed. When I woke up in the mornings the first thing I'd do would be to think back to what I'd done just before going to bed. If the continuity was there, I still existed. And I think it works the other way . . . there's a space ahead that I can anticipate. It's like a balance. I discovered that memory was like a psychic force behind me, and therefore there must be some kind of life force spreading out in front. The human mind, consciousness, exists at the centre. I know that so long as there is one there will always be the other. While I can remember, I am defined.'

Seri said: 'But when you die in the end, because you will . . . when that happens your identity will cease. When you die you lose your memory with everything else.'

'But that's unconsciousness. I'm not scared of that because I won't experience it.'

'You assume you have no soul.'

'I'm not trying to argue a theory. I'm trying to explain what I *feel*. I know that one day I will die, but that's different from actually believing it. The athanasia treatment exists to cure me of something I don't believe I have. Mortality.'

'You wouldn't say that if you suffered from cancer.'

'So far as I know, I don't. I know it's possible I might contract it, but I don't really believe, deep down, that I will. It doesn't scare me.'

'It does me.'

'What do you mean?'

'I'm scared of death. I don't want to die.'

Her voice had gone very quiet, and her head was bent.

'Is that why you're here with me? Because of that?'

'I just want to know if it's possible. I want to be with you when it happens, I want to see you live forever. I can't help that. You asked me what I would do if I won the prize . . . well, I'd take the treatment and not ask why. You say you have never faced death, but I know all about it.'

'What happened?' I said.

'It was a long time ago.' She leaned towards me and I put my arm around her shoulders. 'I suppose it shouldn't matter anymore. It was when I was a child. My mother was an invalid and she was dying slowly for ten years. They said there was no cure for her, but she knew, and we all knew, that if the Lotterie had admitted her she would be alive now.'

I remembered our walk in the village by the petrifying pool, when Seri had argued the Lotterie's case for turning away the sick. I had had no idea of the degree of her contradictions.

'I took the job because I'd heard a rumour that after some

years the staff qualify for free treatment. It wasn't true, but I had to stay on. These people who win, who turn up at the office . . . I loathe them but I have to be near them. It's a kind of rapture, knowing that they will not die, that they can never be ill. Do you know what it is to be in real pain? I had to watch my mother die, knowing there was something that could save her! Every month my father went out and bought lottery tickets. Hundreds of them, whatever cash he had spare. And all that money came to this place, and the treatment that could have saved her is given to people like you and people like Mankinova, and all the other people who don't really need it.'

I drew away from her, and picked stupidly at the grass with my fingers. I had never known pain, beyond the transient agony of a neglected tooth, of a broken arm in childhood, a twisted ankle, a septic finger. I had never considered it before, never thought about death in any way except the abstract.

I failed to measure the value of the clinic's treatment, but this was only because I did not understand the alternative.

Life seemed long and untroubled because it had been so far. But good health was a deception, a variant from the norm. I remembered the hundreds of prosaic conversations I had heard throughout my life, snatches of dialogue in public transport and restaurants and shops: most of them seemed to be about illness or worries, their own or those of close ones. There had been a little shop near my apartment in Jethra where for a time I bought fruit. After a few weeks I had found somewhere else, because for some reason the shopkeeper encouraged his customers to talk about themselves, and waiting to buy fruit was always attended by nightmare glimpses into other people's lives. An operation, a seizure, an unexpected death.

I had shrunk away from that, as if by contagion I would suffer too.

'Then what do you think I should do?' I said at last.

'I still think you should go ahead. Isn't that obvious?'

133

'Frankly, no. You just contradict yourself. Everything you say makes it worse for me.'

Seri sat in silence, staring at the ground. I realized that she and I were moving away from each other. We had never been close, except for affection and the temporary proximities of sex. I had always had some difficulty in relating to her, sensing that we had landed accidentally in each other's lives. For a time our lives were running parallel, but inevitably they would diverge. Once I had thought it would be the athanasia that would divide us, but perhaps it would take less than that to split us up. She would move on, I would move on.

'Peter, I'm getting cold.' There was a wind from the sea, and the latitude was temperate. Here it was just the beginning of summer, as in Jethra it had been the first weeks of autumn.

'You haven't explained yourself,' I said.

'Do I have to?'

'It would help me if you could. That's all.'

We walked back to our chalet, and Seri linked her hand in my arm. Nothing had been resolved, the decision would have to be mine. Because I looked to Seri for an answer I dodged the uncertainty in my own mind.

Like that house in the village, the chalet felt warm after the relative cool outside. Seri sprawled on one of the two narrow beds and began reading one of the magazines we had found. I went to the other end, where an area was furnished as a writing space. There was a desk and a chair, both well made and modern, a wastepaper basket, a typewriter, a stack of clean paper and a number of different pens and pencils. I had always had an enjoyable appreciation for clean stationery, and I sat at the desk for a few minutes, fingering the keys of the typewriter. It was much more efficiently designed and solidly built than the little portable I had used for my manuscript, and as you sometimes feel when you sit at the controls of an unfamiliar car that you could drive it fast and safely, so I got the impression that were I to work at this desk I could write fluently and well.

'Do you know why they've put all this stuff here?' I said to Seri.

'It's in the brochure,' she said in an irritated voice, not looking up from her magazine.

'I'm not disturbing you, am I?'

'Would you just shut up for a while? I want a rest from you.'

I took down my holdall and found the brochure. I flipped through it, glancing again at the photographs. One was of the interior of one of the chalets, brightly lit and unoccupied. There were no sandals scattered on the matting on the floor, no clothes thrown untidily on the ends of the beds, no empty beer cans lined up on the shelf, no shadows on the brilliant white walls.

In the caption to this photograph it said: '. . . each of our chalets includes modern facilities for the writing of your private account, which is a crucial part of our exclusive treatment.'

This must mean the questionnaire Seri had told me about. So I was to write of myself, to tell the story of my life, so that afterwards I could be made into the words I had written. No one here at the clinic could have known that this was something I had already done.

I mused for a while, thinking of the sort of people who had been on the ship with us, each tonight sitting at a desk like this one, contemplating their own lives. I wondered what they would find to say.

It was a return to the hubris I felt whenever I thought of the others. What, indeed, had I found worth saying? While writing, I had been humbled by the discovery that very little of interest had happened to me.

Was this perhaps the real reason I had invented so much? Was it not, after all, that truth was best found through metaphor, but that self-deceit and self-embellishment were the principal motives?

I looked along the cabin at the top of Seri's head, bent over the magazine while she read. Her pale blonde hair fell forward, concealing her face. She was bored with me, wanted a break. I had become self-obsessed, introspective, endlessly questioning. My inner life was constantly externalizing itself, and Seri had always been there to bear the brunt of it. I had spent too much time in my inner world; I too was tiring of it, wanted an end to it all.

Seri ignored me as I undressed and climbed into the other bed. Some time later she turned off the lights and crawled into her own bed. I listened to the sound of her breathing until I drifted off into sleep.

In the middle of the night, Seri came to lie with me. She held me tightly, kissed my face and neck and ear until I wakened, and then we made love.

CHAPTER 14

The following morning, while Seri was taking a shower, the counsellor arrived at the chalet. Almost at once it was as if my doubts were focused.

Her name was Lareen Dobey; she introduced herself, invited me to use her first name, and sat down in the chair behind the desk. I was on my guard from the moment she arrived, sensing the momentum of the Lotterie's system behind her. She was here to counsel me, implying she was trained to persuade me.

She was middle-aged, married, and reminded me of a teacher I had had in my first year at senior school. This alone gave me the instinct to resist her influence, but on a more rational level it was clear she took it for granted that I would be going ahead to take the treatment. I now had an object for my doubts, and my thoughts clarified.

There was a brief, irrelevant conversation: Lareen asked me about my journey, what islands I had visited. I found myself taking a mental step back from her, secure in my new objectivity. Lareen was here to counsel me through the treatment, and I had at last reached my decision.

'Have you had breakfast yet, Peter?' she said.

'No.'

She reached behind a curtain beside the desk and pulled forward a telephone receiver I had not known was there.

'Two breakfasts for Chalet 24, please.'

'Would you make that three?' I said.

Lareen looked at me inquisitively, and I explained briefly about Seri. She changed the order, then hung up.

'Is she a close friend?' Lareen said.

'Fairly close. Why?'

'We sometimes find that the presence of someone else can be distressing. Most people come here alone.'

'Well, I haven't decided—'

'On the other hand, from our point of view the rehabilitation process can be greatly assisted. How long have you known Seri?'

'A few weeks.'

'And do you expect the relationship to go on?'

Annoyed by the frankness of the question, I said nothing. Seri was within earshot, had she chosen to listen, and anyway I could not see what it had to do with this woman. She stared at me, until I looked away. In the shower cubicle I heard Seri turn off the water.

'All right, I understand,' Lareen said. 'Maybe you find it difficult to trust me.'

'Are you trying to psychoanalyse me?'

'No. I'm trying to learn what I can about you, so I can help you later.'

I knew I was wasting this woman's time. Whether or not I 'trusted' her was not the issue; the confidence I lacked was in myself. I no longer wanted what her organization offered me.

Just then, Seri came in from the shower cubicle. She had a towel wrapped around her body and another about her head. She glanced at Lareen, then went to the other end of the chalet and pulled the screen across.

Knowing that Seri could hear me, I said: 'I might as well be honest with you, Lareen. I've decided not to accept the treatment.'

'Yes, I see. Are your reasons ethical or religious?'

'Neither . . . well, ethical I suppose.' The promptness of the question had again taken me by surprise.

'Did you have these feelings when you bought the ticket?' Her tone was interested, not inquisitive.

'No, they came later.' Lareen was waiting, so I went on, noting subconsciously that she was expert at manipulating a response out of me. Now that I had stated my decision I felt a strong compulsion to explain myself. 'I can't really describe what it is, except that my being here feels wrong. I keep thinking of other people who need the treatment more urgently than I do, and that I don't really deserve it. I don't know what I'm going to do with athanasia. I'm just going to waste it, I think.' Still Lareen said nothing. 'Then yesterday, when we arrived here. It's like a hospital, and I'm not ill.'

'Yes, I know what you mean.'

'Don't try to talk me into it, please. I've made up my mind.'

I could hear Seri moving around behind the screen, brushing her hair out.

'You know you are dying, Peter?'

'Yes, but that doesn't mean anything to me. We're all dying.'

'Some of us sooner than others.'

'That's why it doesn't seem to matter. I'll die in the end, whether or not I take the treatment.'

Lareen had made a note on the pad of paper she carried. Somehow it indicated that she had not accepted my rejection of the treatment.

'Have you ever heard of a writer called Deloinne?' she said.

'Yes, of course. *Renunciation.*'

'Have you read the book recently?'

'When I was at school.'

'We've got copies here. Why don't you borrow one?'

'I wouldn't have thought that was approved reading here,' I said. 'It doesn't exactly agree with your treatment.'

'You said you didn't want to be talked out of your decision. If you're not going to change your mind, I want you to be sure you've not made a mistake.'

'All right,' I said. 'Why did you mention it?'

'Because the central point of Deloinne's argument is that the irony of life is its finite nature, and that the terror of death is caused by its infinitude. When death comes, there is no reversing it. A human being can therefore only achieve whatever it is he aspires to in a relatively brief time. Deloinne argues – mistakenly, in my personal opinion – that it is the temporary nature of life that makes it worth living. If life is prolonged, as we can prolong it here, then life's achievements become attenuated. Deloinne also points out, correctly, that Lotterie-Collago has never made guarantees against eventual death. He therefore comes to the conclusion that a short, rich life is preferable to a long and impoverished one.'

'That's how I see it,' I said.

'So you prefer to live your normal span?'

'Until I won the prize, I'd never even thought about it.'

'What would you call a normal span? Thirty years? Forty?'

'More than that, of course,' I said. 'Isn't normal life expectancy somewhere around seventy-five years?'

'On average, yes. How old are you, Peter? Thirty-one, isn't it?'

'No. Twenty-nine.'

'Your records say thirty-one. But it doesn't matter.'

Seri came out from behind the screen, fully dressed but with her hair hanging loose and wet. She had a towel around her shoulders, and a comb in her hand. Lareen took no notice of her as she sat down in the other seat, but instead unclipped a large fold of computer print-out paper and examined the top sheet.

'Peter, I'm afraid I've got some rather hard news for you. Deloinne was a philosopher but you try to take him literally. Whatever you *say*, you believe instinctively that you will live forever. The facts are rather different.' She was moving her pencil over the sheet. 'Here we are. Your life expectancy, at present, is put at just under four and a half years.'

I looked at Seri. 'That's nonsense!'

'I'm sorry, but it's not. I know you find it difficult to believe, but I'm afraid it's extremely likely.'

'But I'm not ill. I've never been ill in my life.'

'That's not what your medical records say. You were hospitalized when you were eight, and you were under treatment for several weeks.'

'That was just a childhood illness. Kidney trouble, they said, but the doctors told my parents I was all right and I've never had any trouble since.' Again I looked at Seri, seeking reassurance, but she was staring at Lareen.

'When you were in your early twenties, you went to your GP several times. Headaches.'

'This is ridiculous! That was just a minor thing. The doctor said it was because I was working too hard. I was at university. Everybody gets headaches! Anyway, how do you know all this? Are you a doctor?'

'No, I'm just a counsellor. If it was as minor as you say, then perhaps our computer prognosis is wrong. You can be examined if you wish. At the moment, all we have to go on is your records.'

'Let me see that,' I said, pointing at the sheet of paper. Lareen hesitated, and for a moment I thought she was going to refuse. But then she passed it over.

I read through it quickly. It was in detail accurate, though selectively. It listed my birth date, parents, sister, addresses, schools, medical treatment. Further on were more unexpected details. There was a list (incomplete) of my friends, places I had often visited, and, disturbingly, details of how I had voted, the tithes I had paid, the political society I joined at university, my contacts with a fringe theatre group, my connections with people who were monitoring the Covenant. There was a section on what the computer called 'imbalance indications': that I drank frequently, had friends of dubious political affiliation, was fickle with women, was given to unreasonable rages when younger, was described as 'moody and introverted' by one of my tutors, was described as 'only 80 per cent reliable' by a former employer, had been granted deferment of the draft on 'psychological' grounds, and that for a time I had been involved with a young woman descended from Glaundian immigrants.

'Where the hell does this stuff come from?' I said, brandishing the sheet.

'Isn't it accurate?'

'Never mind that! It's a complete distortion!'

'But is it factually accurate?'

'Yes . . . but it misses out a lot of things.'

'We didn't ask for these details. This is just what came out of the computer.'

'Do they have files like this on everyone?'

'I've no idea,' Lareen said. 'You must ask your own government that. All we're concerned with is your life expectancy, although this extra information can have a bearing. Have you read the medical summary?'

'Where is it?'

Lareen left her seat and stood beside me. She pointed with her pencil. 'These figures are our codes. Don't worry about them. This is where your life expectancy is printed.'

The computer had printed 35.46 years.

'I don't believe it,' I said. 'It must be a mistake.'

'We're not often wrong.'

'What does the figure mean? Is that how long I have to live?'

'That's the age at which the computer says you are most likely to die.'

'But what am I suffering from? I don't *feel* ill!'

Beside me, Seri took my hand. 'Listen to her, Peter.'

Lareen had returned to her seat behind the desk. 'I can arrange for a medical examination, if you like.'

'Is there something wrong with my heart? Is it something like that?'

'The computer doesn't say. But you can be cured here.'

I was hardly listening. All of a sudden my body felt as if it were a mass of previously unnoticed symptoms. I remembered the numerous aches and pains I had felt: indigestion, bruises, stiff legs, a sore back after working too long, the hangovers I sometimes suffered, the headaches at university, the coughing with head colds. All seemed innocuous and explicable at the time, but now I wondered. Did they hint at something worse? I imagined clotted arteries and neoplasms and gallstones and ruptures, lurking within me, destroying me. Yet it still had a faintly ridiculous aspect: in spite of everything I continued to feel as healthy as ever.

I resented utterly the fact that the Lotterie had thrust this on me. I stood up, looked out of the window, and across the lawns towards the sea. I was free, under no compulsion; Seri and I could leave immediately.

But then the realization: no matter what was wrong with me, there was a cure for it! If I took the athanasia treatment I should never again be ill, I should live forever. Illness thwarted.

It was an exhilarating feeling, one that seemed to give me great power and freedom. I suddenly realized how inhibiting was the prospect of illness: that one was cautious with food, or wary of too little exercise, or too much, aware of the signs of advancing age, shortage of wind, not getting enough sleep, or drinking or smoking too much. I would never need worry about such things again: I could abuse my body as I wished, or ignore it. I should never weaken, never decline.

Already, at the advanced age of twenty-nine, I had felt the first stirrings of envy of those younger than me. I saw the effortlessly agile bodies of younger men, the slender unsupported bodies of girls. They all looked so fit, as if good health were something to be taken for granted. Perhaps someone older than myself would find this amusing to contemplate, but from my point of view I had already noticed myself slowing up. After the athanasia treatment I would remain forever twenty-nine. In a few years' time, those young adults I secretly envied would be my physical equals, yet I would have extra years of insight. And with every new generation I would acquire a greater mental stature.

Given the jolt, the news of my life expectancy, I began to recognize that the Lotterie's treatment was subtly different from Deloinne's interpretation. Because I read his book at an impressionable age, Deloinne had influenced me too much. I made his ideas my own, without questioning them. Deloinne saw athanasia as an abnegation of life, yet really it was an affirmation.

As Seri had pointed out, the coming of death brings the destruction of memory. But life *is* memory. As long as I am alive, as long as I wake every morning, I remember my life, and as the years pass my memory becomes enriched. Old men are wise, not by nature but by absorption and retention, and by the accumulation of sufficient memories to be able to select what is important.

Memory is continuity too, a sense of identity and place and consequence. I am what I am because I can remember how I became it.

Memory was the psychic force I had described to Seri: the momentum of life, driving from behind and anticipating what is to come.

With increased lifespan the quantity of memory would increase, but a mind can fine-tune this into quality.

As memory is enhanced, so is one's perception of life.

This is the fear of death. Because it is unconsciousness, the obliteration of all physical and mental processes, the memory dies with the body. The human mind, at pivot of past and future, vanishes with its memories. Thus, from death there is no remembering.

The fear of dying is not just the terror of pain, the humiliation of the loss of faculties, the fall into the abyss . . . but the primeval fear that afterwards one might *remember* it.

The act of dying is the only experience of the dead. Those who are living cannot be alive if memory includes that of the state of death.

I was aware, beyond my new introspection, that Seri and Lareen were speaking to each other: polite exchanges and pleasantries, places for Seri to visit on the island, an hotel she might stay in. And I was also aware that a man had brought a large tray bearing breakfast, but I was not interested in food.

Lareen's computer print-out lay on the desk, the prediction

of my life expectancy visible on the face I could see. 35.46 years . . . a statistical probability, not really a prediction.

A young man in his early twenties would have an expectancy of half a century. Of course, he might only live another three weeks, but the statistics were against this.

My own expectation was said to be another six years. I could live to be ninety, but the statistics were against this too.

However, I had no way of knowing if the figures were reliable. I looked again at the print-out, stamped with all the implacable neatness of a computer, and read again through the sundry evidence against me. It was a biased picture, saying almost nothing about me that could be construed in my favour. I was said to drink a lot, was moody, had a certain political dubiety. This was supposed to influence my general health and well-being; from this the computer had estimated my life span.

Why had it not taken other facts into account? For instance, that I often went swimming in summer, that I enjoyed well-cooked fresh food and ate plenty of fruit, that I had given up smoking, had attended church until I was fourteen, was generous to charities, kind to animals and had blue eyes?

They all seemed just as relevant or irrelevant to me, yet each would presumably influence the computer, and some might predicate a few extra years for me.

I felt suspicious. These figures had been produced by an organization that sold a product. No secret was made of the fact that Lotterie-Collago was profit-making, that its principal source of revenue was the sales of its tickets, and that every healthy athanasian who emerged from the clinic was a walking advertisement for their business. It was in their interests that winners of the lottery accept the treatment, and therefore they would offer any inducement they could.

I reserved judgement on the treatment, but I resolved that I would make a decision only after an independent medical examination. I continued to feel healthy; I was suspicious of the computer; I found athanasia a challenge.

I turned back to the other two. They had started on the toast and cereals the man had brought. As I sat down, I saw Seri looking at me, and she knew I had changed my mind.

CHAPTER 15

The clinic's medical centre occupied one wing of the main building. Here all recipients of the athanasia treatment were given a screening before progressing further. I had never before undergone a complete medical, and found the experience in turn tiring, alarming, boring, humiliating and interesting. I was readily impressed by the array of modern diagnostic equipment, but I was intended not to understand the functions of most of it. The preliminary screening was by direct interaction with a computer; later I was placed in a machine I took to be a whole-body scanner; after further more detailed X-raying of specific parts of my body – my head, my lower back, my left forearm and my chest – I was briefly interviewed by a doctor, then told to dress and return to my chalet.

Seri had left to find an hotel, and there was no sign of Lareen. I sat on my bed in the cabin, reflecting on the psychological factors in hospitals, in which the removal of the patient's clothing is only the first step of many by which he is reduced to an animated slab of meat. In this condition, individuality is suppressed for the greater glory of symptoms, the former presumably interfering with the appreciation of the latter.

I read my manuscript for a while, to remind me of who I was, but then I was interrupted by the arrival of Lareen Dobey and the man who had interviewed me, Doctor Corrob. Lareen smiled wanly at me, and went to sit in the chair by the desk.

I stood up, sensing something.

'Mrs Dobey tells me you are in doubt as to whether or not you will accept the treatment,' Corrob said.

'That's right. But I wanted to hear what you had to say.'

'My advice is that you should accept the treatment without delay. Your life is in great danger without it.'

I glanced at Lareen, but she was looking away. 'What's wrong with me?'

'We have detected an anomaly in one of the main blood vessels leading to your brain. It's called a cerebro-vascular aneurysm. It's a weakness in the wall of the vessel, and it could burst at any time.'

'You're making it up!'

'Why do you think that?' Corrob at least looked surprised.

'You're trying to frighten me into having the treatment.'

Corrob said: 'I'm only telling you what we've diagnosed. I'm retained by the Lotterie as a consultant. What I'm telling you is that you have a serious condition, which if left unattended will certainly kill you.'

'But why has this never been found before?'

'Perhaps you have not been examined recently. We know that when you were a child you suffered a kidney condition. Although this was dealt with at the time, it has left you with a higher than average blood pressure. You also admit to a drinking habit.'

'Just a normal amount!' I said.

'In your case the normal amount should be none at all, if you care for your health. You say you are a regular drinker, taking the equivalent of a bottle of wine a day. In your condition this is extremely foolish.'

Again I looked at Lareen, and now she was watching me.

'This is crazy!' I said to her. 'I'm not ill!'

'This isn't really for you to decide,' Corrob said. 'According to the results from the cerebral angiogram, you are a very sick man.' He stood with his hand on the door, as if anxious to leave. 'Of course, the decision is yours, but my advice is that you should take the treatment immediately.'

'Would that cure this?'

Corrob said: 'Your counsellor will explain.'

'And there's no danger?'

'No . . . the treatment is perfectly safe.'

'Then that settles it,' I said. 'If you're sure—'

Corrob was holding a small file I had thought must be the case notes on a patient; now I realized it must be on me. He passed it to Lareen. 'Mr Sinclair should be admitted to the athanasia unit immediately. How much time do you require for the rehabilitation profile?'

'At least another day, perhaps two.'

'Sinclair is to be given priority. The aneurysm is a severe one. There's no question that we can allow an attack to happen while he's in the clinic. If he tries to cause delays, he must be off the island tonight.'

'I'll clear him by this evening.'

All this had been said as if I were not there. Corrob turned back to me.

'You must take no solids after four this afternoon,' he said. 'If you're thirsty, you may drink water or light fruit juice. But no alcohol. Mrs Dobey will visit you in the morning, and then you'll be admitted for the treatment. Do you understand?'

'Yes, but I want to know—'

'Mrs Dobey will explain what will happen.' He went through the door, and closed it quickly behind him. He left a whirling air space.

I sat on my bed, ignoring Lareen. I accepted what the doctor had said, even though I continued to feel as well as ever. There was something about the medical manner, the way a symptom was made to be inferior to the doctor's knowledge. I remembered visiting my GP a few years before, complaining of blocked sinuses. After examining me he had discovered that I had been sleeping in a centrally heated bedroom, and, worse, I had been using a proprietary brand of decongestant nose drops. Suddenly, the sinusitis was the consequence of my own misdeeds, I was to blame. I left the surgery that day feeling guilty and humbled. Now, with the departure of Corrob, I felt that I was again guilty in some way of inflicting a weakened blood vessel on myself. I had been a patient as a child, I was a drinker when an adult. For the first time in my life I felt defensive about drinking, felt the need to deny or explain or justify.

It must have been something to do with the clinic's own defensiveness; the staff, acutely conscious of the controversy surrounding the treatment, made the recipients a party to the system. The willing were inducted smoothly and conspiratorially; the unwilling or the reluctant were psychologically manipulated then medically intimidated.

I wished Seri were with me, and I wondered how long she would be gone. I wanted the chance to be a human being again: perhaps go for a walk with her, or make love, or just sit around doing nothing.

Lareen closed the file she had been reading. 'How do you feel, Peter?'

'How do you think I feel?'

'I'm sorry . . . there's no satisfaction for me in the computer being right. If it's any consolation, at least we can do something for you here. If you were still at home, it probably wouldn't have been diagnosed.'

'I can still hardly believe it.' Outside, a man was mowing the lawn; in the distance I could see a part of Collago Town, and behind it the headland by the harbour. I moved away from the window by the bed, and went to sit with Lareen. 'The doctor said you would explain the treatment.'

'For the aneurysm?'

'Yes, and the athanasia.'

'Tomorrow you'll go in for conventional surgery on the diseased artery. What the surgeon will probably do is implant a temporary by-pass until the artery regenerates itself. This should happen quite quickly.'

'What do you mean by regenerate?' I said.

'You'll be given a number of hormonal and enzymal injections. These stimulate cell replication in parts of the body where it doesn't normally take place, such as the brain. In other parts, the enzymes control replication, preventing malignancies and keeping your organs in good condition. After the treatment, in other words, your body will constantly renew itself.'

150

'I've heard that I have to have a check-up every year,' I said.

'No, but you can if you wish. What the surgeons will also do is implant a number of microprocessor monitors. These can be checked at any of the Lotterie's offices, and if anything is going wrong you will be given advice on what to do. In some cases you can be re-admitted here.'

'Lareen, either the treatment is permanent, or it isn't.'

'It's permanent, but in a particular way. All we can do here is prevent organic decay. For instance, do you smoke?'

'No. I used to.'

'Suppose you were to start again. You could smoke as many cigarettes as you wished, and you would never develop lung cancer. That's definite. But you could still contract bronchitis or emphysema, and carbon monoxide would put a strain on your heart. The treatment won't prevent you from being killed in a road accident, and it won't stop you drowning, and you can still get hernias and chilblains, and you can still break your neck. We can stop the body degenerating, and we can help you build immunity to infections, but if you abuse yourself you can still find ways of causing damage.'

Reminders of a body's frailties: ruptures and fractures and bruises. The weaknesses one knew about, tried not to think about, observed in other people, overheard in shop conversations. I was developing sensibilities about health I had never had before. Did the acquisition of immortality simply make one more aware of death?

I said to Lareen: 'How long does this take?'

'Altogether, about two or three weeks. There'll be a short recovery period after the operation tomorrow. As soon as the consultant thinks you're ready, the enzyme injections will start.'

'I can't stand injections,' I said.

'They don't use hypodermic needles. It's a bit more sophisticated than that. Anyway, you won't be aware of the treatment.'

'You mean I'll be anaesthetized?' A sudden dread.

'No, but once the first injections are made you'll become

semi-conscious. It probably sounds frightening, but most patients have said they found it pleasant.'

I valued my hold on consciousness. Once, when I was twelve, I was knocked off my bicycle by a bully, and suffered concussion and three days' retrospective amnesia. The loss of those three days was the central mystery of my childhood. Although I was unconscious for less than half an hour, my return to awareness was accompanied by a sense of oblivion behind me. When I returned to school, sporting a black eye and a splendidly lurid bandage around my forehead, I was brought face to face with the fact that those three days had not only existed, but that *I* had existed within them. There had been lessons and games and written exercises, and presumably conversations and arguments, yet I could remember none of them. During those days I must have been alert, conscious and self-aware, feeling the continuity of memory, sure of my identity and existence. An event that *followed* them, though, eradicated them, just as one day death would erase all memory. It was my first experience of a kind of death, and since then, although unconsciousness itself was not to be feared, I saw memory as the key to sentience. I existed as long as I remembered.

'Lareen, are you an athanasian?'

'No, I'm not.'

'Then you've never experienced the treatment.'

'I've worked with patients for nearly twenty years. I can't claim any more than that.'

'But you don't know what it feels like,' I said.

'Not directly, no.'

'The truth is, I'm scared of losing my memory.'

'I understand that. My job here is to help you regain it afterwards. But it's inevitable that you must lose what you now have as your memory.'

'Why is it inevitable?'

'It's a chemical process. To give you longevity we must stop the brain deteriorating. In the normal thanatic body brain cells never replicate, so your mental ability steadily declines.

Every day you lose thousands of brain cells. What we do here is induce replication in the cells, so that however long you live your mental capacity is unimpaired. But when the replication begins, the new cellular activity brings almost total amnesia.'

'That's precisely what frightens me,' I said. A mind sliding away, life receding, continuity lost.

'You'll experience nothing that will scare you. You will enter the fugue state, which is like being in a continuous dream. In this, you'll see images from your life, remember journeys and meetings, people will seem to speak to you, you will feel able to touch, experience emotions. Your mind will be giving up what it contains. It's just your own life.'

The hold released, sentience dying. Entry into fugue, where the only reality was dream.

'And when I come round I'll remember nothing about it.'

'Why do you say that?'

'It's what surgeons always say, isn't it? They believe it comforts people.'

'It's true. You'll wake up here in this chalet. I'll be here, and your friend, Seri.'

I wanted to see Seri. I wanted Lareen to go away.

'But I'll have no memory,' I said. 'They'll destroy my memory.'

'It can be replaced. That's my job.'

In the fugue the dream dispersed, leaving a void. Life returned later, in the form of this calm-eyed, patient woman, returning my memories to me as if she were a hand writing words on blank paper.

I said: 'Lareen, how can I know that afterwards I'll be the same?'

'Because nothing in you will be changed, except your capacity to live.'

'But I am what I remember. If you take that away I cannot be the same person again.'

'I'm trained to restore your memory, Peter. To do that, you've got to help me now.'

153

She produced an attractively packaged folder, containing a thick wad of partially printed pages.

'There isn't as much time as we would normally have, but you should be able to manage this during the evening.'

'Let me see it.'

'You must be as frank and truthful as possible,' Lareen said, passing the folder to me. 'Use as much space as you like. There's spare paper in the desk.'

The papers felt heavy, auguring hours of work. I glanced at the first page, where I could write my name and address. Later, the questions dealt with school. Later, with friendships, sex and love. There seemed no end to the questions, each phrased carefully so as to promote frankness in my answer. I found that I could not read them, that the words blurred as I flicked the pages across.

For the first time since sentence of death had been pronounced on me, I felt the stirrings of revolt. I had no intention of answering these questions.

'I don't need this,' I said to Lareen. I tossed the questionnaire on to the desk. 'I've already written my autobiography, and you'll have to use that.'

I turned away from her, feeling angry.

'You heard what the doctor said, Peter. If you don't co-operate they'll make you leave the island tonight.'

'I'm co-operating, but I'm not going to answer those questions. It's all written down already.'

'Where is it? Can I see it?'

My manuscript was on my bed, where I had left it. I gave it to her. For some reason I was unable to look at her. As it was briefly in my hands the manuscript had transmitted a sense of reassurance, a link with what was soon to become my forgotten past.

I heard Lareen turn a few of the pages, and when I looked back at her she was reading quickly from the third or fourth page. She glanced at the last page, then set it aside.

'When did you write this?'

'Two years ago.'

Lareen stared at the pages. 'I don't like working without the questionnaire. How do I know you've left nothing out?'

'Surely that's my risk?' I said. 'Anyway, it's complete.' I described the way I had written, how I had set myself the task of expressing wholeness and truth on paper.

She turned again to the last page. 'It isn't finished. Do you realize that?'

'I was interrupted, but it doesn't matter. I was almost at the end, and although I did try to finish it later, it seemed better the way it is.' Lareen said nothing, watching me and manipulating more from me. Resisting her, I said: 'It's unfinished because my life is unfinished.'

'If you wrote it two years ago, what's happened since?'

'That's the point, isn't it?' I was still feeling hostile to her, yet in spite of this her strategic silences continued to influence me. Another came, and I was unable to resist it. 'When I wrote the manuscript I found that my life formed into patterns, and that everything I had done fitted into them. Since I finished writing I've found that it's still true, that all I've done in the last two years has just added details to a shape.'

'I'll have to take this away and read it,' Lareen said.

'All right. But take care of it.'

'Of course I'll be careful.'

'I feel it's a part of me, something that can't be replaced.'

'I could replicate it for you,' Lareen said, and laughed as if she had made a joke. 'I mean, I'll get it photocopied for you. Then you can have the original back and I'll work with the copy.'

I said: 'That's what they're going to do to me, isn't it? I'm going to be photocopied. The only difference is that I won't get the original back. I'll be given the copy, but the original will be blank.'

'It was only a joke, Peter.'

'I know, but you made me think.'

'Do you want to reconsider filling out my questionnaire? If you don't trust the manuscript—'

'It's not that I distrust,' I said. 'I live by what I wrote, because I *am* what I wrote.'

I closed my eyes, turning away from her again. How could I ever forget that obsessive writing and rewriting, the warm summer, the hillside view of Jethra? I particularly remembered being on the verandah of the villa I had borrowed from Colan the evening I made my most exciting discovery: that recollection was only partial, that the artistic recreation of the past constituted a higher truth than mere memory. Life could be rendered in metaphorical terms; these were the patterns I mentioned to Lareen. The actual details of, for instance, my years at school were only of incidental interest, yet considered metaphorically, as an experience of learning and growing, they became a larger, higher event. I related to them directly, because they had been my own experiences, but they were also related to the larger body of human experience because they dealt with the verities. Had I merely recounted the humdrum narrative, the catalogue of anecdotal details in literal memory, I should have been telling only half the story.

I could not separate myself from my context, and in this my manuscript became a wholeness, describing my living, describing my life.

I therefore knew that to answer Lareen's questionnaire would produce only half-truths. There was no room for elaboration in literal answers, no capacity for metaphor, or for *story*.

Lareen was glancing at her wristwatch.

'Do you know it's after three?' she said. 'You missed lunch, and you're not allowed food after four.'

'Can I get a meal at this time?'

'At the refectory. Tell the staff you're starting treatment tomorrow, and they'll know what to give you.'

'Where's Seri? Shouldn't she be back by now?'

'I told her not to be back before five.'

'I want her with me tonight,' I said.

'That's up to you and her. She mustn't be here when you go up to the clinic.'

I said: 'But afterwards, can I see her then?'

'Of course you can. We'll both need her.' Lareen had tucked my manuscript under her arm, ready to take it away, but now she pulled it out again. 'How much does Seri know about you, about your background?'

'We've talked a bit while we were travelling. We both talked about ourselves.'

'Look, I've had an idea.' Lareen held out the manuscript for me to take. 'I'll read this later, while you're in the clinic. Tonight, let Seri read this, and talk to her about it. The more she knows about you the better. It could be very important.'

I took the manuscript back, thinking of the way my life and privacy were being invaded. In writing of myself I had exposed myself; in the manuscript I was naked. I had not written to promote or excuse myself; I had just been honest, and in the process had found myself frequently unlikable. For this reason, the very idea of someone else reading the manuscript would have been unthinkable a few weeks before. Yet two women I hardly knew were now to read my work, and presumably would know me as well as I knew myself.

Even as I resented the intrusion a part of me rushed towards them, urging them to close scrutiny of my identity. In their interpretation, passed back to me, I would become myself again.

After Lareen had left I walked across the sloping lawns to the refectory, and was given the authorized pre-treatment meal. The condemned man ate a light salad, and afterwards was still hungry.

Seri reappeared in the evening, tired from being in the sun all day and walking too far. She had eaten before returning, and again I glimpsed the effect of what was happening. Already our temporary liaison was disrupted: we spent a day apart, ate meals at different times. Afterwards our lives would proceed at different paces. I talked to her about what had happened during the day, what I had learned.

'Do you believe them?' she said.

'I do now.'

Seri placed her hands on the sides of my face, touching my temples with light fingertips. 'They think you will die.'

'They're hoping it won't happen tonight,' I said. 'Very bad for publicity.'

'You mustn't excite yourself.'

'What does that mean?'

'Separate beds tonight.'

'The doctor said nothing about sex.'

'No, but I did.'

The energy had gone out of her teasing, and I sensed a growing silence within her. She was acting like a concerned relative before an operation, making bad-taste jokes about bedpans and enemas, covering up a darker fear.

I said: 'Lareen wants you to help with the rehabilitation.'

'Do you want me to?'

'I can't imagine it without you. That's why you came, isn't it?'

'You know why I'm here, Peter.' She hugged me then, but turned away after a few seconds, looking down.

'I want you to read something this evening,' I said. 'Lareen suggested it.'

'What is it?'

'I haven't enough time to answer her questionnaire,' I said, fudging the answer. 'But before I left home I wrote a manuscript. My life story. Lareen's seen it, and she's going to use it for the rehabilitation. If you read it this evening, I can talk to you about it.'

'How long is it?'

'Quite long. More than two hundred pages, but it's typewritten. It shouldn't take too long.'

'Where is it?'

I passed it to her.

'Why don't you just talk to me, like you did on the boat?' She was holding the manuscript loosely, letting the pages spread. 'I feel this is, well, something you wrote for yourself, something private.'

'It's what you've got to use.' I started to explain my motives for writing it, what I had been trying to do, but Seri moved away to the other bed and began to read. She turned the pages quickly, as if she was only skimming, and I wondered how much of it she could take in with such a superficial reading.

I watched her as she went through the first chapter, the long explanatory passage where I was working out my then dilemma, my series of misfortunes, my justification for self-examination. She reached the second chapter, and because I was watching closely I noticed that she paused on the first page and read the opening paragraph again. She looked back to the first chapter.

She said: 'Can I ask you something?'

'Shouldn't you read a bit more?'

'I don't understand.' She put down the pages and looked at me over them. 'I thought you said you came from Jethra?'

'That's right.'

'Then why do you say you were born somewhere else?' She looked again at the word. ' "London" . . . where's that?'

'Oh, that,' I said. 'That's an invented name . . . it's difficult to explain. It's Jethra really, but I was trying to convey the idea that as you grow up the place you're in seems to change. "London" is a state of mind. It describes my parents, I suppose, what they were like and where they were living when I was born.'

'Let me read,' Seri said, not looking at me, staring down at the page.

She read more slowly now, checking back several times. I began to feel uncomfortable, interpreting her difficulties as a form of criticism. Because I had defined myself to myself, because I had never imagined that anyone else would ever read it, I had taken for granted that my method would be obvious. Seri, the first person in the world to read my book, frowned and read haltingly, turning the pages forward and back.

'Give it back to me,' I said at last. 'I don't want you to read any more.'

'I've got to,' she said. 'I've got to understand.'

But time passed and not much was clear to her. She started asking me questions:

'Who is Felicity?'

'What are the Beatles?'

'Where is Manchester, Sheffield, Piraeus?'

'What is England, and which island is it on?'

'Who is Gracia, and why has she tried to kill herself?'

'Who was Hitler, what war are you talking about, which cities had they bombed?'

'Who is Alice Dowden?'

'Why was Kennedy assassinated?'

'When were the sixties, what is marijuana, what is a psychedelic rock?'

'You've mentioned London again . . . I thought it was a state of mind?'

'Why do you keep talking about Gracia?'

'What happened at Watergate?'

I said, but Seri did not seem to hear: 'There's a deeper truth in fiction, because memory is faulty.'

'Who *is* Gracia?'

'I love you, Seri,' I said, but the words sounded hollow and unconvincing, even to me.

CHAPTER 16

'I love you, Gracia,' I said, kneeling on the threadbare carpet beside her. She was sprawled against the bed, half on, half off, no longer crying but silent. I was always uncomfortable when she said nothing, because it became impossible to comprehend her. Sometimes she was silent because she was hurt, sometimes because she simply had nothing to say, but sometimes because it was her way of taking revenge on me. She said my own silences were manipulative of her. Thus the complexities doubled, and I no longer knew how to behave. Even her anger was sometimes false, leading me to a response that she would call predictable; inevitably when her anger was real I took her less seriously, infuriating her more.

A declaration of love was the only common language left, yet it was spoken more by me than by her. The context of our rows made it sound hollow, even to me.

Tonight's row had been genuine, albeit trivial in origin. I had promised to keep the evening free to go with her to see some friends for dinner. Unfortunately I had forgotten my promise and bought some tickets for a play I knew she wanted to see. It was my fault, I was absent-minded, I admitted it all, but she blamed me all the same. Her friends could not be telephoned; we had wasted money on the seats. Whichever way we acted something was wrong.

It was just the start. The impasse led to tension, and this in its turn brought out the deeper differences. I was unloving, took her for granted, the flat was always in a mess, I was moody and withdrawn. She was neurotic and mercurial, slovenly, flirtatious with other men. It all came out, spreading through the room like a damp cloud of recrimination, making us less well defined to each other, colder and further away, more likely to hurt by blundering into places we could only dimly see.

I was holding her hand, but she was unresponsive and cool. She lay with her face turned away from me, staring into the pillows. She was breathing steadily; the tears were past.

I kissed the back of her neck. 'I do love you, Gracia.'

'Don't say that. Not now.'

'Why not? Isn't it the only thing that's still true?'

'You're just trying to intimidate me.'

I grunted with exasperation and moved away from her. Her hand fell limp. I stood up and went to the window.

'Where are you going?'

'I'm just pulling the curtains.'

'Leave them alone.'

'I don't want people looking in.'

Gracia was careless of curtains. The bedroom was at the front of the house, and although the flat was in the basement the room could be clearly seen from the road. If Gracia went to bed before me she often undressed with the lights on and the curtains open. Once I had walked into the bedroom to find her sitting naked on the bed, drinking coffee and reading a book. Outside, people leaving the pub were walking down the road.

'You're a prude, Peter.'

'I just don't want people to see us rowing.' I drew the curtains anyway, and returned to the bed. Gracia had sat up, and was lighting a cigarette.

'What are we going to do?'

I said: 'We'll do what I suggested half an hour ago. You drive to Dave and Shirley's, and I'll go on the Underground to try to change the tickets. I'll meet you later.'

'All right.'

Earlier, the same proposal had been far from all right; it had reduced her to tears. I was trying to cover up my mistake, trying to get out of seeing Dave and Shirley. Now Gracia's mood had abruptly changed. I was forgiven and soon we would be making love.

I went into the kitchen and ran a glass of water. It was cold and clear but it tasted flat. I had become used to the sweet Welsh water in Herefordshire, the soft Pennine water in Sheffield; in London it was the Thames, chemically neutralized and endlessly recycled, tasting like an imitation of the real thing. I emptied the glass, rinsed it and left it to drain on the side. The dishes from yesterday's evening meal were still stacked there, greasy and odorous.

Gracia's flat was in a street typical of many inner London suburbs. Some of the houses were privately owned, others were council property. The house we lived in was due for modernization, but until then Camden Council was renting out the flats it contained on short leases at subsidized rents. It was sub-standard housing, but no worse than the expensive privately let flat I had lived in before. On the corner of the street was a take-away kebab house run by Cypriots; a number of bus routes went down the main street, from Kentish Town to King's Cross; there were two cinemas in Camden Town, one of which showed minority-interest films by foreign directors; in Tufnell Park, about a mile away, a Shakespearean theatre company had taken over and converted an old church. These were the principal amenities of the area, and it was being slowly converted from low-grade working-class residential to desirable inner-London middle class. The pseudo-Georgian doors, Banham locks, pinewood kitchen tables and Welsh dressers were arriving in many previously neglected houses, and already a number of craft shops and delicatessens were appearing in the main street to serve this discriminating and affluent group.

Gracia had come up behind me. She put her arm around my chest, pulling me against her, and she kissed me behind my ear.

'Let's go to bed,' she said. 'We've got time.'

I resisted her because of the inevitability of it. Gracia was able to use sex for healing, and never really understood that rows were anaphrodisiac to me. I wanted to be alone afterwards, to walk the streets or go for a drink. She knew this because I had explained it, and, by inability to respond, sometimes demonstrated it. She realized now that I was resisting her, and I felt her go taut. Because of that, not wanting to renew the trouble, I turned around and kissed her very quickly, hoping it would be enough.

Soon we were undressed and in bed, and Gracia, her change of mood now complete, became an expert, sensitive lover. She sucked me until I was ready, then a little longer. We only became explicable to each other in bed. I liked to kiss and caress her breasts: they were small and soft and rolled in my hands. Her nipples were pliant, rarely erecting to my touch. I was loving Gracia, truly, but then I remembered Seri, and suddenly it was wrong.

Seri in bed beside me, her pale hair folded untidily across her brow, her lips parted, her eyes closed and her breath sweet. We always made love on our side, she with one knee raised, the other tucked beneath me. I liked to kiss and caress her breasts: they were small but firm, filling my hands, the little stud nipples stiff against my palms. Gracia, dark hair tousled on the pillow, unwashed in four days, was holding my head against hers; I was on top of her, trying to roll to the side, breathing her scents. It was wrong and I could not think why. Gracia felt me withdraw; her instinct for my loss of desire was unerring.

'Peter, don't stop!'

She arched her back, thrusting herself against me, then moved suddenly to clasp my penis at the base, jerking it up and down a few times, then leading me to her. I went on, physically capable but emotionally distant. I felt her nails gripping my shoulder blades, and I kept my eyes closed, hair in mouth and nose. I finished, but it was Seri who was there with me, turned to the side so I lay on her leg. Gracia gradually relaxed, still sensing my emotional withdrawal from her, but because she was physically satisfied the tension faded from her too. I pretended she was Gracia, even though she really was, and held her close while she smoked another cigarette.

Later, when Gracia had driven to Dave and Shirley's flat in Fulham, I walked down to the Underground station in Kentish Town, and caught a train to the West End. The exchange of tickets was simply done; seats were available for the following night's performance, and tonight people were waiting for cancellations. Sure that I had at last done the right thing, I caught a second train to Fulham.

Dave and Shirley were teachers, and they were into wholefood. Shirley thought she might be pregnant, and Gracia got drunk and flirted with Dave. We left before midnight.

That night, while Gracia was asleep, I thought about Seri.

I had once believed that she and Gracia were complementary to each other, but now the differences between them were becoming obvious. That day in Castleton I had used my knowledge of Seri to try to understand Gracia. But the fallacy in this was the assumption that I had consciously created Seri.

Remembering the way I had written my manuscript, blending conscious invention with unconscious discovery, I knew that Seri must be more than a fictional analogue of Gracia. She was too real, too complete, too motivated by her own personality. She lived in her own right. Every time I saw her, or spoke to her, I felt this growing in her.

But so long as Gracia was there, Seri was in the background.

Sometimes I would wake in the night to find Seri in bed with me. She would pretend to be asleep, but my first touch would rouse her. Then she would become, sexually, everything Gracia was not. Lovemaking with Seri was exciting and spontaneous, never predictable. Gracia knew I found her sexually irresistible, and became lazy; Seri took nothing for granted, but found new ways to excite me. Gracia was sexually adept, an expert lover; Seri had innocence and originality. Yet after making love with Seri, when we were fully awake and had the light on, Gracia would sit up to smoke a cigarette, or get out of bed to go to the loo, and I would have to adjust to Seri's withdrawal.

During the days, while Gracia was at work, Seri was an occasional companion. She was often in the next room, where I would be aware of her, or she would wait for me in the street outside. When I could get her near me I would talk to her and explain myself. Our excursions were the times when we came closest to each other. Then she would talk to me of the islands: of Ia and Quy, Muriseay, Seevl and Paneron. She had been born on Seevl, had married once, and since then had travelled widely in the islands. Sometimes, we walked together through the boulevards of Jethra, or took a tram ride to the coast, and I would show her the Seignior's Palace, and the Guards in their exotic, medieval costumes.

But Seri only came to me when she wanted to, and sometimes I needed more of her.

Suddenly, Gracia said: 'You're still awake.'

I waited several seconds before answering. 'Yes.'

'What are you thinking about?'

'All sorts of things.'

'I can't sleep. I'm too hot.' She sat up and switched on the light. Blinking in the sudden brightness, I waited for her to light a cigarette, which she did. 'Peter, it's not working, is it?'

'You mean my living here?'

'Yes, you hate it. Can't you be honest about it?'

'I don't hate it.'

'Then it's me. There's something wrong. Don't you remember what we agreed in Castleton? If it went wrong again we'd be straight with each other about it?'

'I am being straight.' I noticed that Seri had unexpectedly appeared, sitting on the end of our bed with her back turned and her head tilted slightly to one side, listening. 'I've got to adjust to what happened last year. Do you know what I mean?'

'I think so.' She turned her face away, then played with the end of the cigarette in the ashtray, twisting it to make the ash shape into a cone. 'So you ever know what *I* mean?'

166

'Sometimes.'

'Thanks a lot. The rest of the time I just waste my breath?'

'Don't start another row, Gracia. Please.'

'I'm not starting a row. I'm just trying to get through to you. Do you ever listen to what I say? You forget things, you contradict yourself, you look through me as if I'm a pane of glass. You were never like this before.'

'Yes, all right.'

It was easier to concur. I wanted to explain, but feared her anger.

I thought of the times Gracia was at her most difficult, when she was tired after work or something had happened to upset her. When it first happened I had tried to meet her halfway, and offer her something of myself. I wanted her to expend her frustrations so that they became something that united us, rather than divided us, but she put up emotional barriers that I found impassable. She would dismiss me with a petulant gesture, or flare with anger, or retreat from me in some other way. She was extremely neurotic, and although I tried to accept this sometimes it was very difficult.

When I had first started sleeping with her in London, a few months after Greece, I noticed that she kept a little pot of liquid detergent by the bedside. She told me it was in case she needed to remove her finger rings in the night. (I asked her why she did not take them off before getting into bed, but she said that was supposed to be unlucky.) When I knew her better she explained, half embarrassed, that she sometimes suffered claustrophobia of the extremities. I thought it was a joke, but it was not. When tensions mounted in her she could not wear shoes, rings, gloves. One evening, shortly after Castleton, I came in from the pub and discovered Gracia lying on the bed sobbing. The seam of her blouse, beneath the armpit, was torn apart, and my first thought was that some-one must have attacked her in the street. I tried to console her, but she was hysterical. The zip fastener on her boot had jammed, the blouse had torn as she writhed on the bed, the boot was stuck fast on her foot. She had broken her fingernails, smashed a glass. It took me just a few seconds to free the fastener and remove the boot, but by then she had withdrawn completely into herself. For the rest of that evening she walked around the flat barefoot, the torn blouse flapping by her breast. A terror, blank and unapproachable, put silence in her swollen eyes.

Now Gracia stubbed out her cigarette and pressed herself to me.

'Peter, I don't want it like this. We both need it to work.'

'Then what's wrong? I've tried everything.'

'I want you to care for me. You're so distant. Sometimes it's as if I don't exist. You act . . . no, it doesn't matter.'

'It does. Go on.'

Gracia said nothing for several seconds, and the silence spread mistily around us. Then: 'Are you seeing someone else?'

'No, of course not.'

'Is that true?'

'Gracia, there's no one. I love *you* . . . why should I need someone else?'

'You act as if you do. You always seem to be dreaming, and when I talk to you what you say comes out as if you've rehearsed it with someone else. Do you realize you're doing that?'

'Give me an example.'

'How can I? I don't take notes. But there's no spontaneity in you. Everything has been made ready for me. It's as if you've worked me out in your mind, how you think I should be. As long as I do what you expect, I'm reading the script you wrote for me. And then I don't, because I'm upset or tired, or because I'm me . . . and you can't cope with it. It's not fair, Peter. I can't just become what you imagine I am.'

'I'm sorry,' I said, and slipped my arm around her back and pulled her closer against me. 'I didn't know. I don't mean to do that. You're the only person I know, the only one I want to know. I went away last year because of you. There were other reasons, but it was mostly because we'd split up and I was upset. Now I've got you back, and everything I do and think is about you. I don't want anything to go wrong again. Do you believe that?'

'Yes . . . but can you show it more?'

'I'm trying, and I'll try again. But I've got to do it my way, the only way I know.' At the end of the bed I could feel Seri's weight, pressing down the bedclothes over my feet.

'Kiss me, Peter.' Gracia drew my hand to her breast, and brought her legs across my thigh. The nervous energy in her was exciting; I responded to it, sensing the same charge in myself. So we made love, and Seri was not there. Afterwards, drifting into sleep, I wanted to tell Gracia about her, explain that Seri was just a part of my orientation around her, remind her of the rapture of islands, but it was too late for that.

Later there was dawn light beyond the curtains. I was woken by Gracia moving. Her breath was quick. The bed shook as if trembling, and I heard her rings clatter lightly on to the bedside table.

CHAPTER 17

The next day, while Gracia was at work, I felt listless. There were small cleaning jobs to do around the flat, and I did these with my usual lack of enthusiasm. Seri did not appear, and after I had been to the local pub for lunch, I found my manuscript and went through it, seeking references to Seri in the hope of separating her from Gracia. It seemed to me I was confusing Gracia in my mind; Seri distracted me. In the night I had learned that Gracia was more important than anything.

But I was tired, and the only tensions eased by sex were physical. Both Gracia and I were unsure of our identities, and in seeking them we were damaging each other. My manuscript was a danger. It contained Seri, but it also contained myself as protagonist. I needed it still, but it drove me inwards.

Inevitably, Seri appeared. She was real, independent, tanned from the islands.

'You didn't help me last night,' I said. 'I needed you then, to reassure Gracia of what I am trying to do.'

Seri said – I was upset and felt lonely. I couldn't interfere.

She was remote from me, drifting on the periphery. I said: 'But can't you help me?'

Seri said – I can be with you, and help restore you to yourself. I can't say anything to you about Gracia. You're in love with her, and that excludes me.

'If you came closer I might be able to love you both. I don't want to hurt Gracia. What shall I do?'

Seri said – Let's go out, Peter.

I left my manuscript scattered on the bed, and followed her to the streets.

It was spring in the city, and along the boulevards the cafés had put their tables out beneath the canopies. It was the time I liked best in Jethra, and to leave the flat to enjoy the mild air and sunshine was like a tonic to me. I bought a newspaper. We went to one of the cafés I liked best, situated on the corner of a large, busy intersection. Here there was a tram crossing, and I enjoyed the distinctive clang of the bells, the clatter of the wheels on the crossings and the overhead tracery of the power lines. The pavements were crowded with people, conveying a sense of collective bustle and purpose, yet individually most of them seemed merely to be enjoying the sunshine. Faces were upturned after winter. While Seri ordered some drinks I glanced over the headlines of the newspaper. More troops were to be sent to the south; the early thaw had brought avalanches to the mountain passes, and a patrol of the Border Police had been wiped out; the Seigniory had announced further grain embargoes to the so-called non-aligned states. It was depressing news, discordant with the reality of the Jethran day around me. Seri and I sat in the warm light, watching the passers-by and the trams and the horse traffic, and aware of the people at the other tables. There was a predominance of unaccompanied young women; an intimation of the social effect of the draft.

'I love it here in Jethra,' I said. 'At this time of year it's the best place in the world.'

Seri said – Are you going to stay here for the rest of your life?

'Probably.' I saw the sun in her hair, and she was coming closer.

Seri said – 'Don't you feel the urge to travel?'

'Where to? It's difficult while the war's on.'

Seri said: 'Let's go to the islands. Once we're out of Faiandland we can go anywhere we please.'

'I'd love to,' I said. 'But what can I do about Gracia? I can't just run away from her. She's everything to me.'

'You did it once before.'

'Yes, and she tried to kill herself. That's why I have to stay with her. I can't risk that happening again.'

'Don't you think you might be the cause of her unhappiness?' Seri said. 'I've watched the way you two destroy each other. Don't you remember what Gracia was like when you met her in Castleton? She was confident, positive, building her life. Can you still recognize her as the same woman?'

'Sometimes. But she has changed, I know.'

'And it's because of you!' Seri said, flicking back her hair over her right ear, as she sometimes did when she became agitated. 'Peter, for her sake and yours, you've got to get out.'

'But I've nowhere to go.'

'Come with me to the islands.'

'Why is it always the islands?' I said. 'Couldn't I just get out of Jethra, like I did last year?'

I became aware that someone was standing beside my table, and I looked up. The waiter was standing there.

'Would you mind keeping your voice down, sir?' he said. 'You're disturbing the other customers.'

'I'm sorry,' I said, looking around. The other people seemed unaware of me, busy in their own lives. Two pretty girls walked past the tables; a tram clattered by; on the far side of the boulevard a council employee was sweeping up horse droppings. 'Would you bring the same again, please?'

I looked back to Seri. She had turned away while the waiter was there, receding from me. I reached over and found her wrist, gripping it lightly, feeling the substance of it.

'Don't leave me,' I said.

Seri said – I can't help it. You're rejecting me.

'No! Please . . . you were really helping me then.'

Seri said – 'I'm scared you will forget who I am. I'll lose you.'

'Please tell me about the islands, Seri,' I said. I noticed the waiter was watching me, so I kept my voice quiet.

'They're an escape from all this, your own private escape. Last year, when you went to your friend's house, you thought you could define yourself by exploring your past. You tried to remember yourself. But identity exists in the *present*. Memory is behind you, and if you depend on that alone you will be only half defined. You must seek balance, and embrace your future. The Dream Archipelago *is* your future. Here, in Jethra, you will just stagnate with Gracia, and damage her.'

'But I don't believe in the islands,' I said.

'Then you must discover them for yourself. The islands are as real as I am. They exist and you can visit them, just as you can speak to me. But they're also a state of mind, an attitude to life. Everything you've done in your life so far has been inward-looking, selfish, hurtful to others. You must go outward and affirm your life.'

The waiter returned and put down our drinks: a glass of beer for myself and an orange juice for Seri. 'Please settle your bill as soon as you have finished, sir.'

'What do you mean?'

'Just be as quick as possible. Thank you.'

Seri had receded again, and for an instant I glimpsed another café: a dingy interior, plastic-topped tables stained with old tea, steamed-up windows, a milk cooler and a placard for Pepsi-Cola . . . but then a tram went by with a flash of brilliant blue sparks from its conducting antenna, and I saw the pink blossom in the trees, the crowds of Jethrans.

Seri said, returning – 'You can live forever in the Archipelago.'

'The Lotterie, you mean.'

'No . . . the islands are timeless. Those who go there never return. They find themselves.'

'It sounds unhealthy to me,' I said. 'An escape fantasy.'

'No more than anything else you have ever done. For you, the islands will be a redemption. An escape from escape, a return to outwardness. You must go deeper inside yourself to find your way out. I'll take you there.'

I fell silent, staring down at the paving stones beneath the tables. A sparrow hopped between the customers' feet, looking for crumbs. I wanted to stay there forever.

'I can't leave Gracia,' I said at last. 'Not yet.'

Seri said, receding – 'Then I'll go without you.'

'Do you mean that?'

Seri said – I'm not sure, Peter. I'm jealous of Gracia because as long as you're with her you're just using me as conscience. I'm forced to watch you destroy her, and damage yourself. In the end you would destroy me too.

She looked so young and attractive in the sun, her fair hair glowing, her skin mellow from the south, her youthful, unsupported body glimpsed through thin clothes. She sat close beside me, exciting me, and I longed for the day when I could be with her alone.

I paid my bill and caught a tram heading north. As the streets closed in and the rain began, I felt a familiar depression growing in me. Seri, sitting beside me, said nothing. I got off the bus in Kentish Town Road and walked through the mean side streets to Gracia's flat. Her car was parked outside, crammed between a builder's skip and a Dormobile with an Australian flag in the window.

It was getting dark, but no lights showed at the window.

Seri said – There's something wrong, Peter. Hurry!

I left her there and went down the steps to the door. I was going to put the key in, but the door had been left ajar.

'Gracia!' I switched on the lights in the hall, hurried into the kitchen. Her shoulder bag was in the middle of the floor, its contents spilling out over the worn linoleum: cigarettes, a crumpled tissue, a mirror, a packet of Polos, a comb. I scooped them up and put the bag on the table. 'Where are you, Gracia?'

The sitting room was empty and cool, but the door to the bedroom was closed. I tried the handle, and pushed, but something had been jammed against it.

'Gracia! Are you in there?' I shoved at the door with my shoulder; it moved slightly, but something heavy grated on the floor beyond. 'Gracia! Let me in!'

I was trembling, and I felt the cartilage of my knees shaking uncontrollably. With a dread certainty I knew what Gracia had done. I put my weight against the door and pushed as hard as I could. The door moved an inch or two, and I was able to reach inside and switch on the light. Peering round towards the bed I saw one of Gracia's legs dangling down towards the floor. I shoved the door a third time, and then whatever had been pushed against it toppled over with a crash. I forced my way in.

Gracia lay in blood. She was supine, half on the bed. Her skirt had ridden up as she had thrashed on the bed, revealing the unhealthy pallor of her stockingless legs. One of her boots was pulled uncomfortably over her foot, stuck halfway; the other lay on the floor. There was a metallic glint from a blade, lying on the carpet. Blood pulsed from her wrist.

Gasping with the shock I lifted her head and slapped her face. She was unconscious, and barely breathing. I groped for her heart, but I could feel nothing. I glanced helplessly around the room in terrified anguish. I was certain she was dying. Stupidly, I moved to make her comfortable, resting her head on a cushion.

Then scything through the shock, sense sliced my immobility away. I lifted her savaged arm and tied my handkerchief as tightly as I could above the wound. Again, I felt for her heart, and this time I found its beat.

I dashed back into the hall, picked up the pay phone and rang for an ambulance. Soon as possible. Three minutes.

I returned to the bedroom. Gracia had rolled from the position I had left her in, and was in danger of sliding to the floor. I lowered her, trying not to bruise her, so that she was propped up by the bed. I paced the room, mentally urging the ambulance to arrive. I cleared the chest of drawers from where Gracia had moved it against the door, I propped the front door open, and stood in the street.

Three minutes. At last the distant city sound: the two repeated siren notes, approaching. A blue light flashing; neighbours at windows, someone holding back the traffic.

The ambulance driver was a woman. Two men hurried into the flat: an aluminium trolley left by the vehicle, a stretcher carried in, two bright red blankets.

Curt questions: her name, did she live here, how long before I had discovered her? My own: is she going to live, where are you taking her, please hurry. Then the departure: turning in the street with agonizing slowness, accelerating away, the blue lamp electric, the siren receding.

Inside the flat I used the phone again to call a taxi. While I was waiting I went to the bedroom to tidy up.

I pushed the chest of drawers back to its place, straightened the bed cover, stood stupidly and numbly in the centre of the room. There was blood on the carpet; splashes on the wall. I found a mop and some cloths, cleaned the worst of it away. It was awful to do.

The cab still did not arrive.

Back in the bedroom I at last confronted what I had so far avoided. On the bed where Gracia had been lying were the scattered pages of my manuscript, the typewritten sides facing upwards.

Was it to this my writing had led?

Blood spattered many of the pages. I knew what was written on them, even without reading the words. They were the passages about Seri; her name came out of the pages as if underlined by red.

Gracia must have read the manuscript, she must have understood.

The taxi arrived. I picked up Gracia's shoulder bag, and went out to the cab. We drove through the evening rush hour to the Royal Free in Hampstead. Inside, I found my way to the Casualty Ward.

After a long wait a social worker came to see me. Gracia was still unconscious, but she would survive. If I wished I could visit her in the morning, but first there were a few questions.

'Has she ever done this before?'

'I told the ambulance crew. No. It must have been an accident.' I looked away to divert the lie. Wouldn't they have records? Wouldn't they have contacted her GP?

'And you say you live with her?'

'Yes. I've known her for three or four years.'

'Has she ever shown any suicidal tendency before?'

'No, of course not.'

The social worker had other cases to go to; he said the doctor had been talking about making out a Section on her, but if I would vouch for her . . .

'It won't possibly happen again,' I said. 'I'm sure it wasn't deliberate.'

Felicity had told me that after Gracia's last attempt she had been sent for a month's compulsory psychiatric treatment, but she had been released at the end of it. That was in another hospital, another part of London. Given time, the people here would find that out, but hospital casualty wards and the social services were constantly overworked.

I gave the address to the social worker, and asked him to let Gracia have her shoulder bag when she came round. I said I would visit her in the morning. I wanted to leave; I was finding the modern building oppressively neutral and disinterested. What I perversely wanted was some kind of authoritative recrimination, a charge from this social worker that I was somehow to blame. But he was preoccupied and harassed: he wanted Gracia's case to be a straightforward one.

I went outside, into the drizzling rain.

I needed Seri as never before I had needed her, but I no longer knew how to find her. Gracia's act had jolted me; Seri, Jethra, the islands . . . these were the luxuries of idle inwardness.

Yet by the same token, I was less able than ever to cope with the complex real world. Gracia's terrible attempt on her life, my complicity in it, the destruction Seri had warned of. I shied away from them, appalled at the thought of what I might find in myself.

I walked down Rosslyn Hill for a few minutes, then a bus came along and I caught it, getting off at Baker Street Station. I stood for a while outside the entrance to the Underground, staring across Marylebone Road at the corner where Gracia and I had once before reached an ending. On an impulse I walked through the pedestrian subway, and stood in the place. There was an employment agency on the corner, offering positions for filing clerks, legal secretaries and PAs; the high advertised salaries surprised me. It had been a night like this the last time: Gracia and I at an impasse, Seri waiting somewhere around. From there I had found the islands, yet now they seemed to be beyond reach.

The evocations of place: it was as if Gracia were there with me again, rejecting me, willing me to leave her and propelling me towards Seri.

I stood there in the drizzle, watching the late rush-hour traffic accelerate away from the lights, heading for Westway and the Oxford road, the countryside far beyond. Out there I had first found Seri, and I wondered if I would have to go there to find her again.

Feeling cold, I paced to and fro, waiting for Seri, waiting for the islands.

Chapter 18

This much I knew for sure.

My name was Peter Sinclair. I was thirty-one years old, and I was safe. Beyond this, all was uncertain.

There were people looking after me, and they went to great lengths to reassure me about myself. I was totally dependent on them, and I was devoted to them all. There were two women and a man. One of them was an attractive, fair-haired young woman called Seri Fulten. She and I were extremely fond of each other because she was always kissing me, and, when no one else was around, she played with my genitals. The other woman was older; her name was Lareen Dobey, and although she tried to be kind to me I was a little frightened of her. The man was a doctor named Corrob. He visited me twice a day, but I never grew to know him very well. I felt rejected by him.

I had been seriously ill but now I was recovering. They told me that as soon as I was better I should be able to lead a normal life, and there was no chance of a relapse. This was very reassuring to know, because I was in pain for a lot of the time. At first my head was bandaged, my heart rate and blood pressure were constantly monitored, and a number of smaller surgical scars on other parts of my body were protected by plasters; later, one by one, these were removed and the pain began to ease.

My state of mind, described broadly, was one of intense curiosity. It was a most extraordinary feeling, a mental appetite that seemed insatiable. I was an extremely *interested* person. There was nothing that bored me or alarmed me or seemed irrelevant to my interests. When I awoke in the mornings, for just one example, the sheer novelty of the feeling of sheets around me was enough to hold my full attention. Sensations flooded in. The experiences of Warmth and Comfort and Weight and Fabric and Friction were enough sensations to entertain my untrained mind with all the permutations and nuances of a symphony. (Music was played to me every day, exhausting me.) Bodily functions were an astonishment! Just to breathe or to swallow was a miracle of pleasure, and when I discovered farting, and that I could imitate the noise with my mouth, it became my funniest diversion. I quickly worked out how to masturbate, but this was just a phase which ended when Seri took over. Going to the lavatory was a source of pride.

Gradually I became aware of my physical surroundings.

My universe, as I perceived it, was a bed in a room in a small chalet in a garden on an island in a sea. My awareness spread around me like a ripple of consciousness. The weather was warm and sunny, and during most days the windows by my bed were opened, and when I was allowed to sit up in a chair I was put either by the open door or on a small, pleasant verandah outside. I quickly learned the names of flowers, insects and birds, and saw how subtle were the ways in which each depended on the other. I loved the scent of honeysuckle, which came most pleasantly at night. I could remember the names of everyone I met: friends of Seri and Lareen, other patients, orderlies, the doctors, the man who every few days mowed the grass that surrounded the little white-painted room in which I lived.

I hungered for information, for news, and I devoured every morsel that came my way.

As the physical pain receded I became aware that I lived in ignorance. Fortunately, it seemed that Seri and Lareen were there to supply me information. Either or both of them were there with me throughout the days, at first nursing me while I was most ill, later answering the primitive questions I framed, later still spending painstaking hours with me, explaining me to myself.

This was the more complex, intangible, *inner* universe, and it was infinitely more difficult to perceive.

My principal difficulty was that Seri and Lareen could only speak to me from outside. My sole question – 'Who am I?' – was the only one they could not answer directly. Their explanations came to me from without my inner universe, confusing me utterly. (An early puzzle: they addressed me in the second person, and for some time I thought of myself as 'you'.)

And because everything was spoken, so first I had to understand what they *said* before I could work out what they meant, it lacked conviction. My experience was wholly vicarious.

Because I had no choice I had to trust them, and in fact I depended on them for everything. But it was inevitable I would soon start thinking for myself, and as I did, as my questions were directed inwards, two things emerged which threatened to betray that trust.

They crept up on me, bringing insidious doubts. They might have been connected, they might have been quite distinct; I had no way of knowing. Because of my passive role, endlessly learning, it took me days even to identify them. By then it was too late. I had ceased to respond, and a counter-reaction had been set up in me.

The first of the two came from the way in which we worked.

A typical day would begin with either Seri or Lareen waking me. They would give me food, and in the early days help me wash and dress, and use the lavatory. When I was sitting up, either in bed or in one of the chairs, Doctor Corrob would call to make one of his perfunctory examinations of me. After that, the two women would settle down to the serious work of the day.

To teach me they used large files of papers, which were

frequently consulted. Some of these papers were handwritten, but the majority, in a large and rather dog-eared heap, were typewritten.

Of course I listened with close attention: my craving for knowledge was rarely satisfied in one of these sessions. But simply because I was listening so attentively, I kept noticing inconsistencies.

They showed themselves in different ways between the two women.

Lareen was the one of whom I was more wary. She seemed strict and demanding, and there was often a sense of strain in her. She appeared to be doubtful of many of the things she talked to me about, and naturally this colouration transferred itself to my understanding. Where she doubted, I doubted. She rarely referred to the typewritten pages.

Seri, though, transmitted uncertainties in another way. Whenever she spoke I became aware of contradictions. It was as if she was *inventing* something for me. She almost always used the typewritten sheets, but she never actually read from them. She would sit with them before her, and use them as notes for what she was saying. Sometimes she would lose track, or would correct herself; sometimes she would even stop what she was saying and tell me to ignore it. When she worked with Lareen beside her she was tense and anxious, and her corrections and ambiguities came more often. Lareen several times interceded while Seri was speaking, drawing my attention to her instead. Once, in a state of obvious tension, the two women left me abruptly and walked together across the lawns, speaking intently; when they returned, Seri was red-eyed and subdued.

But because Seri was kind to me, and kissed me, and stayed with me until I fell asleep, I believed her more. Seri had her own uncertainties, and so she seemed more human. I was devoted to them both, but Seri I loved.

These contradictions, which I carefully stored in my mind and thought about when I was alone, interested me more than all the bare facts I was learning. I failed to understand them, though.

Only when the second kind of distraction grew in importance was I able to make patterns.

Because soon I started having fragmentary memories of my illness.

I still knew very little about what had been done to me. That I had undergone some form of major surgery was obvious. My head had been shaved, and there was an ugly pattern of scar tissue on my neck and lower skull, behind my left ear. Smaller operation scars were on my chest, back and lower abdomen. In an exact parallel with my mental state, I was weak but I *felt* fit and energetic.

Certain mental images haunted me. They did so from the time I was first aware, but only when I found out what was real in the world could I identify these images as phantasms. After much thought I concluded that at some point in my illness I must have been delirious.

These images therefore had to be flashing memories of my life before my illness!

I saw and recognized faces, I heard familiar voices, I felt myself to be in certain places. I could not identify any of them, but they nevertheless had a quality of total authenticity.

What was confusing about them was that they were utterly different, in tone and feeling, from the so-called facts about myself coming from Lareen and Seri.

What was compelling about them, though, was that they were congruent with the discrepancies I was picking up from Seri.

When she stuttered or hesitated, when she contradicted herself, when Lareen interrupted her, then it was I felt Seri was telling the truth about me.

At times like these I wanted her to say more, to repeat her mistake. It was much more interesting! When we were alone I tried to urge her to be frank with me, but she would never admit to her errors. I was incapable of pressing her too far: my doubts were too great, I was still too confused.

Even so, after several days of this, I knew two separate versions of myself.

The authorized version, according to Lareen and Seri, went like this: I had been born in a city called Jethra in a country called Faiandland. My mother's name was Cotheran Gilmoor, changed to Sinclair on her marriage to my father, Franford Sinclair. My mother was now dead. I had a sister named Kalia. She was married to a man named Yallow; this was his first name only. Kalia and Yallow lived in Jethra, and they were childless. After school I had gone to university, obtaining a good degree in chemistry. I worked for some years in industry as a formulation chemist. In the recent past I had contracted a serious brain condition, and had travelled to the island of Collago in the Dream Archipelago to receive specialist treatment. On the way to Collago I had met Seri and we had become lovers. As a consequence of the surgery I had suffered amnesia, and now Seri was working with Lareen to restore my memory.

On one level of my mind I accepted this. The two women painted a convincing picture of the world: they told me of the war, of the neutrality of the islands, of the upheavals in most people's lives because of the war. The geography of the world, its politics, economy, history, societies, all these were described to me plausibly and evocatively.

The ripple of my external awareness spread to the horizon, and beyond.

But then there was my preservation, based on the inconsistencies, and in my inner universe the ripples collided and collapsed.

They told me I had been born in Jethra. They showed it to me on a map, there were photographs I could look at. I was a Jethran. However, one day, describing Jethra while she glanced at the typewritten pages, Seri had accidentally said 'London'. It shocked me. (In my delirium I had experienced a sensation that was located and described by the word. It was certainly a place, it might or might not have been where I was born, but it existed in my life and it was called 'London'.)

My parents. Seri and Lareen said my mother was dead. I felt no shock or surprise, because this I had known. But they told me, quite emphatically, that my father was alive. (This was an anomaly. I was confused, within my other confusions. My father was alive, my father was dead . . . which was it? Even Seri seemed unsure.)

My sister. She was Kalia, two years older than me, married to Yallow. Yet once, quickly corrected by Lareen, Seri had called her 'Felicity'. Another unexpected jolt: in my delirious images the sister was called 'Felicity'. (And other doubts within doubts. When Lareen or Seri spoke of Kalia, they imparted a feeling of sibling warmth to our relationship. From Seri I sensed friction, and in my delirium I had experienced hostility and competitiveness.)

My sister's husband and family. Yallow featured only peripherally in my life, but when he was mentioned it was in the same terms of comforting warmth as Kalia. (I knew Yallow by another name, but I could not find it. I waited for Seri to make another slip, but in this she was consistent. I knew that 'Felicity' and her husband, whom I thought of as 'Yallow', had children; they were never mentioned.)

My illness. Something inconsistent here, but I could not trace it. (Deep inside me I was convinced I had never been ill.)

Then, finally, Seri herself. Of all her contradictions this was the least explicable. I saw her every day for hours at a time. She was daily explaining to me, in effect, both herself and her relationship with me. In an ocean of cross-currents and hidden depths, she was the only rock of reality on to which I could crawl. Yet by her words, her sudden frowns, her gestures, her hesitations, she created doubt in me that she existed at all. (Behind her was another woman, a complement. I had no name for her, just a total belief in her existence. This other Seri, the *doppelgänger*, had haunted my delirium. She, 'Seri', was fraught and fickle, unreliable and temperamental, affectionate and very sexual. She invoked in me strong passions of love and protectiveness, but also of anxiety and self-interest. Her existence in my underlife was so deep-rooted that sometimes it was as if I could touch her, sense her fragrance, hold her thin hands in mine.)

CHAPTER 19

The doubts about my identity became a permanent and familiar part of my life. If I dwelt on them I saw myself in reverse image, subtly different, like a black-and-white photograph printed from the wrong side of the negative. But my central preoccupation was my return to health, because with every day that passed I felt stronger, fitter, more equipped to return to the normal world.

Seri and I would often go for long walks through the grounds of the clinic. Once, we went with Lareen to Collago Town and watched the bustle of the traffic and the ships in the harbour. There was a swimming pool at the clinic, as well as courts for squash and tennis. I exercised every day, enjoying the sensation of my body returning to co-ordination and fitness. I started regaining the weight I had lost, my hair grew again. I tanned in the warm sunshine, and even the operation scars began to fade. (Doctor Corrob told me they would vanish altogether within a few weeks.)

Meanwhile, other skills returned. I learned to read and write quite quickly, and although I had difficulty with vocabulary, Lareen lent me one of the clinic's retraining books, and after a few hours I was in command of the language. My mental receptivity continued: anything I came across that was novel to me could be learned – or relearned, as Lareen insisted – with speed and thoroughness.

Soon I developed taste. Music, for instance, had been at first an intimidating scramble of noises, but later I was able to detect melody, then harmony, and then, with a sense of triumph, I discovered that some kinds of music were more enjoyable than others. Food was another area where I developed likes and dislikes. My sense of humour became tuned: I discovered that bodily functions had a limited scope for fun, and that some jokes were more amusing than others. Seri moved back from her hotel to live in the chalet with me.

I was restless to be leaving the clinic. I thought I was back to normal and was tired of being treated like a child. Lareen often angered me, with her pedantic insistence that my lessons continue; my sense of taste was developing here too, and I was resenting the fact that things were still being explained to me. Now that I could read I did not see why she could not merely give me the notes she worked from, nor let me read those typewritten sheets.

A breakthrough of sorts came with a paradox. One evening, while having dinner in the refectory with Lareen and Seri, I happened to mention I had lost the pen I had been using.

Seri said: 'It's on the desk. I gave it to you this afternoon.'

I remembered then, and said: 'Yes, of course.'

It was a trivial exchange, but one that made Lareen look sharply at me.

'Had you forgotten?' she said.

'Yes . . . but it doesn't matter.'

Suddenly, Lareen was smiling, and this in itself was so welcome a change that I smiled too, without understanding.

'What's funny?' I said.

'I was beginning to think we had made you into a super-man. It's good to know you can be absent-minded.'

Seri leaned over the table and kissed me on the cheek.

'Congratulations,' she said. 'Welcome back.'

I stared at them both, feeling aggressive. They were exchanging glances, as if they had been waiting for me to do something like this.

'Have you set me up for this?' I said to Seri.

She laughed, but it was happily. 'It just means you're normal again. You can forget.'

For some reason I felt sulky about this; I was a domestic pet that had learned a trick, or a child who could dress himself. Later, though, I understood better. To be able to forget – or rather, to be able to remember selectively – is an attribute of normal memory. While I was learning voraciously, accumulating facts, remembering everything, I was abnormal. Once I began to forget, I became fallible. I recalled my restlessness of the past few days, and I knew that my capacity for learning was nearly full.

After the meal we returned to the chalet, and Lareen collected her papers.

'I'll recommend your discharge soon, Peter,' she said. 'Perhaps by the end of the week.'

I watched her sort her papers into a neat pile, and slip them into her folder. She put the typewritten pages into her bag.

'I'll be back in the morning,' she said to Seri. 'I think you can tell Peter the truth about his illness.'

The two women exchanged smiles, and again I felt that paranoia. The sense that they knew more about me than I did was grating on me.

As soon as Lareen had left, I said: 'Now what did that mean?'

'Calm down, Peter. It's very simple.'

'You've been keeping things back from me.' And more, which I could not say: the constant awareness of the contradictions. 'Why don't you just tell me the truth?'

'Because the truth is never clear-cut.'

Before I could contest that she told me quickly about the treatment: I had won a lottery, and the clinic had changed me so that I would live forever.

I received this information without questioning it; I had no scepticism against which to test it, and anyway it was secondary to my real interest. From the revelatory manner in which Seri spoke, I was expecting something that might explain her contradictions . . . but nothing came.

As far as my inner universe was concerned I had learned nothing.

By not telling me this before, the two women had been indirectly lying. How could I ever know what *other* omissions and evasions there were?

I said: 'Seri, you've got to tell me the truth.'

'I have done.'

'There's nothing else you should tell me?'

'What else is there?'

'How the devil do I know?'

'Don't lose your temper.'

'Is that like being absent-minded? If I get angry, does that make me less than perfect? If so, I'm going to be doing it much more often.'

'Peter, you're an athanasian now. Doesn't that mean anything to you?'

'Not really, no.'

'It means that one day I'm going to die, but that you never will. That almost anyone you meet will die before you do. You'll live forever.'

'I thought we'd agreed I was less than perfect.'

'Oh, you're just being stupid now!'

She pushed past me and went out on to the verandah. I heard her walking to and fro on the wooden boards, but then she slumped into one of the chairs.

I suppose, in spite of my resistance to the idea, that I was psychologically child-like still, because I was incapable of keeping my anger. A few moments later, full of contrition, I went out to her and put my arms around her shoulders. Seri was stiff with frustration at me and she resisted at first, but after a while she turned her head and rested her face against my shoulder. She said nothing. I listened to the night insects, and watched the flashing lights on the distant sea.

When her breathing had steadied, I said: 'I'm sorry, Seri. I love you, and I've no reason to be angry with you.'

'Don't say any more about it.'

'I've got to, because I want to explain. All I can be is what you and Lareen have made me. I've no idea who I am or where I came from. If there's something you haven't shown me, or told me about, or given me to read, then I can never become that.'

'But why should it make you angry?'

190

'Because it's frightening. If you've told me something untrue I've no power to resist it. If you've left something out I've no way of replacing it.'

She drew away from me and sat facing me. The soft light from the window lit her face. She looked tired.

'The opposite is true, Peter.'

'The opposite of what?'

'That we're keeping something from you. We've done everything we can to be honest with you, but it's been almost impossible.'

'Why?'

'Just now . . . I told you that you've been made into an athanasian. You hardly reacted.'

'It means nothing to me. I don't *feel* I'm immortal. I am what you've made me believe I am.'

'Then believe me about this. I was with you before you took the treatment, and we talked about now, about what would happen after the operation. How can I convince you? You didn't want the treatment because you were scared of losing your identity.'

I suddenly had an insight into myself before this had happened: frightened of what might happen, frightened of *this*. Like those delirious images it was temptingly coherent. How much of him, myself, remained?

I said: 'Does everyone go through this?'

'Yes, it's exactly the same. The athanasia treatment causes amnesia, and all the patients have to be rehabilitated afterwards. This is what Lareen does here, but your case has given her special problems. Before you came here you wrote an account of your life. I don't know why you wrote it, or when . . . but you insisted that we use it as the basis for restoring your identity. It was all a rush, there was no time. The night before the operation I read your manuscript, and I found you hadn't written an autobiography at all! I don't know what you would call it. I suppose it's a novel, really.'

'You say *I* wrote this?'

'So you claimed. You said it was the only thing that told the truth about you, that you were defined by it.'

'Is this manuscript typewritten?' I said.

'Yes. But you see, Lareen normally works with—'

'Is that the manuscript Lareen brings every morning?'

'Yes.'

'Then why haven't I been allowed to read it?' Something I had written before my illness; a message to myself. I had to see it!

'It would only confuse you. It doesn't make sense . . . it's a sort of fantasy.'

'But if I wrote it then surely I would understand it!'

'Peter, calm down.' Seri turned away from me for a few seconds, but she reached back to take my hand. Her palm was moist. Then she said: 'The manuscript, by itself, doesn't make sense. But we've been able to improvise. While we were together, before you and I got to this island, you told me a few things about yourself, and the Lotterie has some details on file. There are a few clues in the manuscript. From all this we've pieced together your background, but it's not completely satisfactory.'

I said: 'I've got to read the manuscript.'

'Lareen won't let you. Not yet, anyhow.'

'But if I wrote it, it's my property.'

'You wrote it before the treatment.' Seri was looking away from me, across the dark grounds and into the warm scents of flowers. 'I'll talk to her tomorrow.'

I said: 'If I can't actually read it, will you tell me what it's about?'

'It's a sort of fictionalized autobiography. It's about you, or someone with your name. It deals with childhood, going to school, growing up, your family.'

'What's fictional about that?'

'I can't tell you.'

I thought for a moment. 'Where does it say I was born? In Jethra?'

'Yes.'

'Is it called Jethra in the manuscript?'

Seri said nothing.

'Or is it called "London"?'

Still she said nothing.

'Seri?'

'The name you give it is "London", but we know this means Jethra. You give it other names, too.'

'What are they?'

'I can't tell you.' At last she looked at me. 'How did you know about London?'

'You let it slip once.' I was going to tell her about the ghost memories of the delirium, but somehow it seemed too difficult, too unreliable, even in my own mind. 'Do you know where London is?'

'Of course not! You made the name up!'

'What other names did I make up?'

'I don't know . . . I can't remember. Lareen and I went through the manuscript trying to change everything to places we knew. But it was very difficult.'

'Then how much of what you've taught me is true?'

'As much as possible. When you came back from the clinic you were like a vegetable. I *wanted* you to be who you were before the treatment, but I couldn't just will it. Everything you are now is the result of Lareen's training.'

'That's what scares me,' I said.

I stared up the rising lawn to the other chalets; most were in darkness, but lights showed in a few of them. There were my fellow athanasians, my fellow vegetables. I wondered how many of them were suffering the same doubts. Were they even yet aware that somehow their heads had been emptied of all the dusty possessions of a lifetime, then refurbished with someone else's idea of a better arrangement? I was frightened of what I had been made to think, because I was the product of my mind and I acted accordingly. What had Lareen told me before I acquired taste? Had she and Seri somehow acted in well-intended concert to instil in me beliefs I had not held before the treatment? How would I ever know?

The only link with my past was that manuscript; I could not ever be complete until I read my own definition of myself.

There was a wan moon, misted by high clouds, and the gardens of the clinic had a still, monochrome quality. Seri and I walked along the familiar paths, postponing the moment when we went inside the chalet, but at last we headed back.

I said: 'If I get the manuscript, I want to read it on my own. That's my right, I think.'

'Don't mention it again. I'll do my best to get it. All right?'

'Yes.'

We kissed briefly as we walked, but there was still a remoteness in her.

When we were inside the chalet, she said: 'You won't remember, but before all this we were planning to visit a few islands. Would you still like to?'

'Just you and me?'

'Yes.'

'But what about you? Haven't you changed your mind about me?'

'I don't like your hair as short as that,' she said, and ruffled her fingers through my new stubble.

That night, when Seri was asleep beside me, I was wakeful. There was a quietness and solitude on the island that in a sense I had grown up with. The picture drawn by Seri and Lareen of the world outside was one of noise and activity, ships and traffic and crowded towns. I was curious to experience this, to see the stately boulevards of Jethra and the clustered old buildings of Muriseay. As I lay there I could imagine the world disposed around Collago, the endless Midway Sea and the innumerable islands. Imagining them I created them, a mental landscape that I could take on trust. I could go out from Collago, island-hop with Seri, invent the scenery and customs and peoples of each island as we came to it. An imaginative challenge lay before me.

What I knew of the world outside was similar to what I knew of myself. From the verandah of the chalet Seri could point out the neighbouring islands, and name them, and show them to me on a map, and describe their agriculture, industries and customs, but until I actually went to them they could only ever be distant objects drawn to my attention.

Thus was I to myself: a distant object, charted and described and thoroughly identified, but one which so far I had been unable to visit.

Before I went out to the islands I had some exploring of my own to do.

Chapter 20

Lareen returned in the morning, and brought the welcome news that I was to be discharged from the clinic in five days' time. I thanked her, but I was watching to see if she produced the typewritten manuscript. If she had it with her, it remained in her bag.

Although I was restless, I settled down to a morning's work with her and Seri. Now I knew that fallibility was a virtue, I used it to strategic effect. During lunch the two women spoke quietly together, and it seemed for a moment that Seri had put my request to her. Later, though, Lareen announced that she had work to do in the main building, and left us in the refectory.

'Why don't you go for a swim this afternoon?' Seri said. 'Take your mind off all this.'

'Are you going to ask her?'

'I told you – leave it to me.'

So I left her alone and went to the swimming pool. Afterwards, I returned to the chalet but there was no sign of either of them. I felt useless and wasted, so I signed for a pass from one of the security guards and walked down to Collago Town. It was a warm afternoon, and the streets were crowded with people and traffic. I relished the noise and confusion, a bustling, discordant contrast with the solipsism and seclusion of my memories. Seri had told me that Collago was a small island, not densely populated and well off the main shipping routes, yet it seemed in my unpractised life to be the very hub of the world. If this was a sample of modern life, I could not wait to join the rest!

I wandered through the streets for a while, then walked

down to the harbour. Here I noticed a number of temporary stalls and shops, erected in a position overlooking the water, where patent elixirs could be purchased. I walked slowly along the row, admiring the photographically enlarged letters of testimonial, the exciting claims, the pictures of successful purchasers. The profusion of bottles, pills and other preparations – herbal remedies, powders, salts for drinking water, isometric exercises, thermal garments, royal jelly, meditational tracts, and every other conceivable kind of patent remedy – was such as to make me think, for a moment or two at least, that I had undergone my ordeal unnecessarily. Business along the row was not brisk, yet curiously none of the vendors solicited my business.

On the far side of the harbour a large steamer was docking, and I assumed that it was this arrival that had caused the congestion in town. Passengers were disembarking and cargo was being unloaded. I walked as close as I could without crossing the barrier, and watched these people from the world beyond mine as they went through the routines of handing in their tickets and collecting their baggage. I wondered when the ship would be sailing again, and where it was next headed. Would it be to one of the islands Seri had named?

Later, when I was walking back to the town, I noticed a small passenger bus loading up by the quay. A sign on the side announced that it belonged to the Lotterie-Collago, and I looked with interest at the people sitting inside. They seemed apprehensive, staring silently through the windows at the activity around them. I wanted to talk to them. Because they came, so to speak, from a world of the mind that existed before the treatment, I saw them as an important link with my own past. Their perception of the world was undoctored; what they took for granted was all that I had lost. If this was consistent with what I had learned, then many of my doubts would be allayed. And for my part, there was much I could suggest to them.

I had experienced what they had not. If they knew in

advance what the after-effects would be, it might help them to a speedier recovery. I wanted to urge them to use these last few days of individual consciousness to leave some record of themselves, some personal definition or memento by which they might rediscover themselves.

I moved in closer, peering in through the windows of the coach. A girl in an attractive, tailored uniform was checking names against a list, while the driver was stowing luggage in the back. A middle-aged man sitting by a window was nearest to me, so I tapped on the glass. He turned, saw me there, then quite deliberately looked away.

The girl noticed me, and leaned through the door.

'What are you doing?' she called to me.

'I can help these people! Let me speak to them!'

The girl narrowed her eyes. 'You're from the clinic, aren't you? Mr . . . Sinclair.'

I said nothing, sensing that she knew my motives and would try to stop me. The driver came round from the back of the vehicle, shouldered past me and climbed up to the driving seat. The girl spoke briefly to him, and without further delay he started the engine and drove off. The coach moved slowly through the traffic, then turned into the narrow avenue that led up the hill towards the clinic.

I walked away, running my fingers over my newly regrown hair, realizing that it marked me out in the town. On the far side of the harbour, passengers from the ship were clustering around the elixir stalls.

I reached the quieter side streets and wandered slowly past the shop fronts. I was beginning to understand the mistake I had made with those people: anything I said to them now would of course be forgotten as soon as their treatment began. And their role as representatives of my past was a fallacy. Everyone else had the same undoctored quality: the passers-by in the street, the staff at the clinic, Seri.

I walked until I felt footsore, then made my way up the hill to the clinic.

Seri was waiting for me in the chalet. She had an untidy pile of papers on her knee, and was reading through them. It took me a few seconds to realize it was the manuscript.

'You've got it!' I said, and sat down beside her.

'Yes . . . but conditionally. Lareen says you're not to read it alone. I'll go through it with you.'

'I thought you agreed to let me read it by myself.'

'I agreed only to get it back from Lareen. She thinks you've recovered well, and so long as I explain the manuscript to you she has no objection to you knowing what it's about.'

'All right,' I said. 'Let's get started.'

'This instant?'

'I've been waiting all day for this.'

Seri flashed a look of anger at me, and threw her pencil on the floor. She stood up, letting the pages slide into a curling heap by her feet.

'What's the matter?' I said.

'Nothing, Peter. Not a damned thing.'

'Come on . . . what is it?'

'God, you're so selfish! You forget I have a life too! I've spent the last eight weeks in this place, worrying about you, thinking about you, talking to you, teaching you, being with you. Don't you think there might be other things I want to do? You never ask how I am, what I'm thinking, what I'd like to do . . . you just take it for granted I'm going to go on being here indefinitely. Sometimes, I couldn't give a damn about you and your wretched life!'

She turned away from me, staring out of the window.

'I'm sorry,' I said. I was stunned by her vehemence.

'I'm going to leave soon. There are things I want to do.'

'What sort of things?'

'I want to see a few islands.' She turned back to me. 'I've got my own life, you know. There are other people I can be with.'

There was nothing I could say to this. I knew almost nothing about Seri or her life, and indeed had never asked about it. She was right: I took her for granted, and because it was so true I was speechless. My only defence, one I could not bring myself to summon at that moment was that as far as I knew I had not asked her to be with me, that from the first days of my new consciousness she had always been there, and because I had not been taught to question it I never had.

I stared down at the untidy pile that was the manuscript, wondering if I should ever know what secrets it contained.

We left the chalet, went for one of our curative walks through the grounds. Later, we ate supper in the refectory, and I encouraged Seri to talk about herself. It was not a token gesture prompted by her frustration: by losing her temper with me Seri had opened my mind to yet another area of my ignorance.

I was beginning to appreciate the scale of the sacrifice Seri had made for me: for nearly two months she had done all the things she said, while I, petulant and child-like, rewarded her with affection and trust, seeking only myself.

Quite suddenly, because I had never thought of it before, I became scared she would abandon me.

Feeling chastened by this I walked back with her to the chalet and watched as she tidied up the scattered manuscript pages. She checked through them to make sure they were in correct order. We sat down next to each other on my bed, and Seri riffled the corners, counting.

'All right, these first few pages are not too important. They explain the circumstances in which you started writing. London is mentioned once or twice, and a few other places. A friend was helping you out after you had had some bad luck. It's not very interesting.'

'Do you mind if I look?' I took the sheets from her. It was as she had said: the man who had written this was a stranger to me, and his self-justifications seemed elaborate and laboured. I put the pages to one side. 'What's next?'

'We get into difficulties straight away,' Seri said, holding the page for me to see and pointing with her pencil. ' "I was born in 1947, the second child of Frederick and Catherine Sinclair". I've never even heard of names like that!'

'Why have you changed them?' I said, seeing that pencil

lines had been scored through the names. Above them she, or Lareen, had pencilled in the names I knew as being my parents' correct ones: Franford and Cotheran Sinclair.

'We could check those. The Lotterie has them on file.'

I frowned, appreciating the difficulties I had made for the two women. In the same paragraph there were several more deletions or substitutions. Kalia, my elder sister, had been named as 'Felicity', a word which I had learned meant happiness or joy, but which I had never heard used as a name. Later, I discovered that my father had been 'wounded in the desert' – an extraordinary phrase – while my mother had been operating a switchboard in 'government offices' in somewhere called 'Bletchley'. After the 'war with Hitler', my father had been among the first men to return home, and he and my mother had rented a house on the outskirts of 'London'. It was here that I had been born. Most of these obscure references had been crossed out by Seri, but 'London' had been changed to 'Jethra', giving me a pleasant feeling of reassurance and familiarity.

Seri led me through a couple of dozen pages, explaining each separate difficulty she had found and telling me the reasons for the substitutions she had made. I agreed with them all, because they so obviously made sense.

The narrative continued in its mundane yet enigmatic way: this family had continued to live outside 'London' for the first year of 'my' life, and then they had moved to a northern city called 'Manchester'. (This too had been changed to Jethra.) Once in 'Manchester' we reached descriptions of 'my' first memories, and with this the confusions came thick and fast.

'I had no idea,' I said. 'How on earth did you manage to make sense of this?'

'I'm not sure we have. We've had to leave a lot of it out. Lareen was extremely angry with you.'

'Why? It's hardly my fault.'

'She wanted you to fill out her questionnaire, but you refused. You said that everything we needed to know about you was in this.'

I must have sincerely believed that at the time. At some stage of my life I had written this incomprehensible manuscript, devoutly believing that it described myself and my background. I tried to imagine the sort of mentality that could have held such a belief, against all reason. Yet my name was on the first page. Once, before the treatment, I had written this and I had known what I was doing.

I felt a poignant loneliness for myself. Behind me, as if beyond an unscalable wall, was an identity, purpose and intelligence that I had lost. I needed that mind to explain to me what had been written.

I glanced through the rest of the pages. Seri's deletions and substitutions continued. What *had* I intended?

The question was more interesting to me than the details. In answering it I should gain an insight into myself, and thus into the world I had lost. Had it been these fictitious names and places – the Felicitys, the Manchesters, the Gracias – that had come to me in my delirium, haunting me afterwards? Those delirious images remained a part of my consciousness, were a fundamental if inexplicable part of what I had become. To ignore them would be to turn my back on understanding more.

I was still mentally receptive, still urging to learn.

After a while I said to Seri: 'Can we go on?'

'It doesn't become any clearer.'

'Yes, but I'd like to.'

She took a few pages from me. 'Are you sure this means nothing to you?'

'Not yet.'

'Lareen was certain you would react wrongly to it.' She laughed, shortly. 'It seems a bit silly now, when I think of all the trouble we went to.'

We read a few more pages together, but Seri had spent too long with the manuscript and she grew tired.

'I'll go on by myself,' I said.

'All right. It's not going to do any harm.'

She lay down on the other bed, reading a novel. I continued

with the manuscript, working painstakingly through the inconsistencies, as once, several times, Seri must have done. Occasionally I asked for her help, and she told me what she had had in mind, but each new interpretation only made my curiosity greater. It confirmed what I knew of myself, but it also confirmed my doubts.

Later, Seri undressed and went to bed to sleep. I read on, the manuscript resting on my lap. In the warm evening I was shirtless and barefoot, and as I read I could feel the rush mat abrading pleasantly against the soles of my feet.

It struck me that if there was any truth at all in the manuscript, then it could only be the truth of anecdote. There seemed to be no deeper pattern, no sense of metaphor.

It was the anecdotes that Seri had most frequently deleted. One or two of them she had pointed out to me, explaining that she found them incomprehensible. So they were to me, but because I was making no headway against the shape of the story, I began to look more closely at the details.

One of the longest deleted passages, occupying several pages of the text, dealt with the sudden arrival in 'my' childhood life of a certain 'Uncle William'. He entered the story with all the bravado of a pirate, bringing a scent of the sea and a glimpse of foreign lands. He had captivated me because he was disgraceful and disapproved of, because he smoked a vile pipe and had warts on his hands; yet he also fascinated me while I read of him, because the passage was written with conviction and humour, a plausible-seeming account of an influential experience. I realized that Uncle William, or Billy, as I seemed to remember him, was as attractive a personality to me now as he had been when I was a child. He had really existed, he had really lived.

Yet Seri had deleted him. She knew nothing of him, so she had tried to destroy him.

So far as I was concerned it would take more than a few pencil strokes to remove him. There was a truth to Uncle William, a truth that was far higher than mere anecdote.

I remembered him; I remembered that day.

Suddenly, I knew how to remember the rest. It was not whether the material could be crossed out, or whether names could be substituted. What mattered was the text itself, its shapes and patterns, those meanings that were only alluded to, the metaphors that until then I had been incapable of seeing. The manuscript was full of memories.

I went to the beginning of the text, and started to read it through. Then of course I remembered the events that had taken me to my white room in Edwin's cottage, and all that had gone before. As I remembered I became reassured, united with my real past, but then I became scared. In remembering myself, I discovered how profoundly lost I had become.

Outside the white-painted chalet the grounds of the clinic were quiet. The ripple of my awareness spread outwards: to Collago Town, to the rest of the island, to the Midway Sea and the innumerable islands, to Jethra. Yet where were they?

I read to the end, to the unfinished scene between Gracia and myself on the corner by Baker Street Station, and then I collected the typewritten sheets and shaped them into a tidy stack. I found my holdall beneath the bed and packed the manuscript at the bottom. Quietly, so as not to wake Seri, I packed my clothes and other possessions, checked that I had my money, then prepared to leave.

I looked back at Seri. She was sleeping on her stomach like a child, her head turned to one side. I wanted to kiss her, gently stroke her naked back, but I could not risk waking her. She would stop me if she knew I was leaving. I watched her for two or three silent minutes, wondering who she really was, and knowing that once I left I should never meet her again.

The door eased open quietly; outside was darkness, and the warm sea wind. I returned to my bed to collect my holdall, but as I did so I kicked something that lay on the floor by Seri's shoulder bag, and it clinked against the metal leg of her bed. She stirred, then settled. I crouched down to pick up whatever it was I had kicked. It was a small bottle, made of dark green glass, hexagon shaped. The cork was missing and the label had been removed, but I knew instinctively what it must once have contained, and why Seri had bought it. I sniffed at the neck of the bottle and smelled camphor.

Then I nearly did not go. I stood beside the bed, looking sadly down at the sleeping girl, innocently tired, selfless to me, vulnerably naked, her hair folded untidily across her brow, her lips slightly parted.

At last I put down the empty elixir bottle where I had found it, collected my holdall, then left. In the dark I got through the gate and walked down the hill into Collago Town. Here I waited by the harbour until the town woke up, and as soon as the shipping office opened I inquired when the next steamer would be departing. One had left only the day before; the next would not be for another three days. Anxious to leave the island before Lareen or Seri found me, I took the first small ferry that came, crossing the narrow channel to the next island. Later that day, I moved again. When I was sure no one would find me – I was on the island of Hetta, in an isolated tavern – I bought some timetables and maps, and started to plan my return journey to London. I was haunted by the unfinished manuscript, the unresolved scene with Gracia.

CHAPTER 21

The fact was that Gracia had brought me to an ending. Her suicide attempt was too big to be contained in my life. She swept everything aside, admitting of nothing else. Her drastic act even overshadowed the news that she was not to die as a result. Whether or not she had seriously intended to die was secondary to the gesture she made. She had succeeded in shocking me out of myself.

I was obsessed by an imagined picture of her at that very moment: she would be lying semi-conscious in a hospital bed, with bottles and tubes and unwashed hair. I wanted to be with her.

I had come to a place I knew: the corner where Baker Street crossed Marylebone Road, a part of London forever associated in my mind with Gracia. The rain was intensifying, and the traffic threw up a mist of fine droplets that gusted around me in the city-ducted winds. I remembered the cold moor wind of Castleton, the passing lorries.

It was hours since I had last eaten, and I felt the mild euphoria of low blood sugar. It made me think of the long summer months of the year before, when I had been so intent on writing in my white room that sometimes I went two or three days without proper food. In that state of mental excitement I always imagined best, could perceive the truth more clearly. Then I could make islands.

But Jethra and the islands paled before the reality of London's damp awfulness, just as I paled before my own. For once I was free of myself, for once I looked outwards and thought sorrowfully of Gracia.

At that moment, when I did not hope for her, Seri appeared.

She came up the steps and out of the pedestrian subway on the far side of Marylebone Road. I saw her fair hair, her straight back, the bobbing walk I knew so well. But how could she have entered the subway without my seeing her? I was standing by the only other entrance, and she had not passed me. I watched her, amazed, as she walked quickly into the booking hall of the Underground station.

I ran down the steps, slipping slightly on the rain-glossed treads, and hurried through to the other side. When I reached the booking hall she had passed the ticket barrier and was at the top of the stairs that led down to the Metropolitan Line. I went to follow her, but the inspector at the barrier asked to see my ticket. Angrily, I returned to the ticket office and bought a single fare to anywhere.

A train was standing at one of the platforms; the indicator board said it was going to Amersham. I walked quickly along the curving platform, looking through windows, looking towards the carriages ahead. I could not see her, even though I walked the whole length of the train. Could she have caught another? But this was the evening; there were departures only at ten-minute intervals.

I rushed back as the guard shouted that the doors were about to close.

Then I saw her: she was sitting by the window in a carriage near the back of the train. I could see her face, turned down as if she were reading.

The pneumatic doors hissed loudly and slid towards each other. I leapt aboard the nearest carriage, forcing myself through the closing pressure of the doors. Late commuters glanced up, looked away. Bubbles of isolation surrounded them.

The train pulled away, blue-white discharge sparks flashing on the wet rails as we crossed the points and moved into the long tunnel. I walked to the back of the carriage to be at the door nearest to Seri when we stopped at the next station. I leaned against the heavy, shatterproof window set into the door, watching my reflection against the black wall of the tunnel outside. At last we reached the next station, Finchley Road. I pushed through the doors as soon as they opened, and ran down the platform to the carriage where I had seen her. The doors closed behind me. I went to the place where she had been sitting, but she was no longer there.

Now the train was on the surface, clattering through the crowded, decrepit suburbs of West Hampstead and Kilburn; here the line ran parallel to the street where my old flat had been. I walked the length of the open carriage, looking at all the passengers, making sure Seri had not changed her seat. At the end I looked through the windows of the two connecting doors to the next carriage, and saw her.

She was standing, as I had done, against the sliding doors and staring out at the passing houses. I went through to her carriage – a cold blast of damp air, a moment of swaying peril – and passengers looked up, thinking I must be a ticket inspector. I went quickly to where she had been standing, but once again she had moved. There was no one there who looked even remotely like her, that I might have mistaken for her.

While the train rushed on to the next station, I walked to and fro in the aisle of the carriage, preferring the illusion of doing something to the tensions of idleness. Outside, the rain ran in quick diagonals down the dirty windows. At Wembley Park there was a delay of a few minutes, as here was the interchange with the Bakerloo Line and a train was expected on the other side of the platform. I walked the length of my train, searching for Seri, but she had vanished. When the Bakerloo train arrived she was aboard it! I saw her step down, cross the platform, and climb into the carriage I had first been in.

I returned to the train, but of course she eluded me again.

I found a seat and stared down at the worn and slatted floor, littered with cigarette ends and sweet wrappers. The train moved on, through Harrow, through Pinner, heading out into the countryside. I again felt myself moving into a passive state of mental laziness, content to know that I was supposed to be following Seri. I was lulled by the warmth of the carriage, the motion of the train, and peripherally aware that passengers were getting off as we stopped at stations on the way.

The train was almost empty when we came to a station called Chalfont & Latimer. I glanced out at the station as we drew in, seeing the wet platform and shining overhead lamps, the familiar advertisements for films and language schools. Passengers waited by the carriage doors, and amongst them was Seri. In my somnolent state I barely realized she was there, but when she smiled at me and stepped outside I knew I was to follow.

I was slow and clumsy, and only just got through the doors before they closed. By then, Seri had slipped through the ticket barrier and was again out of sight. I followed, thrusting my ticket at the collector and moving on before he could check it.

The station was next to a main road; as I came out, the train I had been on went noisily over the ironwork bridge. I looked to left and right along the road, seeking Seri. She was already an appreciable distance away, walking briskly along the road in the direction of London. I hurried after her, pacing myself with short bursts of running.

The road was lined with modern detached houses, set back from the traffic with concrete drives, neat lawns and flower-beds, and flagstoned patios. Lighted reproduction carriage lamps glittered their reflections on the rainy ground. Behind curtained windows I could glimpse the hard blue glare of television screens.

Seri stayed effortlessly ahead of me, maintaining her brisk walk without seeming to hurry, yet however much I ran she was always the same distance ahead. I was getting out of breath so I slowed my pace to a moderate walk. It had stopped raining while I was on the train, and already the air was milder, more in keeping with the season.

Seri reached the end of the lighted section of the road, and moved into the strip of countryside between Chalfont and

Chorleywood. I lost sight of her in the dark, so I ran again. In a minute or two I had also passed into the darkness, but I could see Seri whenever cars passed with their headlights on. Farmland lay on either side of the road. Ahead of me, in the south-eastern sky, the sodium radiance of London was lighting the clouds.

Seri halted and turned back to face me, perhaps to be sure I had seen her. Cars passed, throwing spray and light in drifting veils. Thinking she was waiting for me I ran again, splashing in the puddles of the unmade verge. When I was within distance, I shouted: 'Seri, please stay and talk to me!'

Seri said – You've got to see the islands, Peter.

There was a gate where she had waited, and she passed through as I came briefly up to her, but by the time I followed she was already halfway across the field. Her white shirt and pale hair seemed to drift in the dark.

I staggered on again, feeling the turned soil clogging around my shoes. I was tiring, there had been too many upheavals. Seri would wait.

I came to a halt, slithering on the lumpy sods, and leaned forward to catch my breath. I hung my head, resting with my hands on my knees.

When I looked up again I could see Seri's ghostly figure at the bottom of the dip, by what appeared to be a hedge. Behind her, on the gently rising slope of a hill, was the lighted window of a house. Trees stood darkly blurred on the close horizon.

She did not wait: I saw her white movement, sideways along the hedge.

I sucked a deep breath. 'Seri! I've got to rest!'

It made her pause momentarily, but if she called an answer I did not hear it. It was difficult to see: paleness moved like a moth against a curtain, then it was gone.

I looked back. The main road was lights sweeping behind trees, and the distant sounds of wheels and engines. To think made my head hurt. I was in a foreign country, needing translations, but my interpreter had left me. I waited until my breath steadied, then walked on slowly, raising and lowering my feet with the deliberation of a shackled man. The mud made deadweights of my legs, and every time I managed to scrape some of it away more clung on. Somewhere invisible to me, Seri must be watching my ponderous, arm-swinging progress through the clay.

At last I reached the hedge and wiped my feet in the long grass that grew there. I moved on in the direction taken by Seri, and peered towards where I had seen the house with the lighted window, seeking a reference. I must have been mistaken, though, because I could now see no sign of it. A wind, mild and steady, came from beyond the hedge, laden with a familiar tang.

A gate was let into the hedge and I went through. Beyond, the ground continued to drop away in a barely perceptible gradient. I took a few steps in the dark, feeling for the unwelcome cling of waterlogged soil, but here the grass was short and dry.

Ahead was a horizon: distant and flat, flickering with a few tiny lights almost invisible in their remoteness. The sky had cleared, and overhead was a display of stars of such brilliance and clarity as I had rarely seen. I marvelled up at them for a while, then returned to the more earthly business of cleaning the remainder of the mud from my shoes. I found a short branch on the ground and sat down to poke and scrape at the gluey muck. When I had finished I leaned back on my hands to stare down the slope at the sea.

My eyes were adjusting to the starlight, and I made out the low black forms of islands; the lights I had seen were from a town on an island straight ahead. To my right was a shoulder of land, which ran out to sea with an aged, rounded resilience, forming the high end of a small bay. The land to my left was flatter, but I could see rocks and a sand-bar, and beyond these the coastline curved back and out of sight.

I walked on and soon came to the beach, clambering down a small cliff of soil and flints, then running out across dried seaweed and powdery sand that seemed to crush beneath my feet. I ran as far as the water's edge, then stood still in the darkness and listened to the special sound of the sea. I felt utterly reassured and complete, able to face anything, free of worry, cured by the essences of the ocean. The faint pungency of salt, warm sand and drying seaweed held powerful associations with childhood: holidays, parents, minor accidents, and that sense of excitement and adventure which, for me, had always overcome the envies and power struggles between Kalia and myself.

My clothes had dried in the warm air, and I felt invigorated and fit. Seri had vanished, but I knew she would reappear when she was ready. I walked the length of the beach twice, then decided to find somewhere to sleep. I found a place in the dry sand that was sheltered by rocks, and here I scooped out a shallow bowl. It was warm enough to sleep uncovered, so I simply lay on my back, cupped my hands behind my head and stared up at the dazzling stars. It was not long before I fell asleep.

I awoke to the sound of the sea, and to brilliant sunlight, and to the crying of gulls. I was instantly alert, as if the transition from sleep to waking was as easy as turning on a light; for months I had been used to a slow, sleepy recovery, dogged by mental and physical clumsiness.

I sat up, regarded the glistering silver sea and the sweep of bone-white sand, and felt the sun warm on my face. To the side, the headland was yellow with flowers and beyond it was a clean blue sky. Lying on the sand beside me, an arm's length away, was a small pile of clothes. There was a pair of sandals, a denim skirt, a white shirt; resting on the top, in a shallow recess made by a hand, was a small silvery cluster of rings and bracelets.

A small head, black against the light, was bobbing and ducking in the swell. I stood up, narrowing my eyes against the glare, and waved. She must have seen me, because as soon as I was standing she waved back and began to wade out towards me. She came with sand-crusted feet and matted hair, and beads of cold water were dripping from her. She kissed me and undressed me, and we made love. Afterwards, we went for a swim.

By the time we had walked along the coast to the nearest village, the sun was high and the unmade track beside the shore was burning beneath our feet. We ate a meal at an open-air restaurant, while the air was drowsy with insects and distant motorcycles. We were in the village of Paiö on the island of Paneron, but it was too hot for Seri and she wanted to move on. There was no harbour in Paiö, just a shallow river running down to meet the sea, and a few small boats tied to rocks. The bus would arrive in the afternoon, but we could rent bicycles. Paneron Town was a three-hour ride away, on the other side of the central range.

Paneron was the first of several islands we visited. It became a compulsive journey, travelling, travelling. I wanted to slow down, to relish each place as we found it, to discover Seri. But she was discovering herself in a way I barely understood. To her, each island represented a different facet of her personality, each one vested in her a sense of identity. She was incomplete without islands, she was spread across the sea.

'Why don't we stay here?' I said, in the harbour of an island with the odd name of Smuj. We were waiting for the ferry to take us on to yet another island. I was intrigued by Smuj: in the town I had found a map of the interior, where an ancient city lay. But Seri needed to change islands.

'I want to go to Winho,' she said.

'Let's stay one more night.'

She seized my arm and there was the force of determination in her eyes. 'We must go somewhere else.'

It was the eighth day, and already I could hardly distinguish the islands we had visited. 'I'm tired of moving on. Let's not travel for a while.'

'But we hardly know each other. Each island reflects us.'

'I can't tell the difference.'

'Because you don't know how to see. You have to surrender to the islands, become enraptured by them.'

'We don't get a chance. As soon as we land in one place we set off for another.'

Seri gestured impatiently. The boat was approaching the quay, the hot smell of diesel fumes drifting around it.

'I told you,' she said. 'In the islands you can live forever. But you won't know how until you find the right place.'

'At the moment I wouldn't know the right place if we found it.'

We sailed to Winho, and from there to more islands. A few days later we were on Semell, and I noticed that from there ships sailed regularly to Jethra. I was frustrated with the journey, and disappointed with what I had learned about Seri. She transmitted her restlessness to me, and I began to think of Gracia and to wonder how she was. I had been away too long, and should not have abandoned her. Guilt grew in me.

I told Seri my feelings. 'If I go back to Jethra, will you come with me?'

'Don't leave me.'

'I want you to come with me.'

'I'm scared you'll go back to Gracia and forget about me. There are more islands to visit.'

'What happens when we reach the last one?' I said.

'There is no last one. They go on forever.'

'That's what I thought.'

We were in the central square of Semell Town, and it was noon. Old men sat in the shade, the shops were shuttered, in the olive trees growing on the rocky hills behind the town we could hear goat bells, and a donkey braying. We were drinking iced tea, and the timetable from the shipping line lay on the table between us. Seri called the waiter and ordered a spiced pastry.

'Peter, you're not ready to return yet. Don't you see that?'

'I'm worried about Gracia. I shouldn't have left her.'

'You had no choice.' A motorboat started up in the harbour; in the slumbering heat it seemed as if it were the only mechanical sound in all the islands. 'Don't you remember what I told you? You must surrender to the islands, submerge yourself in them. Through them you can escape to find yourself. You've given yourself no chance. It's too soon to return.'

'You're just distracting me,' I said. 'I shouldn't be here. It feels wrong . . . it's not for me. I must go home.'

'And you'll go on destroying Gracia.'

'I don't know.'

In the morning a ship called in Semell, and we boarded her. It was a short voyage – two and a half days, with two ports of call on the way – but as soon as we were on board it was almost as if we were in Jethra itself. The ship was registered there, and the food in the dining saloon had the dull familiarity of home. Most of the other passengers were Jethrans. Seri and I barely spoke to each other. It had been a mistake to go with her to the islands; they were not what I expected.

We docked in Jethra in the late afternoon, and disembarked quickly. We rode the escalator to street level, jostled by the crowds of rush-hour commuters. On the street, traffic rushed past and I glanced at newspaper placards: ambulance drivers were threatening to strike, and the OPEC countries had announced another oil-price increase.

I said: 'Are you going to come with me?'

'Yes, but only as far as Gracia's flat. You don't want me anymore.'

But suddenly I did, and I took her hand and held it tightly. I sensed that she was about to recede from me again, as Jethra had receded even before I had walked in its streets.

'What am I going to do, Seri? I know you're right, but somehow I can't go through with it.'

'I'm not going to try to influence you anymore. You know how to find the islands, and I'll always be there.'

'Does that mean you're going to wait for me?'

'It means you'll always be able to find me.'

We were standing in the centre of the pavement while the crowds pushed by. Now that I was back in London the urgency of my return had left me.

'Let's go to our café,' I said.

'Do you know how to find it?'

We walked along Praed Street, but it was all too emphatic. At the corner with Edgware Road I began to despair.

Then Seri said: 'I'll show you.'

She took my hand, and after we had gone a short distance I heard a tram bell. I sensed that an almost subliminal change had come over the city's appearance. We turned into one of the broad boulevards that ran through the fashionable residential areas, and before long came to the intersection where the pavement café was situated. We sat there for a long time, until after sunset, but then I felt the restlessness growing in me again.

Seri said: 'There's a sailing this evening. We could still catch it.'

I shook my head. 'There's no question of it.'

Without waiting to see what she would do, I left some coins on the table-top and started to walk northwards. It was a warm evening, by London standards, and there were many people about. Many of the pubs had overspilled into the streets, and the restaurants were doing good business.

I was aware that Seri was following me, but she said nothing and I did not look back at her. I had tired of her, had used her up. She offered only escape . . . but escape from, not to, so there was nothing to replace what I left behind.

But in one sense she had been right: I had needed to see the islands to find myself. Something had been purged from me now.

In the emptiness that remained, I recognized my mistake. I had sought to understand Gracia through Seri, whereas in reality she was my own complement. She fulfilled what *I* lacked, became the embodiment of that. I thought she explained Gracia, but in reality she only defined me to myself.

Walking in these streets, which had become ordinary, I saw a new face of reality.

Seri soothed, where Gracia abraded. Seri aroused, where Gracia discouraged. Seri was calm, where Gracia was neurotic. Seri was bland and pale, and Gracia was turbulent, effervescent, moody, eccentric, loving and alive. Seri was bland, above all.

A creation of my manuscript, she was intended to explain Gracia to me. But the events and the places described in the manuscript were imaginative extensions of myself, and so were the characters. I had thought they stood for other people, but now I realized they were all different manifestations of myself.

It was dark when we reached the road where Gracia had her flat. I walked more quickly until I could see the house. I saw a light in the front room of the basement. As usual, the curtains had not been drawn, and I turned away, not wanting to see inside.

'You're going to go in and see her, aren't you?' Seri said.

'Yes, of course.'

'What about me?'

'I don't know, Seri. The islands weren't what I wanted. I can't hide anymore.'

'Do you love Gracia?'

'Yes.'

'You know you're going to destroy her again?'

'I don't think so.'

What I had done to hurt Gracia most of all was to take refuge in my fantasies. I had to reject them.

Seri said: 'You think I don't exist, because you think you created me. But I've got a life of my own, Peter, and if you found me in that you'd know it isn't true. So far you've only seen a part of me.'

'I know,' I said, but she was only a part of myself. She was my embodiment of the urge to run, to hide from others. She represented the idea that my misfortunes came from outside, whereas I was learning that they came from within. I wanted to be strong, but Seri weakened me.

Seri said, and I heard bitterness – 'Then do whatever you want.'

I sensed she was receding from me, and I stretched out to take her hand. She moved it adroitly away.

'Please don't go,' I said.

Seri said – I know you're going to forget me, Peter, and perhaps it's as well. I'll be wherever you find me.

She walked away, her white shirt luminous in the city lights. I watched her, thinking of the islands, thinking of the falsehoods in me she represented. Her slim figure, erect and lithe, the short hair that swung slightly as she walked. She left me, and before she had reached the corner of the street I could see her no more.

Alone with the parked cars I felt a sudden and exhilarating sense of relief. However Seri had intended it, she had released me from my own self-fulfilling escapes. I was free of the definition I had made for myself, and at last I felt able to be strong.

CHAPTER 22

Beyond the parked Australian minibus, Gracia's window shone orange-hued behind palings. I walked forward, determined to reconcile our difficulties.

When I reached the edge of the pavement I could see down into the room, and I saw Gracia for the first time.

She was sitting on the bed in full view of the road. She was upright, with her legs crossed beneath her. She held a cigarette in one hand and was gesticulating with the other as she spoke. It was a pose I had seen her in many times; she was active in conversation, was talking about something that interested her. Surprised, because I had assumed she would be alone, I backed away before she noticed me. I moved to a place from where I could see the rest of the room.

A young woman was there with her, curled up in the only chair in the room. I had no idea who she was. She was about Gracia's age, dressed conventionally, wearing spectacles. She was listening to what Gracia was saying, nodding from time to time, speaking infrequently.

When I was sure neither of them had seen me I moved in a little closer. An ashtray full of cigarette ends was on the floor by the bed. Two empty coffee mugs were beside it. The room looked as if it had been recently tidied: the books on the shelves were upright and in neat rows, there were no clothes in the usual corner and the drawers of the chest were closed. Any remaining signs of Gracia's attempted suicide had long since vanished: the furniture had been repositioned, the damage to the door repaired.

Then I noticed there was a small sticking plaster on the

underside of Gracia's wrist. She seemed totally unaware of it, using the arm as freely as she used the other.

She was talking a lot, but more important she seemed happy. I saw her smile several times, and once she laughed aloud with that sideways tilt to the head that I had seen so often, in the old days.

I wanted to hurry in and see her, but the presence of the other woman held me back. I was gladdened by Gracia's appearance. She was as thin as ever, but that aside she radiated good health and mental animation: she reminded me of Greece and sunbathing and retsina, where we began. She looked five years younger than she had the last time I saw her, her clothes seemed clean and freshly pressed, and her hair had been cut and restyled.

I watched the two women for a few minutes, then, to my relief, the stranger stood up. Gracia smiled, said something, and they both laughed. The woman went to the door.

Not wishing to be seen lurking around, I walked a short distance down the road and stood on the other side. After a minute or two, the woman came up to the road and let herself into one of the parked cars. As soon as she had driven away I walked quickly across the road and slipped my key into the lock.

The lights were on in the hall, and the air smelled of furniture polish.

'Gracia? Where are you?' The bedroom door was open, but she was not there. I heard the lavatory being flushed, and the door was opened.

'Gracia, I'm back!'

I heard her say: 'Jean is that you?' Then she appeared, and saw me.

'Hello, Gracia,' I said.

'I thought – Oh my God, it's you! Where have you been?'

'I had to go away for a few—'

'What have you been doing? You look like a tramp!'

'I've been . . . sleeping rough,' I said. 'I had to get away.'

We were standing a few paces apart, not smiling, not

220

moving to embrace each other. I had an inexplicable thought, that this was Gracia, the real Gracia, and I could hardly believe it. She had assumed an unearthly, *ideal* quality in my mind, something lost and unattainable. And yet she stood there, real and substantial, the very best Gracia, untroubled and beautiful without that haunting terror behind her eyes.

'Where were you? The hospital was trying to trace you, they contacted the police – Where did you go?'

'I left London for a while, because of you.' I wanted to hug her, feel her body against me, but there was something in her that kept me at a distance. 'What about you? You look so much better!'

'I'm all right now, Peter. No thanks to you.' She looked away. 'I shouldn't say that. They told me you saved my life.'

I went to her and tried to kiss her, but she turned her face so that all I could do was touch her cheek. When I put up my arms to hold her, she stepped back. I followed her, and we went into the cool dark sitting room, where the television and hi-fi were, the room we had rarely used.

'What's the matter, Gracia? Why won't you kiss me?'

'Not now. I wasn't expecting you, that's all.'

'Who's Jean?' I said. 'Is that the girl who was here?'

'Oh, she's one of my social workers. She calls every day to make sure I'm not going to do myself in. They look after me, you see. After they discharged me they found out I had tried it before, and now they keep an eye on me. They think it's dangerous for me to live alone.'

'You're looking terrific,' I said.

'I'm all right now. I won't do it again. I've come through all that.'

There was an edge to her voice, an inner hardness, and it repelled me. It felt as if it was intended to repel.

'I'm sorry if I seemed to abandon you,' I said. 'They told me you were being looked after. I thought I knew why you had done it, and I had to get away.'

'You don't have to explain. It doesn't matter anymore.'

'What do you mean? Of course it still matters!'

'To you . . . or to me?'

I stared at her in a futile way, but she gave no hint by her expression that might help me.

'Are you angry with me?' I said.

'Why should I be?'

'Because I ran out on you.'

'No . . . Not angry.'

'What then?'

'I don't know.' She moved about the room, but not in the restless way I used to know. Now she was being evasive. This room, like the bedroom, had been tidied and polished. I hardly recognized it. 'Let's go in the front. I want a cigarette.'

I followed her into the bedroom, and while she sat on the edge of the bed and lit a cigarette, I drew the curtains. She watched me, said nothing. I sat down in the chair the social worker had been in.

'Gracia, tell me what happened to you . . . in the hospital.'

'They patched me up and sent me home. That's all, really. Then the social services found a file on me, and they've been hassling me a bit. Jean's OK, though. She'll be glad you've come back. I'll ring her in the morning and tell her.'

'What about you? Are you glad I'm back?'

Gracia smiled as she reached down to flick ash off her cigarette. I sensed that I had said something ironic.

'What are you smiling at?' I said.

'I needed you when I came home, Peter, but I didn't *want* you. If you had been here you'd only have screwed me up again, but the social people would have left me alone. I was relieved you weren't here. It gave me a chance.'

'Why would I have screwed you up?'

'Because you always did! It's what you've been doing ever since we met.' Gracia was trembling, picking at her fingernails while the cigarette burned upside down in her hand. 'When I came home all I wanted was to be alone, to think for myself and work things out, and you weren't here and it was just what I wanted.'

I said: 'Then I shouldn't have come back at all.'

'I didn't want you here then. There's a difference.'

'So you want me now?'

'No. I mean, I don't know. I needed to be alone and I got that. What happens next is something else.'

We both went silent, probably sensing the same dilemma. We both knew we were dangerous to each other while desperately needing each other. There was no rational way of talking about that: either we acted it out by living together again, or we talked about it in highly charged emotional terms. Gracia was struggling to be calm; I wanted to use my new inner strength.

We were still alike, and perhaps that was what doomed us. I had left her to try to understand myself better, she had needed a space alone. I felt intimidated by the changes around her: the cleaned and tidied flat, the changed hair, the outward rehabilitation. She made me aware of my unkempt, unshaven appearance, my unwashed clothes, my smelly body.

But I too had been through a process of recovery, and because it did not show I needed to tell her about it.

I said eventually: 'I'm stronger too, Gracia. I know you'll think I'm only saying that, but I really mean it. It's why I had to go away.'

Gracia looked up from her silent regard of the freshly vacuumed carpet. 'Go on. I'm listening.'

'I thought you had done it because you hated me.'

'No. I was *scared* of you.'

'All right. But you did it because of me, because of what we had become to each other. I understand that now . . . but there was something else. You had been reading my manuscript.'

'Your what?'

'My manuscript. I wrote my autobiography, and it was here. On the bed, the day I found you. You had obviously been reading it, and I knew you were upset by it.'

'I don't know what you're talking about,' Gracia said.

'You must remember!' I looked around the room, realizing that since returning I had not seen the manuscript anywhere.

I felt a *frisson* of alarm: had Gracia destroyed it or thrown it away? 'It was a heap of paper, which I kept bundled up. Where is it now?'

'I put all your stuff in the other room. I've been cleaning the place.'

I left her and hurried through to the sitting room. Beside the stereo record player, by the records – mine neatly segregated from hers – was a small pile of my books. Underneath, held together with two crossing elastic bands, was my manuscript. I snapped the bands away and turned a few pages: it was all there. A few sheets were out of order, but it was intact. I returned to the bedroom, where Gracia had lit another cigarette.

'This is what I meant,' I said, holding it up for her to see. I was immeasurably relieved that it was safe. 'You were reading this, weren't you? That day.'

Gracia narrowed her eyes, though I sensed it was not to see more clearly. 'I want to ask you about that—'

'Let me explain,' I said. 'It's important. I wrote this while I was in Herefordshire, before I went to Felicity's. I'm sure it's what was causing the trouble between us. You thought I was seeing someone else, but really I was just thinking about what I had written. It was my way of finding myself. But I never really finished it. When you were in hospital, and I knew you were being looked after, *I* went away to try to finish it.'

Gracia said nothing, but continued to stare at me.

'Please say something,' I said.

'What does the manuscript say?'

'But you read it! Or you read some of it.'

'I looked at it, Peter, but I didn't read any of it.'

I put the pages down, automatically reshaping them into a neat pile before letting go. I had not even thought about my writing while I was in the islands. Why was the truth so difficult to tell?

'I want you to read it,' I said. 'You've got to understand.'

Gracia again went silent, staring down at her ashtray.

'Are you hungry?' she said at last.

'Don't change the subject.'

'Let's talk about this later. I'm hungry, and you look as if you haven't had a meal in days.'

'Can't we finish this now?' I said. 'It's very important.'

'No, I'm going to cook something. Why don't you have a bath? Your clothes are still here.'

'All right,' I said.

The bathroom was also fastidiously clean. It was free of the customary heaps of dirty clothes, empty toothpaste tubes and used toilet-roll wrappers. When I flushed the lavatory the bowl filled with fizzy blue water. I bathed quickly, while in the next room I could hear Gracia moving about as she cooked. Afterwards, I shaved and put on clean clothes. I weighed myself on her scales, and found I had lost weight while I was away.

We ate at the table in the back room. It was a simple meal of rice and vegetables, but it was the best food I had eaten in a long time. I was wondering how I had survived while I was away, where I had slept, what I had eaten. Where had I been?

Gracia was eating at a moderate pace, but unlike her old self she finished the meal. She had become like someone I barely knew, yet in the same transformation she had become recognizable. She was the Gracia I had often willed her to be: free of her neuroses, or apparently so, free of the inner tension and unhappiness, free of the turbulence that brought the quicksilver moods. I sensed a new determination in her. She was making an immense effort to straighten herself out, and it made me admire her and feel warm towards her.

As we finished I felt content. The physical novelty of clean body and clothes, of a full stomach, of the belief that I had emerged from a long tunnel of uncertainty, made me feel we could start again.

Not after Castleton; that had been premature for both of us.

Gracia made some coffee, and we took the earthenware mugs through to the bedroom. We both felt more at ease there. Outside, car doors occasionally slammed, and from time to time we heard people passing the window. I sat with Gracia on the bed: she was facing me, her legs crossed beneath her. Our coffee mugs were on the floor beside us, the ashtray was between us.

She was quiet, so I said: 'What are you thinking?'

'About us. You're confusing me.'

'Why?'

'I didn't expect you back. Not yet, anyway.'

'Why does that confuse you?'

'Because you've changed and I'm not sure how. You say you're better, that everything will be all right now. But we've both said that before, we've both heard it.'

'Don't you believe me?'

'I believe you mean it . . . of course I do. But I'm still scared of you, what you could do to me.'

I was lightly stroking the back of her hand; it was the first real intimacy between us, and she had not backed away.

I said: 'Gracia, I love you. Can't you trust me?'

'I'll try.' But she was not looking at me.

'Everything I've done in the last few months has been because of you. It took me away from you, but I've seen I was wrong.'

'What are you talking about?'

'What I wrote in my manuscript, and what it has made me do.'

'I don't want to talk about that, Peter.' She was looking at me now, and again I saw that strange narrowing of her eyes.

'You said you would.'

I swung my legs off the bed, crossed the room and picked up the thick wad of pages from where I had left them. I sat down again opposite her, but she had pulled her hand back.

'I want to read you some of it,' I said. 'Explain what it means.'

While I spoke I was turning the pages, looking for those that had got out of order. They were mostly near the beginning. I noticed that many of the sheets had specks of dried blood on them, and the edges of the pages had a broad smudge of brown down them. Glancing through, I saw Seri's name prominently written, again and again. I would come to that eventually, explain who Seri was, what she had become to me, what I now understood of her. All that, and the state of mind the manuscript represented, the islands, the escapes, the difficult relationship with Felicity. And the higher truths the story contained, the definition of myself, the way it had made me static and inward-looking, emotionally petrified.

Gracia had to be brought into it, so that I could at last be brought out of it.

'Peter, you scare me when you get like this.' She had lit a cigarette, her commonplace action, but this time there was an old tension in her. The match, flung down in the ashtray, continued to burn.

'Get like what?' I said.

'You'll upset me again. Don't go on.'

'What's wrong, Gracia?'

'Put those papers away. I can't stand this!'

'I've got to explain to you.'

She ran her hand across her temple, her fingers wildly combing the hair. The demure new hair style became tangled. Her nervousness was infectious; I reacted to it like I reacted to her sexuality. I could not resist it, yet it rarely satisfied either of us. I saw then what had been missing between us since I returned, because as she moved her arm her blouse lightly compressed her breast, and I wanted her body. It took the madness in us both to bring out the sex.

'What are you explaining, Peter? What's left to say?'

'I've got to read you this.'

'Don't torment me! I'm not mad . . . you've written *nothing*!'

'It's how I defined myself. Last year, when I was away.'

'Peter, are you crazy? Those pages are blank!'

I spread the battered pages across the bed, like a conjuror fans a pack of cards. The words, the story of my life, the definition of my identity, lay before me. It was all there: the lines of typewritten text, the frequent corrections, the pencillings and notes and deletions. Black type, blue ball-point, grey pencil, and brown whale-shaped droplets of dried blood. It was all of me.

'There's nothing there, Peter! For God's sake, it's blank paper!'

'Yes, but—'

I stared down at the pages, remembering my white room in Edwin's cottage. That room had achieved a state of higher reality, of deeper truth, one that transcended literal existence. So too was my manuscript. The words were there, inscribed indelibly on the paper, exactly as I had written them. Yet for Gracia, unseeing of the mind that had made them, they were non-existent. I had written and I had not written.

The story was there, but the words were not.

'What are you looking at?' Gracia cried, her voice rising as if frantic. She was twisting one of the rings on her right hand.

'I'm reading.'

I had found the page I wanted to show her: it was in Chapter Seven, where Seri and I first met in Muriseay Town. It paralleled our own first meeting, on the island of Kos, in the Aegean. Seri was said to be working on the staff of the Lotterie-Collago, whereas Gracia had been on holiday; Muriseay Town was a clamorous city, and Kos had just a tiny port. The events differed, but they had the higher truth of feeling. Gracia would recognize it all.

I separated the page from the others and offered it to her. She put it on the bed between us. She had it the wrong way up.

'Why won't you look at it?' I said.

'What are you trying to do to me?'

'I just want you to understand. Please read it.'

She snatched up the page, crumpled it in her hand and threw it across the room. 'I can't read blank paper!'

Her eyes were moist, and she had pulled the ring until it had come off.

Realizing at last that she could not make the necessary imaginative leap, I said, as gently as possible: 'Can I explain?'

'No, don't say anything. I've had enough. Are you living in total fantasy? What else do you imagine? Do you know who I am, who I *really* am? Do you know where you are or what you're doing?'

'You can't read the words,' I said.

'There's nothing there. Nothing.'

I got up from the bed and retrieved the screwed-up page. I flattened it out with the palm of my hand, and returned it to its correct position. I began to collect the sheets, pushing them into their reassuringly familiar bulk.

'You've got to understand this,' I said.

Gracia lowered her head, pressing a hand over her eyes. I heard her say, indistinctly: 'It's happening all over again.'

'What is?'

'We can't go on, you must see that. Nothing's changed.' She wiped her eyes with a tissue. Leaving her cigarette to smoulder in the ashtray, she walked quickly from the room. I heard her in the hallway. She picked up the phone, and she dialled. After a moment she pushed in a coin, with that mechanical, money-box sound.

Although she spoke softly, as if her back were turned against me, I heard her say: 'Steve . . . ? Yes, it's me. Can you put me up tonight? . . . I'm all right, really. Just for tonight . . . Yes, he's back. I don't know what happened. Everything's fine . . . No, I'll come on the Tube. I'm all right, really . . . In about an hour? Thanks.'

I was standing when she came back into the room. She stubbed out her cigarette, and turned to face me. She seemed composed.

'Did you hear any of that?' she said.

'Yes. You're going to Steve's.'

'I'll come back in the morning. Steve will drop me off on his way to work. Will you still be here?'

'Gracia, please don't go. I won't talk about my manuscript.'

'Look, I've just got to calm down a little, talk to Steve. You've upset me. I wasn't expecting you back yet.'

She was moving about the room, collecting her cigarettes

and matches, her bag, a book. She took a bottle of wine from the cupboard, then went to the bathroom. A few moments later she was standing in the hall by the bedroom door, checking her purse for her keys, a supermarket carrier bag swinging from her wrist with her overnight toilet things, and her wine bottle.

I went out and stood with her.

'I can't believe this,' I said. 'Why are you running away from me?'

'Why did *you* run away?'

'That's what I was trying to explain.'

She wore a non-committal expression, avoiding my eyes. I knew she was making an effort to stay in control of herself; in the old days we would have talked ourselves into exhaustion, gone to bed, made love, continued in the morning. Now she had terminated the whole thing: the phone call, the abrupt departure, the bottle of wine.

Even as she stood there, waiting for me to let her go, she was already absent, halfway to the Tube station.

I held her arm. This made her look at me, but then away again.

'Are you still in love with me?' I said.

'How can you ask that?' she said. I waited, deliberately manipulating with silence. 'Nothing's changed, Peter. I tried to kill myself because I loved you, because you didn't take any notice of me, because it was impossible being with you. I don't want to die, but when I get upset I can't control myself. I'm scared of what you might do to me.' She took a deep breath, but it was uneven, and I knew she was suppressing tears. 'There's something deep inside you I can't touch. I feel it most when you retreat, when you were talking about your bloody manuscript. You're going to make me insane!'

'I came home because I have come out of myself,' I said.

'No . . . no, it's not true. You're deceiving yourself, and you're trying to deceive me as well. Don't ever do that, not again. I can't cope!'

She broke down then, and I released her arm. I tried to pull her against me, to hold her and be comforting, but she dragged herself away, weeping. She rushed through the front door, slamming it behind her.

I stood in the hall, listening to the imagined echoes of the slam.

I returned to the bedroom and sat for a long while on the edge of the bed, staring at the carpet, the wall, the curtains. After midnight I bestirred myself and tidied up the flat. I emptied the ashtrays and washed them up with the supper dishes and the coffee mugs, leaving them all to drain on the side. Then I found my old leather holdall, and packed it with as many of my clothes as I could get in. I packed the manuscript last, cramming it down on top. I checked that all the electricity switches were off, that no taps were dripping. As I left, I turned off all the lights.

I walked down to Kentish Town Road, where late traffic went past. I was too tired to want to sleep rough again, and thought I would find a cheap hotel for the night. I remembered a street near Paddington where there were several, but I wanted to get out of London. I stood undecided.

I was numbed by Gracia's rejection of me. I had returned to her with no idea of what I intended to say, or of what might happen, but had felt my new internal strength would solve all that was wrong. Instead, she was stronger than me.

The zip fastener of my holdall was open, and I could see the manuscript inside. I took it out and turned the pages in the light of a street lamp. The story lay there for me to see, but the words had gone. Some of the pages had typewriting on them, but it was always scribbled over. I saw names flip past: Kalia, Muriseay, Seri, Ia, Mulligayn. Gracia's blood splashes remained. The only coherent words, undeleted, were on the last page. These were the words of the sentence I had never completed.

I stuffed the pages back in the bag, and squatted down in the recessed doorway of a shop. If the pages had become unworded, if the story was now untold, then it meant I could start again.

It was now more than a year since I had been in Edwin's cottage, and much had happened in my life that was not described in the manuscript. My stay at the cottage itself, my weeks at Felicity's house, my return to London, my discovery of the islands.

Above all, the manuscript did not contain a description of its own writing, and the discoveries I had made.

Sitting there in the draughty shop doorway, my holdall clutched between my knees, I knew that I had returned prematurely to Gracia. My definition of myself was incomplete. Seri had been right: I needed to immerse myself totally in the islands of the mind.

Excitement coursed through me as I thought of the challenge ahead. I left the shop doorway and walked quickly in the direction of central London. Tomorrow I should make plans, find somewhere to live, perhaps take a job. I would write when I could, construct my inner world and descend into it. There I could find myself, there I could live, there I could find rapture. Gracia would not reject me again.

I felt as if I were alone in the city, with the vacant illuminated shop windows, the darkened homes, the deserted pavements, the glowing advertisements. I felt a ripple of my awareness spreading outwards, encompassing the whole of London, centred on myself. I strode past the rows of parked cars, the uncollected refuse bags, the discarded plastic cartons and drink cans. I hurried through intersections where traffic lights changed for absent cars, past walls defaced with spray-can graffiti, past shuttered offices and gated Underground stations. The buildings stood high and dim around me.

Ahead was the prospect of islands.

CHAPTER 23

I was imagining Seri was on the ship with me. After leaving Hetta, my temporary refuge from the clinic, we had called first at Collago, and I knew it was possible she had boarded there. I stood amidships while we were in the harbour, covertly watching the passengers embark, and I had not seen her among them; even so, I could have missed seeing her.

For the whole of the voyage, from Hetta to Jethra, via Muriseay, I was glimpsing her. Sometimes it was a sight of her at the other end of the ship: a blonde head held in a certain way, a combination of clothes' colours, a distinctive walk. Once it was a particular scent I associated with her, detected almost subliminally in the crowded saloon. A name kept coming distractingly to mind: Mathilde, whom once I had mistaken for Seri. I searched my manuscript for some reference to her.

I prowled the ship obsessively at such times, looking for Seri, although not necessarily wanting to find her. I needed to resolve the uncertainty, because in a contradictory way I both willed her to be on board the ship with me, and not. I was lonely and confused, and she had created me after the treatment; at the same time, I had to reject her worldview to be able to find myself.

This delusion of Seri was part of a larger duality.

I was perceiving with two minds. I was what Seri and Lareen had made me, and I was what I had discovered of myself in the unaltered manuscript.

I accepted the uncomfortable reality of the overcrowded ship, the circuitous passage across the Midway Sea, the islands we called at, the confusion of cultures and dialects, the strange food, the heat and the stunning scenery. All this was solid and tangible around me, yet internally I knew none of it could be real.

It scared me to know there was this dichotomy in the perceived world, as if to stop believing it could cause the ship to vanish from beneath me.

I felt prominent on the ship because I was central to its continued existence. This was my dilemma. I knew I did not belong in the islands. Inside me I recognized a deep and consistent truth about my identity: I had discovered myself through the metaphors of my manuscript. But the outer world, perceived anecdotally, had a plausible solidity and confusion. It was random, it was out of control, it lacked story.

I best understood this when I considered the islands.

It had seemed to me, as I recovered from the operation, that as I learned about the Dream Archipelago I was actually creating it in my mind. I had felt my awareness of it spreading outwards.

At different times I had imagined it differently, as comprehension changed. Because I was limited in my imaginative vocabulary, I had built up my creation slowly. At first the islands were mere shapes. Then colour was added – bold, clashing primaries – then they were bedecked with flowers and swarmed by birds and insects, and encrusted with buildings, impoverished by deserts, crowded with people, choked with jungle, lashed by tropical storms and swept by surging tides. These imagined islands at first bore no relation to Collago, the place of my spiritual birth, then one day Seri had passed the apparently innocuous information that Collago itself was a part of the Archipelago. Instantly, my mental construct of the islands changed: the sea was filled with Collagos. Later, still learning, I continued to modify. As I developed what I called taste, I imagined the islands from aesthetic or moral principles, endowing them with romantic, cultural and historical qualities.

Even so, endlessly modified, there had been a neatness to my concept of the islands.

Their reality, as seen from the ship, was therefore charged with surprise, the true relish of travel.

I was entranced by the ever-changing scenery. The islands changed, one from another, with latitude, with subsea geology, with vegetation, with commercial or industrial or agricultural exploitation. One group of islands, marked on my charts as the Olldus Group, was disfigured by centuries of vulcanism: here the beaches were black, the rising cliffs loose with old basalt and lava, and the mountain peaks jagged and barren. Within the same day we were sailing through a cluster of unnamed islands, low and tangled with mangrove swamps. Here the ship was visited by innumerable flying insects that stayed, biting and stinging, until nightfall. Tamer islands greeted us with harbours, a sight of towns and farmland, and food that could be bought to vary the ship's limited menu.

I spent most of the daylight hours at the rail of the ship, watching this endless passing show, gorging my senses on the gourmanderie of the view. Nor was I alone; many of the other passengers, whom I presumed were native islanders, showed the same fascination. The islands defied interpretation; they could only be experienced.

I knew that I could never have created these islands as a part of my mental imaginings. The very diversity of the visual richness was beyond the making of anything except nature. I discovered the islands and absorbed them, they came to me from outside, they confirmed their real existence to me.

Even so, the duality remained. I knew that the typewritten definition of myself was real, that my life was lived elsewhere. The more I appreciated the scale, variety and sheer beauty of the Dream Archipelago, the less I was able to believe in it.

If Seri was a part of this perception, she too could not exist.

To affirm my knowledge of my inner reality, I read through my manuscript every day. Every time it made more sense, enabling me to see beyond the words, to learn and remember things that were not written.

This ship was a means to an end, taking me on an inner

voyage. Once I left it and stepped ashore, and walked in the city I knew as 'Jethra', I would be home.

My grasp on metaphoric reality increased, and my inner confidence grew. For example, I solved the problem of language.

After the treatment I had been brought to awareness through language. I now spoke the same language as Seri and Lareen. I had never given it a thought. Because I had come to it as to a mother tongue I used it instinctively. That I had also written my manuscript in it was something I took for granted. I knew that it was spoken, as first language, by people like Seri and Lareen, and by the doctors and staff at the clinic, and that one could make oneself understood with it throughout the Archipelago. On the ship, announcements were made in it, and newspapers and signs were printed in it.

(It was not, however, the only language in the islands. There was a confusing number of dialects, and different groups of islands had their own languages. In addition, there was a sort of island patois, spoken throughout the Archipelago, but which had no written form.)

The day after the ship left Muriseay I suddenly realized that my language was called English. That same day, while I was sheltering from the sun on the boat deck, I noticed an ancient sign riveted to the metal wall behind me. It had been painted over a dozen times, but it was still possible to make out the slightly raised lettering. It said: *Défense de cracher*. Not for a moment did I mistake this for an island language; I knew immediately that the ship was, or at some time had been, French.

Yet where were France and England? I searched my charts of the Archipelago, looking for the coastlines, but in vain. Even so, I knew I was English, that somewhere in my perplexing mind I had a few words of French, sufficient to order drinks, ask the way, or refrain from spitting.

How could English spread through the Archipelago as the language of authority, of the professions, of newspapers, of shopkeepers?

Like everything now, it heightened my trust of the inner life, deepened my distrust of external reality.

The further north we sailed, the fewer were the passengers on board. The nights were cool, and I spent more time inside my cabin. On the last day I woke with a feeling that I was now ready to land. I spent the morning in reading through my manuscript for the last time, feeling that at last I could read it with total understanding.

It seemed to me that it could be read on three levels.

The first was contained in the words I had actually written, the typewritten text, describing those anecdotes and experiences which had so confused Seri.

Then there were the pencilled substitutions and deletions made by Seri and Lareen.

Finally there was what I had *not* written: the spaces between the lines, the allusions, the deliberate omissions and the confident assumptions.

I who had been written about. I who had been assumed to have written. I of whom I remembered, for whom I could anticipate.

In my words was the life I had lived before the treatment on Collago. In Seri's amendments was the life I had assumed, existing in quotes and faint pencil markings. In my omissions was the life I would return to.

Where the manuscript was blank, I had defined my future.

CHAPTER 24

There was one last island before Jethra: a high, grim place called Seevl, approached at evening. All I knew of Seevl was that Seri told me she had been born there, that it was the closest island to Jethra. Our call in Seevl seemed unusually long: a lot of people disembarked and a quantity of cargo was loaded. I paced the deck impatiently, wanting to finish my long journey.

Night fell while we were in Seevl Town, but once we had left the confined harbour and rounded a dark, humping head-land, I could see the lights of an immense city on the low coastline ahead. The wind was cold and there was a ground swell.

The ship was quiet; I was one of the few passengers aboard.

Then someone came and stood behind me, and without turning I knew who it was.

Seri said: 'Why did you run away from me?'

'I wanted to go home.'

She slipped her hand around my arm and pressed herself against me. She was shivering.

'Are you angry with me for following you?'

'No, of course not.' I put my arm around her, kissed her on the side of her cold face. She was wearing a thin blouson over her shirt. 'How did you find me?'

'I got to Seevl. All the ships for Jethra stop there. It was just a question of waiting for the right one to come.'

'But why did you follow?'

'I want to be with you. I don't want you to be in Jethra.'

'It's not Jethra I'm going to.'

'Yes it is. Don't delude yourself.'

The city lights were nearer now, sharply visible over the blackly heaving swell. The clouds above were a dark and smudgy orange, reflecting the glow. Behind us, the few islands still in sight were indistinct, neutral shapes. I felt them slipping away from me, a release from the psyche.

'This is where I live,' I said. 'I don't belong in the islands.'

'But you've become a part of them. You can't just put them behind you.'

'That's all I *can* do.'

'Then you'll leave me too.'

'I had already made that decision. I didn't want you to follow.'

She released my arm and moved away. I went after her and held her again. I tried to kiss her, but she turned her face away. 'Seri, don't make it more difficult. I've got to go back to where I came from.'

'It won't be what you expect. You'll find yourself in Jethra, and that's not what you're looking for.'

'I know what I'm doing.' I thought of the emphatic nature of the manuscript: the inarguable blankness of what was to come.

The ship had hove to a long way from the entrance to the harbour. A pilot cutter was coming out, black against the city-bright sea.

'Peter, please don't go on with this.'

'There's someone I'm trying to find.'

'Who is it?'

'You've read the manuscript,' I said. 'Her name is Gracia.'

'Please stop. You're going to hurt yourself. You mustn't believe anything written in that manuscript. You said at the clinic that you understood, that everything it said was a kind of fiction. Gracia doesn't exist, London doesn't exist. You imagined it all.'

'You were with me in London once,' I said. 'You were jealous of Gracia then, you said she upset you.'

'I've never been out of the islands!' She glanced at the glowing city, and the hair flatted across her eyes. 'I've never even been there, to Jethra.'

'I was living with Gracia, and you were there too.'

'Peter, we met in Muriseay, when I was working for the Lotterie.'

'No . . . I can remember everything now,' I said.

She faced me, and I sensed something new. 'If that was so, you wouldn't be looking for Gracia. You know the truth is that Gracia's dead! She killed herself two years ago, when you had a row, before you went away to write your manuscript. When she died you couldn't admit it was your fault. You felt guilty, you were unhappy . . . all right. But you mustn't believe that she's still alive, just because your manuscript says so.'

Her words shocked me; I could feel the earnestness in her.

'How do you know this? ' I said.

'Because you told me in Muriseay. Before we left for Collago.'

'But that's the period I can't remember. It's not in the manuscript.'

'Then you can't remember everything!' Seri said. 'We had to wait a few days for the next ship to Collago. We were staying in Muriseay Town. I had a flat there, and you moved in with me. Because I knew what would happen when you took the treatment, I was getting you to tell me everything about your past. You told me then . . . about Gracia. She committed suicide, and you borrowed a house from a friend and you went there to write everything out of your system.'

'I don't remember,' I said. Behind us the pilot cutter had come alongside, and two men in uniform were boarding the ship. 'Is Gracia her real name? '

'It's the only name you told me . . . the same as in the manuscript.'

'Did I tell you where I went to write the manuscript? '

'In the Murinan Hills. Outside Jethra.'

'The friend who lent me the house . . . was his name Colan? '

'That's right.'

One of Seri's insertions: pencil above typewritten line.

Underneath Colan's name, scored through lightly, Edwin Miller, friend of the family. Between the two names a space, a blankness, a room painted white, a sense of landscape spreading out through the white walls, a sea filled with islands.

'I know Gracia's alive,' I said. 'I know because every page of my story is imbued with her. I wrote it for her, because I wanted to find her again.'

'You wrote it because you blamed yourself for her death.'

'You took me to the islands, Seri, but they were wrong and I had to reject you. You said I had to surrender to the islands to find myself. I did that, and I'm free of them. I've done what you wanted.' Seri seemed not to be listening. She was staring away from me, across the heaving water to the headlands and moors black behind the city. 'Gracia's alive now because you're alive. As long as I can feel you and see you, Gracia's alive.'

'Peter, you're lying to yourself. You know it isn't true.'

'I understand the truth, because I found it once.'

'There's no such thing as truth. You are living by your manuscript, and everything in it is false.'

We stared together towards Jethra, divided by a definition.

There was a delay on the ship, a hoisting of a new flag, then at last we moved forward at half speed, steering a course, avoiding hidden underwater obstacles. I was impatient to land, to discover the city.

Seri went to sit away from me, on one of the slatted deck benches facing to the side. I stayed in the prow of the ship, watching our approach.

We passed a long concrete wall near the mouth of the river and came to smooth water. I heard the ringing of bells and the engines cut back even further. We glided in near silence between the distant banks. I was looking eagerly at the wharves and buildings on either side, seeking familiarity. Cities look different from water.

I heard Seri say: 'It will always be Jethra.'

We were passing through a huge area of dockland, a major

port, quite unlike the simple harbours of the island towns. Cranes and warehouses loomed dark on the bank, and large ships were tied up and deserted. Once, through a gap, I saw traffic on a road, moving silently and quickly; lights and speed and unexplained purpose, glimpsed through buildings. Further along we passed a wildly floodlit complex of hotels and apartment buildings standing about a huge marina, where hundreds of small yachts and cruisers were moored, and dazzling lights of all colours seemed directed straight at us. People stood on concrete quays, watching our ship as we slid by with muted engines.

We came to a broader stretch of river, where on one bank was parkland. Coloured lights and festoons hung in the trees, smoke rose multicoloured through the branches, people clustered around open fires. There was a raised platform made of scaffolding, surrounded by lights, and here people danced. All was silent, eerily hushed against the rhythm of the river.

The ship turned and we moved towards the bank. Ahead of us now was an illuminated sign belonging to the steamship company, and floodlights spread white radiance across a wide, deserted apron. There were a few cars parked on the far side, but they showed no lights and there was no one there to greet us.

I heard the telegraphy bell ringing on the bridge, and a moment later the remaining vibrations of the engines died away. The pilot's judgement was uncanny: now without power or steerage, the ship glided slowly towards the berth. By the time the great steel side pressed against the old tyres and rope buffers it was virtually impossible to detect movement.

The ship was still; the silence of the city spread over us. Beyond the wharf, the lights of the city were too bright to be properly seen, shedding radiance without illumination.

'Peter, wait here with me. The ship will sail in the morning.'

'You know I'm going ashore.' I turned back to look at her. She was slumped on the seat, huddling against the river winds.

'If you find Gracia she'll only reject you, as you reject me.'

'So you admit she's alive?'

'It was you who first told me she wasn't. Now you remember differently.'

'I'm going to find her,' I said.

'Then I'll lose you. Doesn't that mean anything to you?'

In the dazzle from the city I saw her grief. 'Whatever happens, you'll always be with me.'

'You're just saying that. What about all the things we were planning to do together?'

I stared at her, unable to say anything. Seri had created me on Collago, but before then, in my white room, I had created her. She had no life independent of mine. But her desolate unhappiness was real enough, a truth of a poignant sort was there.

'You think I'm not really here,' she said. 'You think I live only for you. An adjunct, a complement . . . I read that in your manuscript. You made me with a life, and now you try to deny it. You think you know what I am, but you can't know *anything* more than what I made you into. I loved you when you were helpless, when you depended on me like a child. I told you about us, that we were lovers, but you read your manuscript and believed something else. Every day I saw you and remembered what you had been, and I just thought of what I had lost. Peter, believe me now . . . you *can't* live in a fiction! Everything we talked about, before you ran away—'

She wept then, and I waited, staring down at the top of her head, rolling my arms around her thin shoulders. In the night her hair was darker, the wind had tousled it, the salt spray had curled it. When she looked up her eyes were wide, and there was a deep, familiar pain behind them.

For that moment I knew who she really was, who she replaced. I held her tight, repenting of all the pain I had caused. But when I kissed her neck she twisted in the seat and faced me.

'Do you love me, Peter?'

She was hurting because of the tenderness I was taking

from her. I knew she was an extension of my wishes, an embodiment of how I had failed Gracia. To love her was to love myself; to deny her was to inflict needless pain. I hesitated, bracing myself for an untruth.

'Yes,' I said, and we kissed. Her mouth on mine, her lithe body pressing against me. She was real, just as the islands were really there, as the ship was solid beneath us, as the shining city waited.

'Then stay with me,' she said.

But we walked aft and found my holdall, then went down through the metal-echoing passages to the place where a gangplank had been slung across from the shore. We walked down, stepped over the raised wooden slats, ducking under one of the hawsers that held the ship to the quay.

We crossed the apron, passed through the line of parked cars, found an alley that led to steps, and these to a road. A tram went past in silence.

I said: 'Have you any idea where we are?'

'No, but that tram was going to the centre.'

I knew it was Jethra, but knew it would change. We set off in the same direction as the tram. This street that served the docks was draughty and ugly, giving an impression that daylight would only underline its dilapidation. We followed it for a long way, then came to a wide intersection where a white marble building, with a pillared edifice, stood back on lawns.

'That's the Seigniory,' Seri said.

'I know.'

I recognized it from before. In the old days it had been the seat of government, then when the Seignior had moved into the country it had become a tourist attraction, then when the war came it was nothing. For all my life in Jethra it had been nothing, just a pillared edifice, its significance gone.

Beside the Palace was a public park, and a pathway bisected it, lit by lamps. Recognizing a short cut, I led the way. The path climbed the hill in the centre of the park, and soon we were looking down across much of the city.

I said: 'This is where I bought my lottery ticket.'

The memory was too vivid to be lost. That day, the wooden franchise stall, the young soldier with the neck brace and the dress uniform. Now there was no one about, and I stared across rooftops to the mouth of the river and the sea beyond. Somewhere out there was the Dream Archipelago: neutral territory, a place to wander, an escape, a divisor of past and present. I felt the dying of island rapture, and sensed that Seri was staring too. She was forever identified with the islands; if the rapture died, would she become ordinary?

I glanced at her, with her drawn face and her wind-blown hair, the thin body, the dilated eyes.

We went on after a few minutes, now descending the hill, joining one of the main boulevards that ran through the heart of Jethra. Here there was more traffic; horse-drawn and automobile, following lanes marked away from the tramlines. The silence was dying. I heard a tram bell, then metal-rimmed wheels grating on the surface of the street. A door to a bar flew open, and light and sound spilled out. I heard glasses and bottles, a cash register, a woman laughing, amplified pop music.

In the street a tram swished past, clattering over an intersection.

'Do you want anything to eat?' I said as we passed a pavement café. The smell of food was irresistible.

'It's up to you,' she said, so we walked on. I had no idea where we were going.

We came to another junction, one I dimly recognized without understanding why, and by unspoken accord we came to a halt. I was tired, and the holdall was weighing on my shoulder. Traffic roared past in both directions, making us raise our voices.

'I don't know why I'm following you,' Seri said. 'You're going to leave me, aren't you?'

I said nothing until I had to: Seri looked exhausted and miserable.

'I've got to find Gracia,' I said at last.

'There is no Gracia.'

'I've got to be sure.' Somewhere here was London, some-where in London was Gracia. I knew I would find her in a white room, one where blank paper lay scattered across the floor, like islands of plain truth, auguring what was to come. She would be there, and she would see how I had emerged from my fantasy. Now I was complete.

'Don't go on believing, Peter. Come back to the islands with me.'

'No, I can't. I've got to find her.'

Seri waited, staring at the litter-strewn pavement.

'You're an athanasian,' she said, and it seemed to me that she said it in desperation, a last attempt. 'Do you know what that means?'

'I'm afraid it means nothing to me now. I don't believe it ever happened.'

Seri reached up to me, touched me high on my neck, behind my ear. There was still a sensitive place there, and I winced away.

'In the islands you will live forever,' she said. 'If you leave the islands you become ordinary. The islands are eternal, you will be timeless.'

I shook my head emphatically. 'I don't believe any more, Seri. I don't belong.'

'Then you disbelieve in me.'

'No, I don't.'

I tried to embrace her but she pushed me away.

Seri said – 'I don't want you to touch me. Go and find Gracia.'

She was crying. I stood there indecisively. I was scared that London was not there, that Gracia would have gone.

'Will I find you again?' I said.

Seri said – When you have learnt where to look.

Too late I realized she had receded from me. I stumbled away from her and stood by the side of the road, waiting for a gap in the traffic. Carts and trams rushed past. Then I saw there was a pedestrian underpass, so I went through, losing sight of Seri. I began to run, clambering up to the surface on the other side. For a moment I thought I knew where I was, but when I looked back